THE MEET CUTE METHOD

PORTIA MACINTOSH

Boldwood

First published in Great Britain in 2022 by Boldwood Books Ltd.

A CIP catalogue record for this book is available from the British Library.

Paperback ISBN 978-1-80048-780-2

Large Print ISBN 978-1-80048-779-6

Hardback ISBN 978-1-80426-234-4

Ebook ISBN 978-1-80048-781-9

Kindle ISBN 978-1-80048-782-6

Audio CD ISBN 978-1-80048-774-1

MP3 CD ISBN 978-1-80048-775-8

Digital audio download ISBN 978-1-80048-777-2

Boldwood Books Ltd
23 Bowerdean Street
London SW6 3TN
www.boldwoodbooks.com

For Joe – my ultimate meet cute

1

I've seen some seriously weird things on my way to work over the years.

It's to be expected, I suppose, given that my office is based in Soho, smack bang between Oxford Circus and Piccadilly Circus – very apt names because, with the sights I'm used to seeing, a circus feels like the right place for them.

I've been caught in the literal crossfire when activists were launching red paint bombs at the HQ of a fashion retailer across the street. I saw a woman use a flash mob to dump her cheating boyfriend. I even saw a woman giving birth on the Tube, which is a sight I won't forget in a hurry, but is still also probably not the strangest thing I've seen on the Underground.

But of all the weird, sick and twisted things I've seen in the nine years (my God, has it been nine years?) I've been living and working in the city, I don't think I've ever seen anything quite like this...

'I'm sorry, I think that might be my skinny cinnamon vanilla decaf latte,' the man says.

He's a twenty-something with a double shot of the Hugh Grants. He's just reached for a coffee at the same time as a young red-headed woman. Now they're both holding it between them, a hand each on the cup, as they stare into one another's eyes. I don't know how to describe it, there's just something between them, an immediate connection.

'You drink a skinny cinnamon vanilla decaf latte?' the woman asks in disbelief.

'Frankie,' the barista calls out, letting me know that my latte macchiato is ready. Normally I'd grab it and get on my way but, honestly, I'm gripped.

'I do,' the man replies. He uses his free hand to run it through his hair while he briefly glances down at the floor, embarrassed. 'I know, it's a bit weird, but—'

'That's exactly what I drink,' she tells him. 'I need the vanilla to take the edge off the cinnamon and the decaf…'

'…to take the edge off the coffee,' the man continues.

'Wow, we're already finishing each other's…'

'…coffee,' the man jokes, finishing her sentence again.

The woman giggles.

I need to get to work, I really do, but I can't take me eyes off them.

I'm hoping today is the day at work – the day I'm *finally* officially made head of my department at *Stylife Magazine*. It's a formality, in a way. I'm already acting head of Love & Dating, since my boss went off on maternity leave and never came back, and they decided that I'd been doing her job just fine while she was off. Jane, the editor at *Stylife*, finally took me to one side last week and told me that, with my ten-year anniversary coming up, she was going to make my promotion official and give me that all-important pay rise I've been fantasising about.

Of course, for all this to happen, I need to actually get to work, but I can't look away. You see, despite being the main features writer of all things Love & Dating, I'm kind of a cynic when it comes to love. I know, that sounds awful, it would be like finding out Ed Sheeran didn't believe in love (on a much smaller scale, obviously, the magazine and website may be the most popular amongst women between the ages of twenty and forty, but I doubt my features have the same size audience as Ed's music).

I wasn't always like this. In fact, I used to love this job, but I'm thirty-four now, and I don't know if it's because my job has been so focused on telling people how to find love, but I've either been too busy to find it myself, or I've seen too much. Deep diving into all things dating has shown me the man behind the curtain, and he is not a catch, he usually has a girlfriend and a penchant for taking pictures of his penis that nobody asked for.

Perhaps that's why I'm so captivated by the scene in the coffee shop this morning. This couple, with the exact same weird drink order, not just finishing each other's sentences but finishing each other's jokes too. It's the perfect romantic scene – like something from a movie – and I'm not the only one who has noticed. Everyone in this coffee shop has their eyes on them. I have to see how this plays out.

'I'm Mark.'

'My dad is called Mark,' she replies, her smile growing. 'I'm Erin.'

'My cat is called Erin,' Mark tells her giddily.

'Really?' she squeaks, her eyes lighting up even more than they were already.

'No, not really,' he says with an awkward but still charming smile. 'I just didn't want to end our streak of amazing coincidences. To be honest, I'm more of a dog person.'

'Me too!' Erin replies, surely maxing out her enthusiasm.

Mark's face falls straight for a moment.

'God, you're beautiful when you smile,' he tells her. 'If I could wake up to that smile every day, I'd be the happiest man in the world.'

Bloody hell, that's a bit intense.

Erin is still smiling, though. I would have run a mile from a line like that.

'I'm supposed to be on my way to work,' she says through a giggle.

Me and you both, girl.

'Me too,' Mark replies. 'But... what if we don't go?'

Erin laughs again.

'I'm serious,' he tells her. 'Something about this just feels so right. Let's just, I don't know, let's just get on a plane and go somewhere.'

I hold my breath as I wait for her reaction.

'You're right,' she tells him. 'There's something between us, I know it, I feel it... Okay, forget work. Let's go.'

Mark grabs Erin and kisses her and, as their lips finally meet, everyone in the café starts to applaud. Finding myself caught up in it all, I can't help but clap too. I can feel my frosty heart thawing out a little and it's nothing to do with the coffee that I'm letting go cold in my head. I am absolutely captivated. This is like something from a movie!

Mark and Erin stop kissing, hold hands, turn to their applauding audience and take a bow. Okay, that's weird.

'Thank you so much,' Erin announces to the room.

'Yes, thank you,' Mark continues. 'And if you enjoyed our performance today, then be sure to check out the screening of our movie *Love and Stuff Like It* over at the Old Picture Place cinema across the street, starting Tuesday.'

Okay, it was literally a movie. Bloody hell, I'm so annoyed I could crush my coffee cup in my hand. I feel like I've been scammed. The one day – the one day – I absolutely want to be at work on time and I've let myself fall for a performance like this. And I let my coffee go cold too. Brilliant.

I take a few swigs before tossing the cup in the café bin and heading outside to catch my bus, dashing to the bus stop just in time to see it pulling away. *Marvellous*. I'm definitely going to be late for work now.

I gently lean against the convenience shop window behind me. I can't believe I let myself get suckered into an act. Honestly, I feel dirty.

My attention is captured by a woman and a man colliding in front of me. His coffee cup crumples between them, spilling coffee all over them both. Now this really is like something out of a movie, it's very *Notting Hill*, although the fallout is more in keeping with what I'm used to seeing on my way to work. He shouts at her, telling her she owes him a coffee. She starts screaming back at him, telling him he owes her a new blouse. Their arguing is only broken by the commotion across the road. Another couple in an embrace and, nope, he's stealing her handbag. Of course he is.

'Ergh,' I say under my breath, although I feel an almost smug satisfaction that my faith in humanity has been, well, whatever the opposite of restored is.

'It's mad out here today, huh?' a man with a Scottish accent says.

I turn to face him. He's talking to me.

'It's mad out here every day,' I reply with a smile.

'I've never really been over this way,' he says. 'Although I haven't been here that long and sometimes it feels like all I do is work.'

Even if it weren't for his accent, you can tell he isn't a Londoner. He's too friendly, too chatty. There's an understanding, among commuters, that you let people get on with what they're doing, leaving them to travel to and from work in peace. No one wants to chat on public transport, or when they are waiting for it, although I have to admit he's a good-looking guy. He reminds me of Prince Harry, just a bit, but you know, a Scottish version who gets the bus.

'Do you like to hang around bus stops?' he asks.

'Erm, only when I'm getting buses,' I point out.

What a bizarre question.

The stranger smiles curiously.

'I thought you'd have more of an accent,' he tells me.

I raise my eyebrows. Really? I just sound like any other thirty-something Londoner. What is he expecting, Dick Van Dyke?

'Nope, this is it,' I say with a shrug and a polite smile.

'I'm not complaining,' he insists. 'You have a lovely voice. So, where are we going?'

'Where are we going?' I repeat back to him.

'I was thinking coffee first,' he says. 'We can have a chat, get to know each other, then maybe a museum?'

I can't help but laugh. Is this man asking me out? Me? Here at this bus stop? After the morning I've had, I refuse to believe it.

'Sorry, is that sad?' he replies. 'Well, we can do whatever you want to do, then. What do you think?'

I think I need to get to work but, wow, he really does seem keen. Ordinarily I'd run a mile but is that my problem? Do I never give people a chance? My instincts are telling me to tell him to piss off and leave me to wait for my bus in peace but...

'Sean?' a petite Irish woman asks.

The first thing I notice is that she's carrying the exact same bright pink Michael Kors handbag as I am.

The man – Sean, I'm assuming – looks at her, then at me, then at her again.

'Saoirse?' he says to her.

'Erm, yeah,' she replies.

Sean turns to me.

'I'm so sorry,' he says. 'I've made a terrible mistake. I'm new in town so a friend said he'd set me up with someone else who was new in town, and all he said was that she'd be outside this shop with a bright pink bag and...'

I don't know who is more embarrassed, me or him. Actually, I do, it's me. It's absolutely me. Of course he wasn't asking me out, he thought I was someone else. Why did I even consider, for a second, that I was having some kind of moment? It's that bloody scene from the café this morning, it's got romance in my head. I suppose it's a good thing, given my job, and my bus is here now, and I've never been so motivated to get on it.

'No worries,' I tell him. 'I need to get to work.'

'Nice to almost meet you,' he calls after me.

'Yep,' I say as I hurry on board.

I find a seat and slump down into it. At least when I finally get to work things will turn around for me. My promotion is imminent, and I've got a pitch for a series of articles that my editor is going to love, where I basically adopt a different personality type on each dating app, and see which one gets me the furthest.

I really need to hurry up and get there now but, it's true, you never know what you're going to see on your way to work on a morning. I just can't believe today, of all days, was the day I let it make me late.

2

I work in a large building nicknamed the Cactus – I'm unsure if it was intentionally modelled on a cactus or not, but it does look like one, thanks to its rounded shape and its green window frames. I like that it's different from all the other blocky buildings that sit alongside it. I do love this part of London. That's why I'm so excited about the idea of moving here – well, that and the commute. Currently it takes me about an hour to get to work. An hour that consists of a bus, a Tube and a couple of fast walks. Don't get me wrong, I know there are people with much longer commutes, but that doesn't make mine any easier. The apartment I viewed last night was in Soho, which not only means I can get to work in minutes, but it's so gorgeous, really. So modern, so sleek, and – most importantly – all mine. Well, I'll be renting it, obviously, and it's small, but I won't be sharing it with anyone like I am now.

It's not that I don't like living with other people, it's just that I live with four other people. There's a bit of a student house vibe, just with the sheer volume and mixture of people living there, which is fine some of the time, but I'm supposed to be a young professional (although I rarely feel like both of those things at the same time). Still, living in Soho is the dream, so I'm trying to make it happen. It finally seems on the horizon, as I'm due a promotion at work, which comes with a nice pay bump – a bump that means I'll be able to finally get my own swanky place.

I'm hoping the pay increase might help me to feel a bit better about my job too – the fact that I'm really not enjoying it any more. Well, it's hard to write about all things love and dating when no one outside your family loves you and you haven't dated anyone in ages. It's just such a demoralising time to be playing the dating game and, given that I'm expected to write all about it too, it forces you to over-analyse everything. Plus, everything is so tech driven these days. It's all apps and algorithms, and while I do prefer to be ghosted on an app than stood up in person, I don't enjoy inputting data into programs that tell me how loveable I am.

But that's the job, doing all of these things in the name of finding love, writing about how it plays out. I still try to keep an optimistic tone to my work – no one would want to read it if I didn't – but for me, finding love is just work, it's not something I'm actively looking for, it's just all part of the day job. I do realise how depressing that sounds, but trust me, no matter how much you enjoy doing something, as soon as it's work, it sucks all the fun out. They say if you do something you love you'll never work a day in your life. I disagree. I sometimes wonder, if I did find someone and then settled down with them, whether or not I could even do my job any more, and I like to think that perhaps for that reason I self-sabotage all my relationships, for the good of my career, but it's not true, I'm a jaded old cynic – and at just thirty-four years old too.

Today I'm an extremely late jaded old cynic. I scan my pass to get through the barriers in the lobby and, as I make my way towards the lifts, I notice that one of them is on the ground floor, the doors just about to close.

I do that painfully awkward fast walk, the kind you see so often in this country, that is more a sign of intent than an actual increase in speed. Sure enough, it does its job. One of the men in the lift sees me hurrying towards them and quickly presses the button to open the doors again.

'Thank you,' I say as I practically dive through them, not unlike a shattered marathon runner charging past the finish line (although clearly in much worse shape because all I have done is hurry from the bus stop to here).

As the doors close behind me, I breathe a huge sigh of relief. I could almost be convinced to smile, were it not for the fact that only a few seconds later the lift grinds to a premature halt.

I feel my eyes widen as I look to my lift mates. There are two of them, the one who held the door for me and another guy who quickly takes a leadership role.

'Hello?' he says as he pushes the alarm button. 'Helloooo?'

Nothing. He glances at his friend, then at me.

'Oi,' he tries again. 'Some of us have got actual work to do.'

The Cactus is home to Mediworldwide, the big bad company which owns *Stylife Magazine*, along with a handful of other news outlets, and a rolling news channel. This building is home to *Yum Things*, the food magazine, as well as ByteBanter, a popular tech website. Somehow, I can tell, just by looking at these two guys, that they are from the tech website. They must be. The guy angrily mashing at the emergency button is wearing a plaid shirt, it doesn't get any more tech than that, does it? They both have a sort of cool vibe about them, which sounds vague, but it's a genuine coolness that can't really be defined. Like the coolest boys at school. They get the girls, get the attention, get away with murder. If only they could get this lift going.

'A different approach might be better,' the man who held the lift for me suggests. He looks more stylish than his friend, in a soft white shirt and jeans. He's got a pair of sunglasses hooked on his shirt, where his top two buttons are undone. He looks like he should be on the deck of a party yacht somewhere off the Amalfi coast, not heading into the office on a baking hot July day – and definitely not trapped in a lift.

'What do you mean, a different approach?' his friend asks.

'Well, a nicer one,' he teases with a smile.

'Oh, yeah, go on then,' he replies. 'Let's see if they pay attention to someone who looks like a young Paul Rudd.'

'Surely that's just a Paul Rudd,' I say, clearly having nothing to offer but a joke in this trying time. They both stare at me. 'Because, you know, he's always looked the same age.'

I explain the joke, not that I think they didn't get it, I'm sure we can all agree Paul Rudd hasn't aged a day in his life, I just don't think they were expecting me to say anything.

The Paul Rudd lookalike smiles. He does kind of look like him, with his short dark hair and his friendly yet cheeky smile. He's clearly younger than I know Paul Rudd to be, though. He looks about my age. His friend is maybe a little older, also with dark hair, but his short, overly neat beard gives them a bit of a good-cop-bad-cop vibe.

'Paul' – the only thing I can think to call him to distinguish between the two – steps forward, turns up his smile a few notches, leans into the keypad camera and pushes the button. He holds his smile as he waits patiently. Still no one replies.

Why, oh why, does stuff like this only happen at the worst possible times? Not that there's ever a good time to be stuck in a lift, but today of all days, when I'm late for work, and when the Monday morning editorial meeting always takes place, which I am mostly certainly going to be walking into the middle of, if I even make it at all.

'Well, there you go,' the first man says with an amused smugness. 'Nice guys really do finish last.'

Right on cue, the lift starts moving again and it's 'Paul' who gets to smile.

'I definitely did that,' 'Paul' says.

'Oh, yeah, of course you did,' his friend replies.

The lift stops on their floor first – the ByteBanter floor, as I predicted. The first man hurries out, but 'Paul' flashes me that grin of his first, an acknowledgement of what we just went through together, and a goodbye too, after the longest (what was probably only) four minutes of my life. It does cross my mind to get out while I can, and take the stairs the rest of the way, but the doors are closed again before I can act on it. It's probably for the best, because I can't even imagine the state I'd be in, after dragging my unfit arse up a few flights of stairs.

It's hard to celebrate (although it is totally appreciated) when the lift finally arrives on the *Stylife* floor, and I have to make the dash of a girl who is so very clearly very late, through reception, down the hallway and into the conference room where we have our editorial meetings.

I burst through the doors – and I don't just mean that in the way people usually do when they're late, I mean that I quite literally (but entirely accidentally) go at them a little too hard, pushing the double doors wide open, banging them on the side tables inside the conference room.

I am not surprised to see everyone staring at me. But I am surprised to see a person who is not my editor leading the meeting.

'Oh,' I blurt unintentionally.

'Oh, indeed,' she repeats back to me.

Suddenly I don't feel like I'm at work. I feel like I'm back at school, being chewed out by an angry teacher in front of a class full of kids, who would all be going 'oooh', like they knew I was in trouble, if they weren't too scared to open their mouths.

I remember being in Year 9, starting a new school, and not

being able to find my humanities classroom for the first time. I flagged a teacher down, asked her for directions, and she told me it was on the corridor adjacent to the one we were standing on. I was thirteen and had no idea what an adjacent corridor was so I was late – a whole seven minutes late – and Ms White gave me one hell of a precedent-setting dressing-down in front of everyone.

The look on her face was the same look as the one on the woman standing in front of me, except it isn't Ms White, who in hindsight was small and squeaky and not all that scary, it's someone who looks like Gwyneth Paltrow's forty-something sister, only a version who takes herself far more seriously. She stands up in her place. She must be 5'10" which means she towers not only above everyone sitting around her but, at 5'5" myself, I definitely feel like a kid again.

'You're our late one, I take it?' she says.

'Yes, sorry, I'm Frankie George, the Love & Dating writer,' I admit, because for some reason it comes out like an admission, rather than a fact.

'Oh, wonderful,' she says, in no way trying to mask her sarcasm. 'It's a wonder we were getting by without you.'

'I'm so sorry I'm late,' I say as I sheepishly take my usual seat next to my friend Cora. She subtly widens her eyes at me. Something is going on. 'I encountered so many delays on my way to work. I missed my bus, saw someone get mugged, I was mistaken for someone else and then, to top it all off, the lift broke down.'

'A quick word of advice,' the new woman starts as she takes her seat again. 'If you're going to make an excuse for your lateness, pick one and stick with it. It will be an easier sell. Now. For those of you who are new to the room...' Me, then. 'My name is Addison Anderson, the new editor of *Stylife Magazine* and website, and I'm here to shake things up. I'm going to be bringing new people in, getting rid of some of the dead wood, you are very much going to have to sing for your supper, so what better way to show me your worth than in this editorial meeting... or so you would think. So far, I am so unimpressed.'

I force a nervous dry swallow, which only makes my throat feel tighter. A new editor? What about Jane? My former editor, I suppose – but she was the one who was promoting me, and while I'm hesitant to say money is everything, that pay rise is everything to me. It's my key to a new apartment where I can live on my own like a real adult, not squashed into a tired old place with four housemates on the other side of the river to where my life is. I need this job. Now it sounds like things are up in the air.

'Next up, Emma, beauty, what have you got for me?' Addison asks.

'Erm, okay, so,' Emma starts, her confidence slowly building with each word. 'I was thinking eyebrows. The evolution of the brow, the thin, the thick, HD, laminated – basically a timeline of all the trends, maybe a fun look at what might be next.'

Emma's confidence builds to a point before it starts to quickly fade. I've just met Addison, so I don't know how to read her yet, but she doesn't look impressed. Perhaps that's just her face?

'Trash,' Addison says simply. 'I tell you what you're going to do, you're going to write me a piece on botched cosmetic procedures, the kind everyone and their bestie is getting, fillers, Botox. If you want to throw eyebrows in, go ahead, perhaps some microblade horror stories, but I do want them to be horror stories, I want gory pictures, I want readers who don't want to look but can't look away – I'm sorry, are we here to eat breakfast, or are we here to try to justify our jobs and hopefully put out something worth reading?'

Addison switches from destroying Emma's idea to calling out Lauren from Travel for having the audacity to eat the croissant on the table in front of her.

Fuck, this is bad. This is so bad.

'You think you can handle that, Emma?' Addison asks her, getting back on track.

Emma nods.

'Right, finally,' Addison continues. 'Frankie, Love & Dating, department of one. I'm supposed to work out if we're hiring above or below you so go on, dazzle me. But it better not be the usual, the online dating bore, "I went on Matcher and only matched with people who reminded me of my dad" or "Ten ways to tell if you're a Tinder tease" or some equally dull, depressing, demoralising drivel.'

Wow. I look down at my notepad and blink a few times. My first idea, Matcher-maker, involves swapping phones with a friend and working the dating apps on behalf of one another, to see if we're better at selling our friends than ourselves. My other ideas are all similar. Of course they are. That's all I've been allowed to write since online and app dating became so big. What else is there to talk about? People don't meet people like they used to, not without tech, and my trip to work this morning only proved that to me.

'Oh, nothing like that,' I insist as I rummage around in my brain for an idea I shelved years ago, or something, anything. The events of this morning buzz around my head like an annoying fly.

'Come on, Frankie, we're all on the edge of our seats,' Addison presses me. I'm starting to think her sarcastic nature is her most obvious characteristic.

'So, the dating app things have been done to death,' I start, basically saying what she said, and she's frowning at me like I'm stating the obvious, but I just need to buy myself some time, time to think of an idea. 'People don't meet like they used to, right? Well, that got me thinking, how did people used to meet, before they had apps, and the answer is... meet cutes.'

Addison cocks her head.

'Er, what's meet cutes?' Lauren asks. I notice she's managed to eat her croissant while Addison has been distracted.

'You know, in TV shows and movies, when two love interests meet for the first time, that's a meet cute. It's a popular romcom trope. Think *Notting Hill* when Hugh Grant literally bumps into Julia Roberts and spills a drink down her, or in *What Happens in Vegas* where Cameron Diaz and Ashton Kutcher accidentally check in to the same hotel room,' I explain.

For the first time, Addison displays something that resembles interest.

'Go on,' she prompts me.

'What I'm thinking,' I start and, yes, I am making this up as I go along, 'is that I could take a bunch of these classic meet cutes and try to put myself in those positions, to see if it helps trigger a romantic connection. No apps, no websites, just real people, out in the real world, in real situations – real in that they're in real life, obviously they'll be set-up scenarios.'

My pitch doesn't finish as strong as it started but cut me some slack, I am making this up on the spot.

'An idea that doesn't suck,' Addison says simply. 'There's hope for us yet.'

Suddenly it feels like summer is over before it's even begun. Ordinarily it would take more than a frosty reception from an ice-cold new boss to bring about climate change, but it's more than that. Summers in this office are usually a delight. The heat outside is kept at bay by a combination of good air conditioning and ice-cream runs, the beautiful weather and long days keep everyone smiling, and for those weeks while the sun is out, you'd be surprised how many afternoons are cut short to go and sit in beer gardens. Now it's seeming like it's going to be a season of stress, of proving our worth, of fighting for our jobs.

I sigh heavily as I make my way back to my desk. Everyone disperses in silence and slinks back in a similar manner.

Considering the fact I was late, it's a miracle that I somehow came out of that meeting on top. Well, sort of on top. I don't know, she didn't tell me that my idea was trash or scream at me for eating a pastry, but it's hard to consider it a win. Especially because now, when it comes to this big idea Addison loves so much, I'm going to have to come up with the damn thing and hope it works. I can kiss goodbye to my new apartment if I don't.

3

Addison Andrews is going to be a massive pain in my arse – I can already tell.

It sounds like she is bad news for everyone here too.

Our office space is all open-plan, apart from the conference rooms and – of course – Addison's office. When Jane was in charge, the door to that office was almost always kept open. Jane would close it if she needed to take a call, so we all kind of knew not to bother her when it was closed, but when it was open, we would wander in and out, and she would pop out for a chat or to take our Friday afternoon ice-cream orders. It was nice and relaxed. A genuinely wonderful environment to work in.

Addison's office door is closed – but Addison isn't behind it. Instead, what she has opted to do, to get a feel for how we work, is wander around our desks like an exam invigilator, watching us, breathing down our necks. I feel like she's looking for us doing something – anything – wrong so that she can yell at us.

So, when she has briefly stepped into her office to make a call, or popped to the break room, or wandered off for any reason, that's when we jump at the chance to talk about her. I don't know if all of what people are saying is true, or if it's like that game we used to play as kids, where you would sit in a circle and whisper things to the person next to you, except it would change as the game went on and become something completely different by the end of the game.

Information about Addison that has reached my ears so far includes all the different publications she's edited, rock stars she has dated, and people she has fired. One thing that is crystal clear is that it's sort of Addison's thing, that she takes up a job as editor, cleans house, hires new people, generally shakes things up, and then leaves. Ultimately, she leaves the publication in better shape than she found it, but not without leaving a pile of casualties in her wake, and considering the fact that one of the bits of info to hit my desk earlier today was that Addison fired her own cousin at one newspaper she worked at, no one is safe, are they?

My friend Cora, who writes for the Home section, sits at the desk facing mine. It's been a long morning and we're bursting to talk, but we make do with exchanging glances, rolling our eyes, biting lips, scrunching noses – when you're friends with someone for a long time, you develop these ways of communicating without exchanging a single word.

'I'm going out to get a coffee,' Addison announces. 'I'll be back shortly.'

She disappears out of the door next to us. Cora and I give her a couple of safety minutes, to make sure she's gone, before we both start talking at the same time. I pause to let her go first.

'Oh my God, what a nightmare,' Cora says. 'What the hell has happened to Jane?'

'I messaged her,' I reply. 'They've sacked her. Poor sales and hits on the decline, apparently. They didn't even want her to work her notice, they just asked her not to come back, I can't believe it.'

'I've been working on some new pitches but now I feel like all my ideas are crap – you missed me pitching. It was not pretty.'

The look on Cora's face tells me everything I need to know.

I love Cora. We started working here around the same time, so we initially bonded over our newbie status, but then we realised we had everything in common – including our birthday. You would think we were twins, were it not for the fact we look nothing alike. Cora is so stylish. Her long dark-brown hair is so straight and so neat it almost doesn't resemble the texture of hair any more. I, on the other hand, have my long hair with a dark root, mostly blonde lengths, but with a few little flashes of purple, and I usually wear it wavy to hide the fact that years of peroxide and heated styling tools have left it a little frizzy.

Cora has really good cheekbones. I assume I must have cheekbones, given that I have a face, but there's no sign of them. I have more of a round face, which I try to fix with contouring and highlighting. I like my make-up to be bold, to make a statement. I know that Cora wears a ton of make-up, I've watched her get ready for nights out enough times now, but I'm sure you'll know what I mean when I say that you can't actually see any of it on her face.

'How about I help you with your pitches if you help me with mine – what I need is ideas for these meet cutes,' I tell her.

'I have a few ideas,' Addison says, appearing from... I have no idea where.

We both jump out of our skin.

'Addison, hi,' I say, trying not to sound like she's just caught me out, but I feel like she has. I'm not even sure what she's caught me out with but, still, that's the level of intense authority I'm getting from her.

'Didn't you just say you were going to get a coffee?' Cora says bravely.

Addison bats her hand before pulling up a desk chair to sit next to us.

'An old management trick,' she tells us proudly. 'Pretend to leave the room and see what the workforce are saying about you when they think you're not listening. I heard you talking about your piece. It's a very exciting concept. I'm not sure it's been done before. I've looked over your work here, and I've certainly never seen you do anything like this. I saw lots of millennial bullshit. Although I do admire the savagery of some of your work. That time you only matched with people who you thought were unattractive.'

Addison cackles as she slaps her thigh.

'I, er...' I start, but she doesn't let me finish.

'Absolutely savage,' she says again.

In my defence, that isn't strictly the concept of that article, what I did was only match with people I wasn't instantly attracted to based on their pictures alone. Of course, it turned out that was just most of the men on Matcher, because I've always found it hard to fancy someone based on nothing more than their appearance, and they were all the same usual dating app kind of weirdo/arsehole anyway.

'Thanks,' I say anyway.

'I'm actually really excited about this,' she says. 'You, Cara, was it?'

'Cora,' she politely corrects her.

'Cora, maybe take a bit of time off writing about your candles or whatever and help us devise some meet cutes.'

'Oh, I've got loads of ideas, don't worry,' I insist. It's not that I don't want Cora's help, we always bounce our ideas off one another, it's more the case that I don't want Addison here breathing down my neck while I try to pretend that I know what I'm doing.

'It sounds like fun,' Addison insists. 'So, let's talk romcoms.'

'Maybe if we start with our favourites?' Cora suggests.

'That's a great idea,' Addison replies. I can see Cora's relief, to have said something right, to have impressed the new boss in even just a small way. 'Mine is *Pretty Woman*.'

I stare at her for a second but she's not kidding.

'Oh, okay,' I say. 'Well, to be honest, if I can avoid prostitution, I would prefer it.'

'What about *What Happens in Vegas*?' Cora suggests.

Yes, absolutely, send the two of us to Vegas, I'm begging you!

'We could maybe do a local version, or something similar-ish,' Addison says thoughtfully. 'Maybe you could just hang around at a hotel bar and wait for a man to pick you up.'

'I'm not sure the tone of that is all that meet cute,' Cora chimes in. 'Getting "picked up".'

'I'm sure it would work,' I offer politely. 'But, yes, the tone is still a bit *Pretty Woman*, possibly.'

'Okay. *Sleepless in Seattle*. Maybe a tourist destination,' Addison continues. 'You could ask a man to take you up the Shard?'

'Well, that would definitely work,' I joke cheekily.

'Hmm, I'll have a think about it,' Addison says thoughtfully. 'I really will go and get that coffee. Or find someone to go get it for me, I suppose. But you keep working on this. We'll have a strategy meeting tomorrow, see what we each come up with overnight.'

'I really appreciate your help,' I lie. 'But I've got loads of ideas, I'll get to them right away. I might even try one tonight.'

Also a lie.

'Strategy meeting tomorrow,' she says, ignoring me.

I watch her walk away this time, waiting until she's clearly out of earshot before I open my mouth again.

'Wow, she's hands-on,' I whisper.

'I hate it,' Cora admits. 'She loves your idea, though. Look at her, she clearly wants to be involved. What are you going to try tonight?'

'Honestly, I have no idea,' I confess. 'I was just trying to get her off my back, to get her to leave me to it.'

'Ah,' she replies with a sympathetic chuckle. 'Well, you might want to think of something, or Addison will be thinking of stuff for you. Cough. *Pretty Woman*. Cough.'

I slump back into my desk chair. She's right. God knows what Addison is going to have lined up for me if I don't come up with something myself. I'll work on it tonight, come up with some sort of plan of attack. I didn't exactly think this through, given the fact that I came up with it on the spot, with the new office dragon breathing down my neck, but I'm starting to realise this idea isn't going to be as easy as I'd hoped. I have to pull it off, though, somehow. My promotion (and therefore my new flat) depends on it.

4

I don't hate any of my flatmates. Hate is a very strong word. I don't exactly get on with all of them, or all of their partners, but nothing is bad enough with any individual that I would use the H word. I do, however, hate that there are four of them. Four flatmates, each with their own partner who often stays the night – there's always at least one extra person here. I know, it sounds like I'm bitter, because I'm the only single one, but it's not that.

The five of us live in a five-bed ground-floor maisonette. I feel like the landlord calls it a maisonette – and we do for the exact same reason – because it sounds better than calling it a flat. But it is a ground-floor flat. The only reason you can call it a maisonette is, basically, I think, because it has a front door, rather than a communal entrance. It's hardly worthy of a special name, especially because it has a real student digs vibe about it. It's old and tired. We have two bathrooms between the five (or sometimes *nine*) of us, one with a shower and one with a bath, except the bath has silverfish so no one ever uses it. The mouldy grouting alone was enough to put me off having a dip, never mind a bug infestation. I was lucky enough (if that's not too strong a term for something so bleak) that my designated toilet is the one in the other bathroom. I don't like the idea of sitting in the bug bathroom for even a minute.

Other than our bedrooms, the only space we have is an L-shaped living-kitchen-dining space. Initially an open-plan space seemed like a great idea but that one room seems pretty small when enough of us are in it. There's a three-seater sofa, a dining table pushed up to the wall with four chairs, and a U-shaped kitchen. When you've got two people trying to cook in the kitchen, two watching TV, and one sitting at the table (and that's without any partners in the mix) you can't move, you can't hear – you can't think straight. I can't face it, spending time in the cramped living room or my tiny bedroom, with only the bug-infested bath to escape to.

It's summer at the moment, which makes things slightly easier. We have a little private paved area just outside a patio door off the living room. It's only small, with a tired material canopy pulled over a mismatched arrangement of furniture (some of it, like the faux leather chair from an old three-piece suite, definitely indoor furniture), which means that on lovely evenings like tonight, the living room extends into the garden.

'We just need to think of genre tropes,' Travis suggests helpfully as he swigs a bottle of cider.

I know you're not supposed to have a favourite flatmate, but Travis Carter is mine. He's an assistant director, most recently working on popular fantasy show *Bragadon Forrest*, one of the only shows we can all agree to get together and watch as a household. He, like me, is also saving up to find somewhere better to live, so he gets it. He's also, lucky for me, one of the best people to talk to about my latest project, because genre theory was his 'thing' when he was at uni.

'Okay, hit me,' I say. I pull my legs up onto the plastic garden chair I'm sitting on.

'*First Love* is an easy one,' he suggests.

'I'm nipping that one in the bud,' I reply quickly. 'I'd need to be pretty desperate before I'd call up an ex-boyfriend for anything, never mind under the pretence of wanting to get something going again.'

'Got it,' he replies. 'This one should be easy: *Coitus Ensues*.'

He wiggles his eyebrows.

'Ha!' I cackle. 'Yes, sure, okay, I'll hit up the long line of men wanting to shag me.'

'What does that mean?' Laila asks, returning with a cider, before plonking herself down on the arm of the faux leather chair Travis is sitting on.

Laila Richardson is Travis's girlfriend. They met on set, where she was playing a 'peripheral fairy' – that's an extra to you and me.

'It's how we got together,' he tells her through a cheeky smile.

'What, banging in a caravan because we were bored waiting for my scene?' she replies with a scoff.

'Yep,' he confirms. 'It's when two people wind up having sex.'

'Oh,' she says with a shrug. 'Cool.'

I can't help but laugh.

'Obviously I'm not doing that one,' I say before taking a sad swig from my drink. Chance would be a fine thing.

'What about *Enemies to Lovers*?' Travis says. 'Anyone who hates your guts?'

'Sascha is in the kitchen, complaining to Marcus and his boyfriend about how you left purple hair dye in the shower,' Laila tells me, lowering her voice. 'She said she would have killed you if it had stained. She said she'd be getting her three grand deposit back from you, one way or another.'

'What an excessively violent overreaction,' I say, not all that fussed by it. That's Sascha through and through. Hilariously, it was her fault I had to abandon rinsing my hair, to go and let the maintenance man in. No one else was answering the door so I assumed she wasn't in, until I got back to the bathroom and found her standing there, with a face almost as purple as the shower flow. I was annoyed at her for not answering the door, she was mad at me for the 'state' of the bathroom – which rinsed away instantly, might I add – but that's just Sascha. There's no love lost between us. I overhear her complaining to Rhys, her boring boyfriend, all the time. Marcus and his boyfriend Alan will be loving it – Marcus is always complaining about anyone who is messier than him, and he is an extreme neat freak. It doesn't bother me, it just motivates me to move ASAP.

'But, no, no enemies that I know of,' I say.

'No pending "will they, won't they"?' he continues.

'No pending anything,' I reply.

Wow, I thought we were brainstorming, not analysing the state of my non-existent love life.

'No unresolved sexual tension? With anyone but me, obviously. Possibly Laila too,' he jokes. I think it's supposed to make me feel better, but it just makes things seem all the more tragic.

'Sadly not,' I reply sarcastically. I mean, it's true, but I'm styling it out.

'Okay, well, let's go for something a bit vaguer,' he says, unwilling to give up yet.

'What are we up to?' Darcy asks.

She and her boyfriend, Tris, sit down on the wooden bench.

I like Darcy. She's in the room next to me and she's a nice, quiet neighbour. She hasn't been with Tris for very long, but he seems cool too.

'I need to come up with offline ways of meeting people for an article I'm writing,' I tell them. 'And try them out.'

'She told her boss she'd be doing one this evening,' Travis tells them. 'But so far we've got nothing.'

'What about something really old-fashioned?' Darcy suggests.

'Like her dad offering her hand in marriage to the local rich fella?' Travis jokes.

'Not that old,' she says with a smile and a roll of her eyes.

'Like *Chitty Chitty Bang Bang*?' I suggest with a laugh. 'I don't have a car and driving one into the Thames wouldn't quite have the same effect anyway.'

'I've got my car with me,' Tris chimes in. 'I'm driving back to Birmingham in the morning but I'm not doing anything with it tonight.'

I cock my head thoughtfully.

'Actually, that could be a great shout,' I say. 'What if I broke down, and stood all helpless at the side of the road? Someone would stop and help me, surely?'

'Ooh, especially if we get you all dolled up,' Darcy suggests.

'I was going to go for a run before dinner,' Tris continues. 'I could leave you somewhere with my car. It's a piece of crap. In fact, it doesn't even start on the first try. I have to turn the key and sit for a few minutes before the engine will start.'

'Are you sure you don't mind?' I ask through a laugh. 'This could be a really good way to kick things off.'

'Yeah, come on, let's do it, it will be funny,' Tris replies.

'Let's go get you looking ladylike and helpless,' Darcy says, jumping to her feet.

'I can help,' Laila adds excitedly.

Now isn't the time to take issue with the fact I am supposedly not ladylike, now is the time for action. Here goes nothing, it's time for my first meet cute.

5

I'm never quite sure how to describe my style.

My mum would probably describe me as 'still a mosher' in reference to my school days when I wore gigantic baggy jeans, a disturbing amount of fishnet, and so much black eye make-up I'm pretty sure some of it is still there. I always made it my own, though, and always moved with the trends. I wore my Elizabeth Duke clown necklace with the best of them.

I suppose I'm still the same. I still very much have my own sense of style, and it's not that I'm not girly, I'm just not the soft, flowery kind of girly. Well, not usually, but today is not a usual day.

I'm currently standing at the side of the road, next to one of those places with the floodlit five-a-side pitches, where people go to play football on evenings and weekends. Well, what better place to happen upon groups of men, or have them happen upon me, technically, than football grounds?

I'm here, next to Tris's old banger of a car, safe in the knowledge that if I were to try to start it, it wouldn't start, so when someone does decide to try to rescue this damsel in distress, it will seem genuine.

What may not come across as genuine is me. In this outfit, I not only don't feel myself, but I feel positively awkward.

Darcy is very much a girly girl. Her long brown naturally curly hair floats down almost as far as her waist. Her clothes always follow a similar theme. Light, loose materials that cascade down her body. Travis always jokes that she looks like someone who appears to you during a dream sequence, but everything is a movie or a TV show to him.

So, in an effort to make me a little more Truly Scrumptious, and a little less truly tragic, Darcy has let me borrow a dress. It's a long cream frilly thing that makes me feel like Miss Havisham, but needs must so I'm trying to style it out. I feel like a total tit, though. It's funny that more material could make me feel more self-conscious. Before I was wearing a short black strapless dress and somehow felt far more at ease.

It's a couple of minutes to seven, which means that the people playing right now should be wrapping up. I'm in the perfect position for catching the eye of anyone leaving, they'll all be coming down this road, so all I need to do is wait.

I practise my pose. First I try leaning against the car, in a sad attempt at sexy, like, who do I think I am, Shania Twain circa 'That Don't Impress Me Much'? I'm certainly not impressing anything with this poor show of posture. I pull myself to my feet. Okay, I need people to know I'm broken down, so maybe I should stand by the bonnet. Tris showed me how to open it, if I needed to, so I'll do that and then, I don't know, stand helplessly next to it? It's ironic that I can't quite seem to figure out how to look stupid next to a car, but in a way I'm pretty sure I'm already doing it.

I notice two sweaty men in shorts carrying boot bags walking this way. Okay, Frankie, here we go. It's showtime.

I try to look forlorn. I make eye contact. I stare expectantly.

'All right?' one of the men says to me, giving me one of those singular nods fellas around my age seem to be so fond of.

I smile, then open my mouth to speak, but that's all I'm getting. They continue on their way.

Okay, fine, they were on foot. Perhaps they don't know anything about cars? Why would they if neither of them drives? I just need to focus my attention on the road.

A car exits the grounds and passes me. Then another one. Then another one. Hmm, maybe this was a stupid idea. It relies on many factors that, realistically, were never going to fall into place for me. For one thing, it depends on the kindness of strangers, and that's not really something I've ever found to be that reliable. It also depends on people either knowing how to help, or finding me attractive enough to try, and here I am looking like the fucking Ghost of Christmas Past.

Right when it seems as though all hope is lost, a minibus grinds to a stop in front of me. Oh my God, it worked, someone has stopped to help me, and not just one man but a whole (admittedly tiny, but still) busload has turned up.

I straighten my big frilly dress and fix my posture, ready to try to sell myself as stranded, wondering what I should look out for someone doing before I turn the key at just the right time to make the car start.

I can't help but laugh to myself softly when it's a women's team that gets off the bus. You can always rely on women and, credit where it's due, they all rally round me right away.

'Having car trouble?' a tall blonde asks.

'Erm, yes,' I reply. 'Don't worry, my boyfriend is on the way to help me.'

I don't want to waste their time. I feel especially bad now that they've stopped to help me. I grab my phone and text Tris, telling him I'm finished when he is.

'Is your boyfriend a mechanic?' she asks with a smile. 'Because Katie is.'

Katie, a petite brunette, steps forward and gives me a wave.

'Oh, honestly, please don't go to any trouble,' I insist.

'It's no trouble at all,' Katie replies. 'Let's have a look.'

The others chat politely to me as Katie gets to work. I keep an eye on her, wondering if perhaps she can tell that I'm basically faking it, or if the problem will just seem like simply that. A problem.

'Try to start it now,' Katie suggests.

I do as I'm told by both her and Tris. The car starts.

I thank everyone multiple times as they're leaving. Seconds later, Tris returns.

'How did it go?' he asks.

'Men suck,' I tell him. 'Present company excluded. It was a minibus full of women who stopped to help. One of them was a mechanic.'

'Well, I feel like I've been taught a valuable lesson in sexism today,' he says with a thoughtful laugh.

'Yeah, at this point, I'm not actually sure what we need men for,' I joke. 'Thanks so much for letting me use the car.'

'You're welcome,' he replies. 'I'm happy whatever is wrong with it could come in useful for once.'

'Oh, that reminds me, Katie, the mechanic, said that you might have something wrong with your transmission, your oil needs topping up, and two of your tyres aren't legal.'

Tris's face falls.

'Wow, expensive experiment for me, then,' he says with a sigh.

'Sorry,' I reply. 'At least the check-up was free.'

That's the only silver lining of this little experiment – if it even counts as a silver lining. Ah well, it's back to the drawing board, I suppose. This really isn't going to be as easy as I'd hoped.

6

I may have gone to bed in a defeatist mood, but I refuse to wake up in one. I have to make this meet cute thing work. I have to impress Addison and I have to get my dream apartment.

I also have to get some better ideas because last night was so bad I'm tempted to not even mention it in my article.

I did come up with an idea to try on my way to work, so that's what I'm doing now.

Every day, my journey to work is the same. I walk to the same coffee shop I go to every day, I catch a bus, then the Tube, then I walk the final stretch to the office. With the exception of me missing the occasional bus, or the bus being delayed, I can always rely on my journey to stay the same. Sure, I see some weird and wonderful things, but even the fact that I see unusual things and people is really quite usual for me now. So, given how predictable my day is, I can also count on seeing the same people too.

There are the people who serve me my coffee – sure, they're on a rota, with different people working on different days, but it's the same people. I even see the same people on public transport. Not just the drivers, but the passengers too. So many people are like me, making the same journey every day, all probably going to their jobs too. We're all just trying to survive the commute, keeping our heads down, listening to music, reading books, sucking down double-shot coffees to feel alive. I know better than to strike up a conversation with someone on the Tube – I would hate it if someone wanted to small-talk me when all I wanted to do was go back to bed – and that wouldn't be much of a meet cute anyway.

There's a man who is always on the same bus as me – sometimes we'll even end up sitting next to each other. I've noticed that, to pass the time, he'll either listen to podcasts on his phone, or he'll read a book.

This man is in his early forties – I don't know if he's tall or short because he gets on the bus before me, and off after me, but I'm going to lean on the side of tall because his body seems quite long. Suddenly I feel like a psycho, saying I notice what he's doing on his phone, and how long his body is. I'm not going to bother him, though, I'm just going to give him the opportunity to talk to me, if he wants to. Well, what could be more meet cute than finally talking to the good-looking man I see on my commute every day?

I laid in bed last night wondering how I could get him to talk to me. No, I'm not going to do anything even slightly similar to the shitshow from last night, I came up with something more subtle instead.

One of the things I couldn't help but notice is that he's been reading the *Dune* novels. He doesn't read every day, and he doesn't read quickly. The last time I spotted him reading one, it was the second book in the series. What I decided to do, to make him think we could have things in common and that he should chat to me, is buy a *Dune* book, but not the one he's reading, the next one in the series, just in case he tries to get all book clubby with me and wants to talk about the plot. If I'm further along than he is, then I can simply say I don't want to talk about the plot in case I spoil it for him and, on the super off-chance that this does result in us falling madly in love, well, I'll just watch the movie and style it out from there.

So, I got up early, I headed to my local bookshop, and I picked up a copy of *Children of Dune*. Then I went for my coffee, caught my usual bus, and here I am, sitting right where he can see me, reading my book. Well, I'm not reading-it reading it. I tried to read a little, but it didn't make a lick of sense to me. I don't know if that's because I'm starting with the third book (possibly) or because it's too complex for someone like me (more than likely). The only problem is that he isn't looking up. His eyes have been firmly fixed on his phone all morning. For goodness' sake, I can't catch a break.

We're nearing my stop now which is just typical. That's eight pounds down the drain, unless I actually plan on reading it, but then I'll need to buy the first two books, which is a bit of a sunk-cost fallacy given that I probably won't read those either.

The bus slows down as it reaches my stop. I need to think. How can I turn this around? I've noticed that, at my stop, the bus usually sits for a minute or two before it sets off again. I need to act now – and I need to cover all bases.

I quickly rummage around in my purse to find something – anything – with my name on it. Years ago, in an attempt to make us seem more professional, there was talk about giving us all business cards. They had prototypes made for everyone before deciding that the lowly writers didn't need them. I've had one business card sitting in my purse for God knows how long. I'm almost hesitant to part with it, but it has my name and where I work on it, this is my only shot. At least if my plan doesn't work, he'll know where to find me – tracking me down at work to return my book would definitely be a meet cute, but I'm hoping he'll run after me. I'm going to give him plenty of time to do so, and given that the bus hovers at this stop briefly, he'll have the time.

I place the business card on a random page, like a bookmark, and then when the bus finally stops I 'accidentally' drop my book on the floor right next to him. It lands with a slap, but I pretend not to notice. I get off the bus, walking slowly, but I don't hear anyone calling after me. I walk a few more steps before standing still on the spot. He'll be able to see me from his seat. Come on, guy, what are you doing? Eventually I turn around, only to see him somehow looking even more settled in his seat, reading my book. My jaw drops as the bus drives away.

Wow. I thought I was bad at meeting men the modern way. It turns out I'm crap at the old-fashioned way too.

7

My latest article is the talk of the office. Well, on the *Stylife* floor, at least. I doubt anyone at ByteBanter gives a damn about me renting out my love life like this.

It's all anyone wants to talk about – to me, at least. Cora is on hand, helping me work through my ideas, and Addison can't keep away, wanting to be involved as much as she can. I know she's the boss, and with that comes a certain level of control, but I feel like I'm a game of *The Sims* to her right now. She is genuinely jazzed at the thought of throwing me into different situations and seeing what happens.

There are some perks to being Addison's favourite project – for example, before our little think-tank session she sent her assistant out to get coffees and cupcakes. We have a great break room here, as well as a really nice canteen that serves the whole building, but Addison likes her coffee from a very specific place (and made by a very specific barista, it turns out) and her cupcakes from a certain bakery. As extra as it sounds, it certainly beats the coffee pods in the break room.

Addison is an interesting character. She's this ball-busting businesswoman, at the top of her game, who can fill any man, woman or child with fear. But, at the same time, you can see the human hiding inside her. She's clearly enjoying chatting to us, coming up with ideas, and I do get this sense that she's enjoying being one of the girls, having a laugh. I wonder what her friends are like in real life – I wonder if she has any who aren't scared of her? I've noticed she doesn't wear a wedding ring. I'd definitely be too scared to date her, and I can't exactly afford to be too fussy these days, can I?

We're currently discussing our favourite love stories to see if that helps us come up with anything.

'Mine is *Titanic*, but it always makes me think of my ex, for obvious reasons,' Cora says.

'Oh my God, did he drown?' Addison asks, clearly horrified.

'No!' Cora, who was looking a little glum thanks to Aaron creeping into her mind, can't help but laugh now. 'It was the movie we were watching together when we started arguing before we broke up later that night.'

When Cora and Aaron broke up after four years together, Cora was heartbroken, obviously. I had to move in with her for a week, comforting her, getting drunk together, cheering her up, giving her the green light to play on my dating apps, easing her back into talking to men and showing her what was out there, but with her using it on my behalf. No one needs another man that quickly.

Addison looks almost embarrassed, but only for a second. I imagine it's hard to feel embarrassed when you have so much self-confidence. That must be nice. Sometimes I feel embarrassed by my own existence.

'*True Romance* is one of my favourites,' Addison says.

'It's a great film,' I reply. 'But it's not as... classically romantic as the title suggests. And, once again, has a prostitute character.'

'Not a method actor, then,' Cora jokes.

'Sorry, I don't mean anything by it,' Addison says with a smile.

Her friendliness is nice but unnerving. I like that she's talking to me more like I'm a friend, I just need to remember that she is a friend who can fire me.

'Come on then, Frankie, what are your favourite romances?' she asks.

I think for a moment, and it becomes quickly apparent that there's a problem with my favourite love stories: they're all sad as hell. There's also largely impossible to replicate for this experiment and ultimately they are all generally quite depressing. *Moulin Rouge*, for example, is too specific (and tonally way off the mark), and *Brokeback Mountain* is off the cards for multiple reasons – the most obvious being that I'm not a cowboy. *Closer* is another film about love that I absolutely adore but, again, it's so depressing. It's more of a what-not-to-do than something I should be attempting to copy. Even *Ghost*, which has a sort of happy ending (well, as happy as you can get, given the circumstances), isn't any good to me either. I'm not going to kill a guy. Not yet, anyway.

'Perhaps my favourite romcoms might be closer to the mark,' I suggest. 'It's a bit late in the day to pull a *When Harry Met Sally*. I'm not a movie star so *Notting Hill* is out. Even my guilty pleasures like *Made of Honour* and *The Wedding Date* are out because, obviously, I don't know anyone who is getting married.'

'Does *The 40-Year-Old Virgin* count as a romcom?' Cora asks.

'Oi, you cheeky cow,' I joke. 'I'm not forty just yet, and that ship sailed a long time ago.'

Why is it suddenly so hard to think of meet cutes that are doable, upbeat and legal? And why are my favourite love stories so depressing? This is why I need to focus on the funny ones, because not only is it more helpful for the project, but it's almost concerning, thinking about how bleak my favourite love stories are. The fact I have work to do is the only thing staving off an existential crisis, but I'm pretty sure that's just true for everyone over thirty anyway.

'What about *13 Going On 30*?' Cora suggests. 'Not the part where you wish you were older and magically skip forward in time. Just, the whole first-love thing, there could be something in that?'

'Nope, I already vetoed this idea last night,' I insist.

'Such a strong response makes me think there might be an ex worth reaching out to?' Addison says thoughtfully.

'Hmm, well, let's see,' I start, before reining it in a little. 'I probably only have one ex of note and that note says that we were together four years before he cheated on me.'

'That note usually has more expletives in it,' Cora jokes, lightening the mood.

Cora held my hand through the whole ordeal. It was a few years ago now, I'm over it – over it to the point where it doesn't upset me or feel like all that much of a loss, but not so over it that I don't hope he's miserably single and will stay that way forever.

'We'll put a pin in that one,' Addison says surprisingly. I would have thought watching me in excruciating pain would be right up her street.

'Perhaps we should look at kids' films,' I say, changing the subject, taking a second cupcake and hoping that no one notices. I remember my gran used to say 'feed a cold, starve a fever' and I don't know how true it is but as far as me being stressed goes, that's definitely a beast I need to feed. People always go one of two ways when they're stressed, don't they? Too stressed to eat or too stressed not to. I wear my feelings on my sleeve in that respect – well, more like my arse, thighs and tummy, but you get my point. I remember someone who used to work in the fashion department telling me I could be a size ten if I just applied myself. Excuse me while I roll my eyes forever.

'*Cinderella* is an obvious one,' Addison offers.

'Except losing a shoe is just going to make me look like an idiot,' I say with a laugh. 'I'm sure it must be almost impossible for a grown adult to lose one shoe while they're going about their business.'

'We can probably rule out a fair chunk of Disney movies,' Cora says. '*Sleeping Beauty, Snow White, Aladdin*.'

'I never knew not being a princess was going to hold me back so much in life,' I muse through a smile.

I think back to the Disney films I loved when I was a kid.

'When I think of Disney movies that don't involve princesses, it's usually because they are about animals,' I point out.

'*Bambi*, anyone?' Addison jokes.

'*The Aristocats*,' Cora adds.

This isn't helpful but it is funny.

I rush through my childhood on fast forward. Eventually, something hits me.

'Oh,' I blurt, before pausing to make sure I'm not barking up the wrong tree – pun intended. 'What about *101 Dalmatians*?'

'I can't see you in a fur coat,' Cora teases.

It doesn't feel like we're getting anywhere, but at least we're having fun.

'I was thinking more along the lines of when Roger and Anita meet,' I say. 'It's their dogs that bring them together. A dog would be a great way to initiate a meet cute.'

'Fantastic idea,' Addison says with a clap of her hands. 'What sort of dog do you have?'

Perhaps now would have been a better time for that second cupcake.

'I don't have one,' I admit. I think for a moment. 'But that might not matter. Maybe I could just pretend that I did?'

'Nothing attracts a man like a woman hallucinating a dog,' Cora says sarcastically.

I gently twirl from side to side in my desk chair while I think my idea through. No more half-baked ideas. No more saying the first thing that pops into my head. I need to figure this thing out fully before I run it by the team. I know that I've probably said this before, but this one might actually work.

'Okay, I've got it,' I start proudly. 'I'll go to the park at lunchtime, walk around for a bit and then *pretend* I've lost my dog. Hopefully there will be lots of people around willing to help me look – and hopefully it will be men wanting to help this time. If any women try to get involved, I'll pretend to get a text saying someone has found the dog safe and sound. I can pretty much do that at any point, to nip things in the bud.'

'Well, if you agree a code word with Cora, you could message her, and she could call you, tell you the dog is home safe with your flatmate, and then that leaves you to hang around with the mystery man who stops to help you,' Addison says. 'You could be *sooo grateful* he offered to help that you just have to repay him.'

Cora and I both stare at her for a second.

'I mean buy him an ice cream or something,' she quickly adds. 'It will give you an excuse to sit and chat. Really get the meet cute going.'

'That's it, then. Finally, a good idea to try,' I say. 'I'll head to the park at lunchtime.'

'Take a longer lunch,' Addison tells me. 'It will be worth walking the extra, to go to Hyde Park, hopefully get a better class of gentleman.'

I'm not about to turn down a long lunch. Wow, there really are perks to being teacher's pet. I'm not under any illusions, I know that

Addison is just having fun with my project, I'm no better than anyone else here.

I'm just so happy that I finally have an idea that is seemingly foolproof.

What could possibly go wrong?

8

Is there anything better than a nice relaxing walk through the park on a hot summer's day?

It's one of those rare perfect days where it is lovely and warm and the sun is shining but there's a nice gentle cool breeze that takes the edge off. We're just not made for any other kind of summer day in this country. The only thing worse than London on a belting hot day is being inside an apartment with no air conditioning in the night that follows, lying on top of the covers, wriggling restlessly as you force warm air into your lungs and sweat the bed.

Today is just wonderful – and made all the more incredible by the fact that the off-the-shoulder dress I decided to wear is perfect for allowing the sun to kiss my skin. I've got a gigantic iced pink lemonade from a pop-up just outside the park, and my boss has pretty much given me the go-ahead to take as long a lunch as I need to, to try to make something happen. What more could I ask for? Aside from a better job, a nicer place to live, a ton of disposable income and a smoking-hot boyfriend. Oh, and an actual dog, obviously. I'm going to try and make it work, though.

After draining the last of my drink, I walk along the path further, looking for my... I want to say 'mark', is that right? Okay, so I'm hardly an internationally renowned con artist, but I am doing something covert, so let me play make-believe just this once. I'm pretty sure mark is the right term, but it's not like I'm going to be using it in the article, so I won't worry too much.

There's a young couple having a picnic – obviously they're not going to be any use to me. A group of friends drinking iced coffees – but they're all women, and I can't make that mistake again, plus, knowing my luck, one of them would probably turn out to be a vet, or a psychiatrist, and would rumble me right away. That's when I spot him – well, how could I not? He's huge. Like, Mr Universe huge. He's wearing shorts and one of those vests with the skinny straps buff fellas seem to like wearing because they show off their back muscles, all topped off with a backwards cap on his head and a pair of AirPods in his ears. He's sweaty, like he's been running, but he's currently standing on the grass doing squats. It looks surprisingly difficult for him, given how jacked he is, but that's probably because his legs are so big they can't make room for one another. I have a similar thing with my thighs if I try to wear a pencil skirt without any stretch, so I feel his pain. We're basically the same, right?

A woman with a pushchair passes him. Something somehow falls from the net pocket on the back of it. A stuffed panda. He notices and quickly grabs it before flagging her down, returning the toy, and then getting back to his exercise. How kind and helpful of him. Oh, he's going to be perfect. Exactly the kind of man I need.

I shudder. Bloody hell, Joe from *You* much? But then I laugh, because it's hardly the same thing, is it? This is just a harmless social experiment to see if meeting people offline is still a viable option. I'm not exactly a crazy stalker.

Right, here we go.

'Buddy,' I call out. 'Here, Buddy, where are you, Buddy?'

I try to sound as natural as possible, but I feel like, if I can't even kid myself, how on earth is anyone else going to fall for this stupid charade?

I purposefully move my one-woman search party in his direction, ramping up the visual dramatics because there's no way he'll be able to hear me if he has his music playing.

Sure enough, when he notices me searching for something, he squeezes the button on one of his pods to stop the noise.

'Hi, is everything all right?' he asks in a strong northern accent – Yorkshire, I think.

Time to make myself seem like a believable pet owner.

'Not really,' I lie. Well, I half lie. It isn't a lie, to say that everything isn't all right, because it's clearly not all right if it's come to this. 'It's my baby, I can't find him.'

'You've lost your baby?' he says, visibly panicked, which is what I should be.

'Oh, God, sorry, no,' I babble. If babbling were an Olympic sport, I would take the gold every time. Why did I say baby? For God's sake. I was trying to sound more like a pet owner, someone with an animal they loved, who was a part of their family, but I didn't stop to think that, you know, baby generally means baby to most people.

'My dog,' I correct myself. 'But he's, like, my baby, you know?'

Oh, *wow*! Give me an Oscar to go with those Olympic medals. What a performance. Not.

'That's okay, pets are important, they can feel like our children, but don't worry, I'll help you find him, okay?' the man replies. 'What does he look like, and where did you see him last?'

Both very good questions and both things I should have figured out before I put this plan into action. Time for some more world-class babbling.

'A pug,' I say, but that's too vague, I need to say something really specific, to make it more believable. I imagine a real dog owner would know exactly what their dog looked like. 'But not a fawn-coloured one, like most pugs are, one of the black and brown speckled ones. He's wearing a blue collar. And I think the last place I saw him was sort of over there.'

Am I nailing specific but vague? I think I might be.

'What, by the café? By the toilets?' he asks, expecting a little more detail, but clearly more than happy to be helping. What a good guy. He has definitely made me feel better after all the fellas at football gave the gender a bad name.

'Yes,' I reply. Now is the time to stay vague.

'Okay, I'll go look for you,' he says. 'You stay here, in case he comes back to where he saw you last, he might be looking for you too. Do you have his lead?'

Shit. Of course I don't. I could have at least bought a lead! Although props do make this feel slightly weirder, and I've already wasted money on the book, so I'd rather not take that extra step if I don't have to.

'I must have lost it somewhere,' I say. 'Actually, I think he might still have it attached to him.'

I should have just said the second thing. That makes the most sense. I'm clearly just a little bit too slow for this malarky.

'Listen, it's going to be okay,' the man reassures me with a squeeze of my shoulder. 'I'm Al, I'm going to help you find him, we're in this together.'

'Thank you,' I reply as he dashes off, before awkwardly calling after him, 'I'm Frankie.'

How is it possible that I've had to audacity to target the fittest man in the park (in both respects) and he's not only helping me but he's introduced himself and established physical contact? Dare I consider that this could be working?

Al charges off out of sight, which gives me the chance to take out my phone and send the code word to Cora. It's not really a word we agreed on, though, it's an emoji. A dog emoji, obviously. I don't even know why we need a code word, it's not like anyone else can see my phone. Anyway, it's definitely time to send it.

My phone makes that little swoosh noise it always makes when a message is successfully sent. Then I look up and see that Al has also been successful. Sort of.

'Here we go,' Al calls out proudly. 'I told you we'd find him!'

How the fuck has this man managed to find a missing dog that *I made up*?

'Erm,' I say quietly to myself.

There he is. A brown and black pug in a blue collar, with a blue lead hanging off his neck. Al has him cradled in his massive arms. It would be quite cute if I weren't panicking about how I'm going to get myself out of this one.

'I thought I'd better carry him,' he says. 'In case he gave me the slip too. Looks like he was looking around the café for food and thankfully his lead got tangled on something.'

I'm speechless. Absolutely speechless.

'Aw, he's a cute one,' Al says. He places the dog down on the floor before making a fuss of him. The dog loves it – at least it's a friendly one. 'Wow, that's an interesting name. How do you pronounce that?'

Luckily, Al didn't hear me calling out the name Buddy when I started looking. I'd say it was a mistake, to commit to a name, but obviously I didn't expect him to find me an actual dog.

Al is holding the dog's ID tag lightly in his fingertips. I quickly lean forward to catch a glimpse. The dog's name is Joachim. Erm...

'Jo-chim,' I say with a confidence I absolutely do not have. Truthfully, I have no idea how his name is pronounced, this is just my best guess, but I'm hopefully styling it out.

'Huh, what does that mean?' he asks curiously. 'Where is it from?'

How the shit should I know? I can't believe how badly I've shagged this up. *Again*.

Right on cue, my phone starts ringing. It's Cora. I need to shut this down ASAP, so I use her as an excuse.

'Oh, sorry, I had better get this, it's my boyfriend calling,' I lie.

'Oh, okay, no worries,' Al says as he hands me Joachim's lead. 'Well, there you go. Nice to meet you both and glad you're safely back together again, and I'm more than happy to have helped.'

I do genuinely believe Al means that. I take the lead from him. Shit. What the fuck am I supposed to do now?

'Erm, yeah, thanks again,' I insist, as sincerely as I can, because I am grateful for his participation in whatever the hell this has been, but obviously I'm majorly freaked out to be randomly in possession of someone else's dog. I turn on my heel and head for the café.

Right, okay, new mission. Find the owner of the dog I seem to have acquired. Yes, I'll be sticking with acquired, even though it's sort of starting to seem like Al may have stolen a dog for me.

Thankfully it doesn't take me too long to spot a worried-looking man searching for something. He's definitely doing a more convincing job than I was. I'd take notes if it weren't for the fact that I am 100 per cent never trying to pull a stunt like this again.

'Are you looking for this little fella?' I call out.

'Oh, Joachim,' the man says, pronouncing it in a completely different way to the stab in the dark I had at it. The man has an accent – German, I think, but I'm as bad with accents as I am with things like pronunciation and not stealing dogs. 'There you are! I've been so worried, thank you, thank you.'

I hand over the lead, but the man is straight on the floor to hug Joachim like he hasn't seen him in a decade. That's what I should have done, when Al brought the dog to me – although, in my defence, I was floored by the fact that I maybe just inadvertently tricked Al into stealing the dog for me.

'I was just ordering drinks in the café,' the man tells me. 'I thought I'd hooked him up safe outside. Thank you so much. How can I repay you?'

'Oh, no, please, nothing,' I insist.

I know it wasn't intentional, but I feel awful for being the reason this poor man thought his dog was missing. I'm definitely not taking credit for returning a dog I had a hand in stealing.

'Oh, she's calling my name,' the man says. 'My drinks must be ready.'

I notice the barista at the café's outdoor serving hatch is calling out the name 'Mirko'.

'That's my coffee – and his puppuccino,' Mirko tells me. 'Listen, I'll have the milk drink, you take my coffee, please, it's the least I can offer.'

I smile. Wait, is *this* a meet cute? Does this count? This totally counts, right?

'Oh, that's very kind of you, are you sure?' I reply, still feeling a bit iffy about the whole thing.

'Of course,' he replies. 'Do you want to collect them? I'll keep my eye on Joachim, in case he tries to escape again.'

Mirko gives me a friendly smile. I'm happy to go and collect his drinks for him – it's the least I can do – but I should probably make my excuses and go. I feel so bloody guilty.

The café hatch is a short walk, and out of earshot, so when I notice Cora calling me again I quickly answer.

'Is everything okay?' she asks me.

'Cora, honestly, I don't think it could be going worse,' I tell her. 'Don't say anything to Addison yet, but the whole fake missing-dog thing has backfired. I met a man who said he would help me look, but then he came back with the dog I described and just handed it to me.'

'No!' she shrieks.

'Yep,' I reply. 'So then I had to go and find the actual owner of the dog, who was clearly worried sick, so now I'm just collecting his drinks from the café for him, and then I'll head back.'

I wedge my phone between my head and my shoulder as I grab the two drinks. The café employee notices me struggling and hands me a cardboard holder so I can carry them in one hand. I quickly grab my phone again, before I drop it, because a smashed iPhone would probably be a perfectly valid karmic response after today's goings on.

'You stole a dog,' she says simply.

'I stole a dog,' I reply, in a similar tone, given the gravity of the words we're saying.

I'm heading back over to Mirko when I notice someone crouched down on the floor, petting his dog. Shit, it's Al. I quickly step behind a tree.

'I've got to go, the man who stole the dog is talking to the guy he stole it from,' I blurt, which makes sense to me, even if it sounds nonsensical.

'Hello again, Jo-chim,' Al says as he ruffles his ears enthusiastically.

Mirko looks beyond puzzled right now.

'It's pronounced yow-uh-keem,' Mirko corrects him, saying it properly. 'But how do you know my dog's name?'

'Oh, I just met your girlfriend, when she was looking for him over there,' Al replies.

'I don't have a girlfriend,' Mirko tells him, confused *and* kind of alarmed now.

'The blonde with the purple bits in her hair,' Al prompts him. 'In the weird dress.'

Oi, my dress is not weird, it's just... individual. Hardly the matter at hand, though. I place the drinks on the table next to the tree I'm hiding behind before running away as fast as my feet will allow.

The last thing I was intending to happen today was me getting arrested for stealing a dog in the park on my lunch hour. Unless, of course, I can trigger some sort of meet cute with the arresting officer – I'm *definitely* kidding. Time to go back to work, and back to the drawing board too.

9

Part of your job, when you work for a publication owned by a massive parent company, is doing a lot of shit that you don't understand, just because someone tells you to. One of those things is attending networking events.

On the top floor of the Cactus, there's a large events space with its own bar and a swanky roof terrace. We get one hell of a view from up here. I'll often default to staring down at the busy world beneath us while I'm waiting for these events to end because they are always so boring it's unreal. It's a great perk to have above the office, especially when it comes to the fancy parties, but it is just a totally different vibe during the day, especially at these dull-as-dirt events.

Another day, another networking event. To be honest, I don't fully understand what this one is for, it seems we're playing host to some kind of company that makes the software we use to write and submit our articles. I imagine someone at some point will come up to me and I'll be expected to talk or listen. In the meantime, it's a case of grabbing a drink from the bar and working the room. At least it gets me out of work for an hour this afternoon.

Today is worse than others because, as well as rounding up a bunch of editorial staff from our building, we're playing host to some of our biggest rivals. I know because I can see mine standing in front of me, over by the window, and they are both beckoning me over with their hands. Yes, it seems friendly, but I know their MO. They're going to roast me while they try to work out a way to push me out of one of the floor-to-ceiling windows. That's how these things usually go. I grab a glass of Prosecco from the bar (genuinely the only redeemable feature of these things) and reluctantly make my way over.

'Hello,' I say brightly.

Standing in front of me are Lise and Gail, the editor and one of the lead writers from *Women's Monthly*. Yep, two birds from a mag that sounds like it's all about periods have the brass neck to try to make fun of me whenever they see me. Lise, the editor, is older. I'm not sure how old, but she's just got this middle-aged vibe about her. And then there is Gail, her minion, who might actually be the dullest person I've ever met. I don't even know how to describe her, she's just a girl with straight brown hair – shapeless, like her personality. Her only defining characteristic is her meanness and, somehow, you can see it all over her, in her narrow eyes, and her tight, thin lips. Her lips may not even be that thin, perhaps her mouth is just imploding after years of spewing out general horribleness – and I'm sure constantly having them on Lise's arse must be taking its toll too.

'We heard Jane got the sack,' Lise says by way of a hello.

'I heard you're getting the sack too,' Gail tells me. 'They don't get Addison Anderson unless they want heads to roll.'

'I do think Addison quite likes me,' I tell them, not quite smugly, but it's definitely a close cousin of smug.

'Well, surely that's all the worse,' Gail replies. 'If Addison likes you – the ice bitch herself – then something must be wrong with you.'

She laughs. Apparently, if you laugh after you say something, it means it's a joke, even if it is just a mean comment, and not actually a joke at all.

I've never really wasted my time trying to retaliate against Lise and Gail, because I almost view them as a sort of parody. Initially, when I didn't rise to their rivalry, it was as though it annoyed them so much that they felt like they needed to try harder. Even when we were up for the same award, and they started pranking us (totally lame stuff, like sending a delivery of raw fish to our office), like we were in rival sororities or something, but then we won – I really thought that would have shut them up, but no. It's always like this now, just snide remarks and general bitchery. Honestly, they are like caricatures of horrible women, which is why it's so easy to just ignore how vile they can be. They really hate that I don't care and that's how I remain the person who comes out on top of all our encounters, even if I'm the only one who believes it.

I just shrug.

'I think she's great,' I tell them. 'And it seems like she turns around every publication she's worked at.'

'What on earth makes you think she likes you?' Lise asks me, as though the concept of someone finding me likeable is beyond belief. 'I heard she doesn't like anyone.'

People always 'hear' these things, don't they?

'We're working together on an article,' I reply. 'And we're having a lot of fun together.'

'What, is she helping you write "How to Stay Single" in 500 very boring words?' Gail asks. Oh, you can tell from the look on her face that she's over the moon with that sick burn.

'Are you still single, Frankie?' Lise asks me.

'I am,' I reply, without an ounce of shame. 'It helps with the job.'

'It won't help when you're fifty and miserable,' Lise says.

'You're doing just fine,' I point out with a smile.

Okay, so I don't *always* rise above it, but they more than ask for it.

'Perhaps you could find a man here?' Gail suggests, I'll bet insincerely. 'We've just been admiring the talent.'

Grim.

'Oh, yeah, who have you got your eye on?' I ask.

'Well, we're both married, as you know,' she tells me, knowing that I know, but clearly wanting to remind me that I am the only unmarried person standing here chatting. 'Given that I head up Love & Marriage. Which is like kind of like what you do, except it's not just for sad singles.'

'Ah, okay, I don't read *Women's Monthlies*,' I tell them with a slight smile.

They either don't get what I just said or don't care. They might not even be listening, to be honest.

I follow Gail's gaze to the other side of the room. There's a man, standing on his own, looking out of the window. What's interesting about this is not the fact that these two married mean girls are perving over him, although that is fascinating, but the fact that I know the man they are staring at. Well, I don't know-him know him. But I've met him. Sort of. He's one of the fellas I got stuck in the lift with – the nice one. The Paul Rudd-alike.

'Him?' I ask through a smug smile. 'I know him.'

'*You* know *him*?' Gail replies.

'Erm, yeah,' I reply, very matter-of-factly.

'He doesn't work with you,' she points out, as though I wouldn't know that, and implying that's the only way I could possibly know him.

'I know him outside of work,' I tell her. Well, I know him from when I was stuck in a lift with him for a few minutes, and I'm classing this as outside of work because everyone knows the lifts are basically like international waters.

'Why don't you go say hello to him, then?' Lise suggests, calling my bluff. Shit, she's on to me.

'Because I'm talking to you,' I tell her with a smile.

'But we don't like you,' she replies. 'And you know him, right?'

She's got me there and I'm not exactly having a good run with the make-believe stuff today, but I can't give her the satisfaction of being right. I'll just go over and ask him something boring. Like if he has the time. Then I'll just fake a phone call or something. They'll never be able to tell the difference.

'Okay, sure, fine,' I reply with a shrug. 'See you both later – it's been pleasant, as always.'

I try to leave with some confidence, heading over to see my man who is not my man. I glance back and unfortunately they're still looking at me, watching, to see if I go through with it, so I guess I'm going to have to go with the 'asking the time' plan. Failing that, or to drag things out, I suppose we could reminisce about the lift or something, otherwise, that's it, that's the extent of our non-existent rapport.

I'm hoping the right thing to say will hit me when I get to him. Unfortunately, he turns around right as I meaningfully arrive next to him, so the only thing that actually hits me is him. Our hands collide and our drinks spill. By some miracle, there isn't a drop on me – which is somehow even more embarrassing because all of my Prosecco and most of his Coke are all over his white shirt.

'Erm, hello again,' the man says through a bemused laugh.

Even if he didn't have a celebrity doppelganger, I'd remember him by his handsome looks. His perfectly styled short dark hair. His friendly eyes. His cheeky smile. And he must remember me, given that he just said 'hello again'.

'Hi,' I reply. What a clown. Hi. Is that really the best I can do?

'Fancy bumping into you here,' he says.

His smile falls for a second when he realises I'm just staring at him.

'It's okay,' he tells me. 'Don't look so worried.'

His smile returns. I try to loosen up, but it's hard when you're the most embarrassed you've ever been in your life – and that's coming from the girl who stole a dog today.

'Sorry,' I say, first apologising for being weird. Now I need to apologise for the drinks that are all down his shirt. 'Sorry. I wasn't looking where I was going.'

'Honestly, it's fine,' he insists. 'I'm bored out of my mind, you've given me something to do. Although I am leading a meeting later, but it just means you've given me something to talk about too. So thank you.'

I smile.

'I think I can help you out with that,' I tell him, finding myself again. 'Come with me.'

I nod towards the exit.

'I don't usually let strangers take me to the toilets,' he jokes.

'Neither do I,' I insist with a smile. 'But I'm not taking you to the toilets, promise.'

I look over at Lise and Gail, who are gripped. I'll bet they were delighted when I swilled the man. Now, obviously I'm not dragging him off the loos to have my wicked way with him, but I'm not upset if that's what it looks like to them.

'Let's do it,' he says. 'I've already been trapped in a lift this week, what could be scarier? That was you, wasn't it?'

'It was,' I reply. 'I had nothing to do with it, though, I promise.'

'I'll believe you,' he replies. 'Depending on what happens next.'

'Disaster doesn't always follow me around,' I say, which is hopefully true, it just doesn't feel like it at the moment.

I stop outside the toilets.

'Wait here,' I tell him. 'I'll be back in a few minutes – lift permitting.'

'I won't hold my breath, then,' he replies with a smile. 'But okay.'

I can see the intrigue in his eyes, and I like it. I wouldn't go as far as to say I'm charming him, but I certainly have my audience captivated.

I pop down to the *Stylife* office which is thankfully empty of people who would stop me to chat or ask me what I was doing. Most people are at lunch or at the event upstairs.

I nip into the storeroom – the place where we keep the masses of freebies we're sent every day. Most things get snapped up pretty quickly, if they're up for grabs, but we always have plenty of clothes. Even men's clothes, which seems surprising, but around Christmas-time when we're writing gifting guides, or we have mixed-gender fashion shoots, it's all useful. I grab a white shirt that looks about his size and make my way back upstairs. Thankfully the lift doesn't get stuck and I find him waiting exactly where I left him.

'Here you are,' I say. 'You can borrow this if you want.'

'Wow, that was fast,' he replies. 'Do you always carry around more costume changes than Katy Perry at the 2017 VMAs?'

I shoot him a look.

'Don't ask me how I know that, because I don't know how I know that,' he insists.

I laugh.

'It's actually from work,' I tell him. 'I write for *Stylife*.'

'Oh, you're one of those,' he says through a scowl. 'A journalist.'

'Guilty,' I reply. 'I get that a lot.'

I really do, even though I write about love and dating, which is not exactly politics, is it?

'I'm just kidding,' he insists. 'I'm one too. I write for ByteBanter. I've always wondered what it's like in *Stylife* HQ.'

'Oh, really?' I reply in disbelief.

'It's all we talk about at ByteBanter,' he replies. 'It's like the girls' changing rooms at school.'

'Traumatic and full of mean girls?' I joke. 'Go change your shirt and then maybe I'll tell you all about it.'

'Okay, deal,' he says, taking the shirt from me. 'Wow, this feels really nice, considering it's just a white shirt.'

'It's a Valentino,' I tell him. 'You wouldn't get much change out of 500 pounds.'

'And you're going to let *me* wear it? The man who spilled his drink on himself minutes ago?'

'I think that one was on me,' I say, holding my hands up.

'No, it was definitely on me,' he jokes, pointing at the stain on his shirt. 'Back in a minute.'

The man disappears inside the gents. I lean back on the wall next to the door, smiling so big it makes my cheeks ache. I catch sight of myself in the full-length mirror on the wall opposite me. Oh my God, look at me, I look like a giddy little girl. What is going on? A few minutes with a handsome man who makes me laugh and I'm melting like a discarded ice lolly on the hot pavement outside.

It's been a long time since a man made me feel this way – it's that instant attraction to someone, like (okay, I'm not officially claiming this is what this is, I'm not getting ahead of myself, but) that love-at-first-sight kind of rush. I feel almost sick with it. Bloody hell, it's clearly been such a long time since I had a man, if I'm getting this crazy over a fella I just spilled a drink on, who did little more than crack a few jokes to make me feel better about it. It's not that I'm easy, or that a handsome face makes me go weak at the knees. It's just something about the way he talks to me. God, I can't wait for him to come back out here and talk to me again.

Eventually, the man of my dreams returns, his drink-stained shirt messily folded in his hand.

'I didn't think I was mad at you,' he starts, his expression giving nothing away. 'But I am. I'm furious. How am I ever supposed to wear a high-street shirt again? This just feels so... wow.'

I must have just tensed up because I feel a wave of relief washing over me, loosening me up again. I exhale deeply, not even realising I must have held my breath for a second or two. Hopefully he doesn't notice.

'Sorry,' I say with a smile. 'It happens to us all. It's the perks and the curse of the job.'

'I'll bet,' he replies.

If it was up to me, I would tell him to keep it, it looks that good on him, but writers at my level aren't allowed to just help themselves to the stuff in there. No one will know if I borrow one for a few days, though.

'We get clothes, make-up, skincare stuff – which is all great,' I continue. 'But we also get loads of weird shit like lollipops that stop you feeling hungry and creams that are supposed to make your boobs grow. No one wants that stuff.'

'Wow,' he blurts. 'I'm currently reviewing a mouse and a preamp, which I thought showed variety, but your stuff is something else. What happens if you put the boob cream on a different body part?' he suddenly asks with a hilarious curiosity.

'Thankfully not my department,' I reply. 'I'll see if I can get you in as a freelancer, you can do it.'

'Thank you,' he jokes. 'All we get are keyboards, monitors, GPUs...'

'I don't even know what that last one is,' I admit.

'It's not as fun as a cream that might make boobs grow on your knees,' he says with a laugh.

Shit. I like him. I like him, I like him, I like him.

He has a big smile on his face too. His cheeks twitch a little, as he seems like he consciously tries to make it smaller.

'Do I need to leave something with you for insurance?' he asks. 'For the shirt, so you know I'm not going to try and skip the country with it.'

'I trust you,' I say with a smile. 'Just bring it to the office when you're done – it will give you an excuse to peep inside the mysterious *Stylife* HQ. You can go back to ByteBanter and tell all the others about your expedition. Just ask for Frankie at reception.'

His face falls for a split second and I wonder whether I've overstepped the mark. Is it because I tried to make plans with him? Because I told him my name? I'm always writing about how easily spooked men are, how something as simple as sending a text too quickly, or just generally seeming too keen, can – confusingly – really put them off. I remember years ago, chatting to a guy I met on Matcher, and me joking something along the lines of 'That's what I like about you' and him spiralling into this panic, replying 'You like me, eh?' and it just seeming like the stupidest reaction to me showing interest in him.

'Frankie,' he repeats back to me as his friendly smile returns. 'I'm Max.'

Our conversation finally feels like it's reached that point: the moment someone has to do something or say something, in the seconds before it's over. If one of us doesn't say or do something, the only natural thing to do will be to go our separate ways.

Obviously, I – the supposed love and dating expert – have no idea what to say, and opening my lips, to see what comes out, doesn't work. Now I'm just silent with my mouth open.

'Can I buy you a drink?' Max asks, nodding towards the function room. Of course, we both know that all the drinks are free. I couldn't be more smitten.

'Go on, then,' I reply. 'That's very generous of you.'

'It's the least I can do,' he insists. 'We could take them out onto the terrace. That way, when whoever is organising this is doing the rounds talking to everyone, we can avoid them.'

'You sound like you've done this before,' I say as I follow him back into the main room.

'You'll be amazed what lengths I go to, to avoid stuff,' he admits. 'I've got some of those fake cigarettes in my drawer – did you ever get one from the joke shop when you were a kid? They're full of powder so that when you blow through them, it looks like smoke. Except it doesn't really look like smoke, obviously. When my desk mates go for their smoking breaks on the terrace I go too, take one with me, pretend to join in. My mates know it's fake, obviously, but no one else has ever questioned it.'

'That's kind of genius,' I say.

'Well, why should smokers get breaks?' he says with an awkward laugh. I wonder if he thinks he sounds crazy.

'I'll have to get some.'

'Do,' he replies. 'But don't tell anyone else. If everyone starts doing it, the whole scam is ruined.'

We make our way to the bar where Max 'buys' me another glass of Prosecco, then we head out onto the terrace and look out across the city while we chat.

Oh, boy. Actually meeting someone outside of the meet cutes was not part of the plan at all.

10

Sometimes the journey home takes forever. Some days there are real delays, others it just feels like it's taking forever because my mind is on other things. Today is a combination of both.

Needless to say, my mind has been on Max all day. So much so that, after our lovely chat earlier, I spent the last part of the workday daydreaming about him. I know, I'm pathetic, but he made quite the first impression. Unfortunately, this means I didn't really get any work done this afternoon, so the plan is to go inside, have a nice cool shower, make something to eat and then just chill out, watch TV, and try to come up with some new meet cutes to try.

I really hope it isn't one of those evenings when *everyone* and their significant others are home. Again, I'm not bitter because I'm single, the flat is just too small and too warm for a houseful today.

The heat isn't as glorious as it was earlier. I can feel the sweat sitting on my skin, underneath my make-up, making it feel like my face is about to slide off. I feel sticky in my clothes too, thanks to a combination of sweaty public transport and my sluggish walk for the last stretch of the journey. But I'm here now, ready for a nice easy night.

I'm only just through the door when I spot Darcy standing in the living room doorway. Oh God, what's happened now? You only get accosted at the door when something bad is going on. Upstairs better not be leaking *again* because it took the landlord months to do something about the damp last time. Another reminder that I *need* my promotion and I *need* my new flat. Unless, of course, I want to take my parents up on their offer, and move back in with them in Surrey, but if I already hate my commute as it is, I can't imagine moving further away is going to make me happier.

'Is something wrong?' I ask her.

'Come in the living room for a minute,' she starts before lowering her voice to a whisper. 'I've got something for you.'

Oh, boy.

I follow Darcy into the living room, where I spot a man sitting on the sofa.

'Frankie, this is Tom.' Darcy makes the introductions. 'Tom, this is Frankie.'

'Hi,' he says with a casual nod – that man-nod I always notice. I don't know why, but it always seems so indifferent.

'Erm, hello,' I reply.

Tom is tall and in sort of average shape. I don't know how else to describe him really, he just looks normal. Don't get me wrong, normal is good, but I suddenly find it impossible not to measure men up against Max. He's got light brown blown-back hair which is held in place with a heavy-duty product. I can see the sunlight bouncing off it.

'Tom is looking for someone to go out for dinner with this evening,' Darcy explains. 'And I thought, who would be perfect for Tom, who loves a good meal out? My beautiful friend Frankie.'

Shit, it's a set-up. On the one hand, I have to be appreciative. Darcy has taken the initiative to force a meet cute on me by fixing me up with an eligible man. This is something I could never do on my own, for obvious reasons, but... on the other hand... ugh. I just want to have an easy night. I don't want to go for dinner with some random man. I'm off the clock, I'm not in the mood for a meet cute, but beggars can't be choosers, I guess.

'Oh, wow,' I blurt.

'I've got a booking at a place not too far from here,' Tom says. 'It's in half an hour so, if you're up for it, you best go get ready now.'

Tom, what an absolute charmer. It's all for a good cause, that's what I need to keep reminding myself.

'Okay, yeah, that would be lovely,' I say, putting on my bravest face.

'Great,' he replies. 'You'd better go get changed, then.'

I definitely wasn't planning on getting changed, even if I have been wearing this dress all day.

'Oh, right, okay,' I babble. Darcy winces at his choice of words. 'Is it a formal place or...?'

'Not especially,' he replies.

I figured as much, given that he's wearing jeans and a T-shirt. Wow, I really must look bad.

'Wonderful,' I reply. 'Back in a sec.'

Tom, the world's most vanilla man, doesn't think I look good enough to go to a casual eatery with him. What a delight.

Once in my room – although tempted to lock the door and refuse to come back out – I whip off my dress, blast my armpits with some deodorant, and pull on a different sundress, just a red one from my bedroom floor that I wore a couple of days ago. That will do. I try to sort my sweaty roots with some dry shampoo and I take off just enough make-up to carefully put some back on. It's the best effort I can make in so little time, no matter how enthusiastic (or unenthusiastic) I am about this date.

I head back into the living room. Tom doesn't look too impressed.

'Well, we'd better get going, if we want to get there in time,' he says as he pulls himself to his feet.

'Okay,' I reply. 'See you later, Darcy.'

'See you,' she replies with a smile.

Bless her, I think she thinks she's done me a huge favour, and she sort of has, it's just I'd really rather it wasn't tonight, and I'd much prefer someone other than Tom. Max, obviously, but it's pathetic how much I'm thinking about him.

'We need to walk quickly,' Tom tells me once we hit the pavement. 'It's not too far, but it's a bit of a walk.'

'Shall we just get a taxi?' I suggest. I know, I'm not exactly made of money right now, but I'm wearing a wedge heel and it's boiling again now the breeze has cleared off.

'Don't be daft,' he says. 'It's good to walk. It does you good, you know.'

Right, wow, okay. Do I look like I missed the memo about exercise and its benefits? To be fair, probably, given how knackered I must look already.

'Tell me a little about yourself,' I suggest, trying to hide how out of breath I am, trying to keep up with him.

'What do you want to know?' he replies.

'Oh, just general stuff,' I say. 'Get-to-know-you kind of things.'

'You have to be more specific,' he insists. 'I can't just talk about myself. You have to ask specific questions.'

Oh, boy, it's going to be a long night.

'Erm...' I wrack my brains for questions to ask. What's his problem? Everyone knows how to say a bit about themselves. Isn't it part of being a grown adult? 'Where did you grow up? What's your favourite food? Do you prefer cats or dogs? Not to eat, obviously, that last question is its own thing.'

Tom turns around to pull a face at me. He doesn't find me charming at all. He thinks I'm stupid.

'I would've thought, from my accent, that it's pretty obvious I grew up in North Wales,' he says, as though he's almost angry I even asked. 'Veal escalope is a food that I enjoy – I'm not six years old, so I don't have a favourite anything. And, I don't know, cats, I suppose.'

Wow. What a tosser. I wouldn't say he had any detectable accent, so I don't know how I would possibly know that, I think veal is absolutely gross, and I'm definitely more of a dog person than a cat person. This really could not be going any worse.

'How old are you?' I ask him. '"Not six" leaves a lot of possibilities.'

'I'm twenty-nine,' he tells me.

Oh my God, he isn't even thirty yet? He's got such middle-aged-man energy.

'You?'

'I'm thirty-four,' I reply.

'Thirty-four?' he repeats back to me.

'Thirty-four,' I say again, for the people at the back.

'I didn't realise you were older.' He sounds quite annoyed by the concept of me being an 'older woman'. The good news is that this means I must not look my age. The bad news would be that this is clearly a turn-off for Tom, were it not for the fact that I do not care one little bit what he thinks of me.

'Yep, I'm a regular granny,' I joke, trying to get things back on track. 'But don't worry, I'm young at heart.'

Tom steps out into the road while there's a break in the traffic. I follow him.

'Do you want kids?' he asks me.

'Not today, thanks,' I reply. 'Usually more of a third-date activity.'

'I mean generally,' he says, ignoring my joke. I obviously know what he meant. 'I just mean, at your age...'

The oncoming traffic is the only thing preventing me from stopping in my tracks. Oh, he did *not* just say that, did he? If this were a real date and not something I was doing for the sake of an article, believe me, I would turn around right now and never look back. I should probably do that anyway, except...

'We're here,' Tom announces.

Hopefully now that we're here, he'll forget about my ovaries. I've come this far. I may as well stick it out. You never know, he might turn on the charm now that he's not worrying about us being late. Or not. But even if he's a crap date, well, it's another failed meet cute to add to the list. Too many more of these and I'm going to need to shift the focus of the article to something along the lines of how *not* to meet men. I'm clearly great at that.

We're at the Guelder Rose, a restaurant that I've heard of, but never been to before, so if all else is a bust, at least I've got to try somewhere new. It seems like a cool place, flamboyant but romantic (it's a shame I'm here with Tom, what a waste), with white flowers everywhere, climbing the walls, hanging from the ceiling. There's a purpose-built flower archway against one of the walls in the entrance, framing a backlit sign with a large flower logo in the centre. The perfect spot for taking a trendy snap for social media. I wonder if Tom would take a photo of me for my Instagram? There's a group of women there at the moment, taking it in turns to snap pictures of one another, having an absolute blast doing so.

'Isn't it pathetic?' Tom says to me, not all that quietly, as we pass them. 'More nonsense for their social networks – they mine your data, you know.'

'Wow, do they?' I reply sarcastically.

Tom is officially joyless. Imagine begrudging strangers taking a photo in a beautiful place. I, like most ancient millennials, love social media. I'd probably be scrolling Instagram right now, if I weren't here.

'I've got a booking for Tom Daley,' Tom tells the hostess.

'Your name is Tom Daley?' I say with a smile.

'Yes, and what's wrong with that?' he asks angrily.

'Oh, no, there's nothing wrong with it,' I quickly insist. 'I just... you have the same name as the famous diver. You must have heard that before?'

'Would you believe you are the first one?' he says with an almost aggressive level of sarcasm. He rolls his eyes before turning back to the hostess.

Oh my God, what a miserable man. I was just trying to be cute. I mean, come on, I'm called Frankie. Do you know how often I get told to relax? Or asked if I've ever been to Hollywood? When I was in Year 10 and my French teacher found out my name, he started singing 'The Power of Love' to me – a reference I didn't even get at the time, but it was the reason one of the meaner boys started a rumour that this particular teacher fancied me. Funnily enough, this was the same kid who used to call me Dettori.

'Let me show you to your table,' the hostess says. She flashes me a sympathetic smile. Suddenly I feel embarrassed, like she's looking at me thinking this must be the best I can do, if I'm still willing to stick it out when Tom is so very clearly a dick. Let it never be said I'm not devoted to my job.

The place is about as busy as you would expect for 7 p.m. on a Tuesday evening. It's a nice big room with lots of space between the tables. I'm glad, because that means no one will be able to hear what I'm subjecting myself to.

'Dinner is on me tonight,' Tom announces.

'That's very generous of you, but I don't mind paying for myself,' I tell him. I don't want to give him any kind of signals that this is a date that is going well, and I definitely don't want to feel like I owe him anything.

'No, I told you, I'm paying,' he insists.

'Can I take your drinks order?' a friendly waiter asks, looking at me first.

'Hmm, I think I might have a glass of wine,' I say as I cast my eyes down the menu.

'We'll get a bottle,' Tom says.

'Oh, I'm fine with just a glass,' I insist. 'I'm not in much of a drinking mood, at work today we had—'

'They have some very good bottles around the thirty-five-pound mark,' he tells me, interrupting me, clearly uninterested in what I was about to say.

'I know, but I'd rather just get a glass of—'

'We'll take a bottle of the Grüner Veltliner,' Tom tells him.

I feel my eyebrows shoot up.

'I'll be back with that in a moment,' the waiter says, minding his own business, doing as he's told.

I pick up my food menu and cast an eye over it. I wonder if he'll order my food for me too, like Patrick Bateman in *American Psycho*. He's certainly got that vibe about him.

'Veal, is it?' I ask him. I can't help myself sometimes.

'They don't offer it,' he replies. 'Not everywhere does. It's ridiculous. I'm made to feel like I'm a cannibal, just for enjoying it.'

I don't say anything. I stare at my menu. It doesn't take me too long to choose what I fancy, but I keep reading, just to avoid having to talk to him.

Eventually our waiter returns with our wine. He pours us a glass each before taking our order.

'Any starters?' he asks.

'Not for me, thank you,' I say. 'I think I'll go straight for my main.'

Anything to make this process go faster.

'Have a starter,' Tom says, and it sounds like an instruction rather than an offer.

'I'm fine.'

'Have one,' he insists.

I just freeze.

'Okay, well, I'll have the truffled wild mushrooms,' Tom says. 'And bring her the salt and pepper chicken too.'

'Okay,' the waiter says, keeping out of it. 'Your main?'

'Can I have the lobster mac and cheese, please?' I say.

'No,' Tom interrupts.

I know I'd phrased it like a question, but that's just what you do when you're ordering, isn't it? I wasn't really seeking permission from Tom.

'No?' I repeat back to him in disbelief.

'No, not that,' he tells me. 'Have something else.'

I'm nearing the end of my patience now.

'What am I allowed?' I ask him, almost sarcastically. 'That might save some time.'

'Anything but the lobster dishes and the steak,' he says rather oddly. I wasn't expecting him to actually give me an answer.

See, this is why I want to pay for my own dinner, so I can get what I want. I imagine this is all because Tom is insisting on paying – not that I'm going to let him.

'I guess I'll have the cheeseburger, then,' I say as I hand over my menu.

As we wait for our starters, I make the terrible mistake of asking Tom about his job. He's currently working as a legal secretary and, other than believing he is severely underpaid, his main complaint seems to be that he works under a woman, and that having 'secretary' in his job title is somehow emasculating too. I'm getting serious small-dick energy from this one.

It feels like forever before our food is placed down in front of us. I *can't wait* to try the chicken I didn't want or order. At least it looks good.

'How is it?' Tom asks me through a mouthful of mushroom. 'Any good?'

'Yeah, it's nice,' I reply.

'Describe it to me,' he persists.

Now I definitely feel like I'm in some kind of horror movie.

'What do you want, an essay?' I reply with a snort.

'No, just thirty to fifty words,' he says.

Erm... thirty to fifty words? That's oddly specific. What the...?

'Hang on a minute,' I start as my mouth catches up with my brain. 'Is this some kind of review thing?'

'Lower your voice,' Tom insists loudly, before lowering his own. 'Yes, I do mystery dining for cash. The food is free, you just have to order certain things, but I don't get paid – or reimbursed – if we don't do it right, so can you just do what I ask you, please?'

Oh my God, this isn't a date at all, it's a job. His job. All I'm getting out of it is some free food that I didn't want, some wine that I don't like, and some misogynist reminding me that my biological clock is ticking. Fantastic. Oh, I can't wait to tell Cora and Addison about this one. Definitely another failure to add to the list.

11

'Have you checked your pockets?' Cora asks me.

'Checked my pockets?' I reply. 'For what?'

'For the freak magnet you appear to be carrying around with you,' she jokes from behind her desk.

I've just told Cora and Addison all about my horrible nightmare date (if we're even calling it that) last night. Naturally they think it's hilarious. I suppose it is – now that it's over, and I never have to see him again.

'Do you think he'll give you half of what he gets paid?' Cora asks.

'Oh, I doubt it,' I reply. 'Not that I'd take it. Eventually he told me how he gets paid for doing these jobs – he doesn't really get anything. Just the free food and a mileage allowance. We walked, so I suppose that's how he gets paid.'

'I'd check for that magnet,' Addison insists. 'Where are all the normal men?'

I think she's speaking rhetorically but I can't resist finally telling them about Max, after managing to keep it to myself for not even twenty-four hours. I could wait until it's just me and Cora, but I'm hoping that if I encourage Addison's friendship, there is no way she could fire me.

'I did meet someone yesterday,' I confess. 'Someone charming and hilarious and absolutely gorgeous.'

'Did you?' Cora replies with a squeak. I don't know if she's surprised I've met someone nice or surprised it's taken me so long to tell her about it. I imagine it's a bit of both.

I nod as I try to mask my grin.

'His name is Max. He's wonderful,' I blurt. 'He works downstairs at ByteBanter. He's a writer, we met—'

'Let me stop you there,' Addison says. 'Workplace romance? That's boring.'

'I know, but I—'

'No,' she interrupts me again. 'I'm working on something much better for you. How do you feel about jumping out of a plane?'

'Honestly?' I reply. Addison nods. 'Really bloody negatively.'

'I'm thinking we have you strapped to some big, buff army man,' she explains, not really explaining all that much. 'See if the adrenaline of jumping out of a plane together makes the two of you fall in love.'

'Erm...'

'I just need to work out who and how,' she continues. 'I'm not sure the army is the right one. Would it be the air force?'

There's no way I'm helping her with this one.

'Do you really think someone is going to fall for Frankie if they jump out of a plane with her?' Cora asks in disbelief.

'Yes – why?' Addison replies.

'Frankie is my friend, and I love her to pieces, but I went on the Hangover ride with her at the Winter Wonderland a few of years ago,' Cora explains. 'Believe me, she is not at her most loveable when she's up high.'

'I was terrified,' I insist, in an attempt to strengthen my case to

Addison. I'm not going to contest what Cora just said, it's true, I was swearing, crying, throwing up, making deals with God. I didn't realise I was quite so scared of heights until I was *that* high up – well, how else would I know? Never again. Never *ever* again.

'Perhaps we need to work on your seduction techniques,' Addison suggest.

Wow, this ought to be good.

I raise my eyebrows in anticipation.

'Oh, yeah?'

'Yes,' she replies. 'Go on, show me your skills, seduce me.'

I snort. She can't be serious. There are people working at their desks. What if they look over?

'They made me sit through a very long, very weird video when I started here,' I tell her. 'One that made clear I should absolutely never try to seduce my boss.'

'What if it's an order?' she replies.

'I'm pretty sure they probably made you watch a video too, telling you never to order your staff to seduce you,' I remind her through a laugh.

Addison thinks this is hilarious.

'Just do it,' she demands. 'We need to work out why you're failing so spectacularly.'

'Seduce your boss, Frankie,' Cora playfully commands me.

I'm actually cackling now – and in a very unsexy way.

'I can't just be sexy,' I insist. 'Can you?'

Addison stands up and sits down *on* my desk. She slowly pushes my pen pot and a small pile of papers off my desk with her feet before dancing on top of my desk, sort of like when the Vandergeld sisters dance on the bar in *White Chicks*. Wait, no, that's a terrible point of reference, maybe Addison has a point. I shouldn't have said that, I should have said *Coyote Ugly* or something similar. Damn, maybe I am terrible when it comes to seduction. If I were to get up and dance on a bar, I would probably look more like Pee-wee Herman busting moves to 'Tequila'.

'Wow, that's pretty good,' Cora admits.

I glance around the room. Addison has caught a few people's attention with her display. No one really seems to find it funny or shocking. There's been a major vibe shift since Addison turned up. No one feels relaxed any more and I'm embarrassed that she's spending so much time with me. I don't want my colleagues thinking I'm teacher's pet and holding it against me.

'It's for work,' she calls out.

'Nothing to see here,' Cora jokes.

'It's not exactly hard,' Addison insists, turning her attention back to me, now that her little performance is over. 'Come on, Frankie, try to pick those pens up, but be sexy about it.'

'Erm, okay,' I say. I push my chair back, hoping I'll know what to do as I'm doing it, but I run over my pens with the wheel of my chair, causing them to crunch. 'Shit.'

It isn't exactly going to be sexy, watching me pick up fragments of plastic from the office floor for fifteen minutes, is it? *Is it?* I clearly have no idea.

'Perhaps practise on a man,' Addison suggest. 'Then it might come a little more naturally.'

I'm absolutely sure it won't.

'Back to the drawing board, then,' I say, scooping up my crushed pens. Some are salvageable – unlike my meet cute ideas.

'Oh, I know who you can practise on,' Addison says as a cheeky grin spreads across her face. 'On my first day, when I was having trouble logging into the system, they sent an absolutely smoking hottie from tech support to get me going.'

'It sounds like he did,' Cora jokes bravely.

'He really did,' she replies. 'We just spent twenty minutes making sexual computer puns. Hard drive this, floppy disk that. I didn't have a clue what we were talking about, but it was pretty hot.'

'I think you might need to watch that sexual harassment video again,' I insist, half joking.

'We were only having a laugh,' she replies with a bat of her hand.

Addison is a hard one to figure out. She's somehow a terrifying ball-buster and a big bag of laughs. Perhaps that's why she's so successful.

'My point is, we should get him up here, to give you a little tech support, and so that you can practise being seductive on him,' she says. 'He seems like the type who would flirt with anyone.'

'Oh, boy,' I say. 'I really can't see that working out well for me. Even if he does "flirt with anyone".'

So charming.

'Come on, you've got to give it a go,' she insists, finally getting up from where she's been sitting on the edge of my desk, so that she can hover next to me and look at my screen. 'How do we make a computer problem?'

I stare at my desktop. Obviously I don't know enough about computers to fix them – which also means I don't know enough to break them either.

'Can you crash it?' Cora suggests.

'I don't know how, not on purpose,' I reply. 'It always does it when I don't want it to.'

Isn't that always the way?

'I know,' Addison says. The light bulb barely has time to switch on in her head before she is actioning her plan, grabbing the cup of coffee I let go cold earlier and pouring the full contents of the cup out onto my keyboard.

I quickly push back in my chair, to avoid it cascading down onto my lap – is she serious?

'Whoa,' Cora says. 'Did that really just happen?'

'I'd better go and call tech support,' Addison says with a satisfied smile.

Addison heads into her office to make the call. Cora throws me a box of tissues from her desk so I can try to mop up some of the coffee.

'She's crazy,' I whisper.

'She really is,' Cora replies. 'I can't work out if it's a good thing or a bad thing.'

'Bad,' I reply in an instant. 'She's going to make me jump out of a plane, strapped to a man, who is apparently going to fall in love with me, even after I coat him in vomit and call him a... what did I call you for talking me into going on that ride?'

'A monster bitch from hell, if memory serves,' she replies through a smile.

I somehow manage to cringe and laugh at the same time.

'See, it's a terrible idea, I'm even uglier up high.'

Cora rolls her eyes.

'Okay,' Addison starts, poking her head out of her office door. 'There's a guy from tech on the way up. Remember to be sexy.'

'I couldn't possibly forget,' I call back.

'Good luck,' Cora tells me.

'Thank you,' I mouth back to her.

I place my eyes on the door, awaiting the entrance of this hottie from tech. I wonder what he looks like – I wonder what he would need to look like, for me to muster up the strength to be sexy. Henry Cavill is good with computers, isn't he? Imagine if he's moonlighting, taking time off from shooting *The Witcher* to tinker with the office tech – he could reboot my RAM any day. I've no idea what that means, or if it even makes sense, but that's why I'm not the tech expert... or any good at flirting.

I watch as people come and go, but I don't see signs of any hotties.

'Are you the one who needs tech support?' I hear a voice say. 'Come on, I've not got all day, who needs me?'

I turn to see a fifty-something man standing behind me. This isn't Addison's hottie, surely? He's definitely a coldie.

'Er, I do,' I say reluctantly.

'Right, what's... is this some kind of joke?'

Eesh, he looks angry.

'No, no, no joke,' I say. 'It's my keyboard, I—'

'I can tell it's your keyboard, darling,' he says, using the term of endearment ever so patronisingly. 'What the hell have you done to it?'

I glance over at Addison's office door. She's peeping out at me. I can just about make out her mouthing the word 'flirt' at me repeatedly.

'My coffee spilt,' I reply.

'And you think I can fix that, do you?'

I shrug.

'If anyone can, you can,' I reply with a flirty smile – or at least what I *think* is one.

'I'm going to have to order you a new one,' he says, sounding the most inconvenienced he's ever been in his life. 'Do you think I just have keyboards lying around for when ditzy blondes somehow spill their entire drink on one?'

Ditzy blonde?

'I need to give you a case number,' he says. 'Write this down.'

I grab one of my pens and take the number down. Then, in a last-ditch, ill-advised attempt at being seductive, I place the top of the pen in my mouth and suck. The ink from the end that I forgot was broken shoots up into my mouth. My eyes widen as I feel it hit my tongue.

The man frowns at me in disgust before leaving.

Addison heads back over as I swill my mouth with water, spitting it back out into my empty coffee cup.

'Do you see what happens when I try to be sexy?' I say.

'Yeah, that wasn't pretty at all,' she replies. 'My God, you're going to need to rinse that again, you've got a blue tongue.'

'Fantastic,' I say with a sigh.

'Perhaps I should let the two of you get on for a bit,' Addison says. 'I'll go get your parachute jump booked in. I just need to pitch it with a different angle, to get them to say yes.'

'How are you going to use your computer?' Cora asks. 'If yours can't be fixed, and everyone seems to be in and at their desk today.'

I smile.

'I know a guy,' I tell her.

I call the building switchboard and ask to be put through to Max at ByteBanter.

'Hello?' he eventually answers.

'Hello,' I reply. 'It's the girl who lent you a shirt when you spilled a drink on it.'

'Erm, I think you'll find you spilled the drink on it,' he reminds me. I can hear him smiling.

'Either way,' I continue. 'I was hoping you might be able do me a favour. In all the tech stuff you have lying around, might you have a keyboard I can borrow?'

'Of course, but why?' he asks.

'I spilled a drink on mine,' I tell him with a giggle. A stupid, giddy, teenage-girl giggle, but that's how he makes me feel. 'Plus, it means you get to see inside the infamous *Stylife*.'

'I'll be there in a couple of minutes,' he says excitedly. I don't know if he's putting the enthusiasm on or not, but it's adorable.

'Okay, what was that?' Addison asks.

'That was me getting a keyboard so I can get on with some work,' I reply. 'What do you mean?'

'*Who* was that?' Cora chimes in.

'That was Max,' I reply. 'The one I was telling you about.'

'That was flirting,' Addison points out. 'See, you can do it.'

'Nooo, I wasn't flirting,' I insist. 'I just... I needed something. He owed me something. Sort of. Maybe. It's nothing.'

'You need to be more helpless,' Addison points out. 'Helpless works for you.'

'I was helpless when I was choking down ink,' I point out. 'And that didn't go all that well.'

'Be vulnerable,' she clarifies. 'Men like it when you need their help.'

'Well, men didn't want to help me when I was broken down at the side of the road,' I start. 'I had to rely on women for that. And that guy last night was only trying to help himself. I suppose there was that big, buff fella in the park, who helped me steal a dog, but he was just helping anyone who needed him, not just me. And that bloke from tech clearly *loved* my helpless act.'

'He was a hard nut to crack, wasn't he?' Addison replies.

We fall silent for a moment, all lost in our thoughts, wondering what the right thing to do next is.

'That wasn't the hottie, was it?' Cora eventually asks. 'It can't have been.'

I suppose that was what was going through her mind.

'Oh, no, the hottie can't have been more than twenty-five,' Addison replies. 'Don't look at me like that.'

I didn't realise we were looking at her like anything.

'My dates aren't that young,' she insists.

'Ooh, your dates,' Cora says, trying to drag a little more information out of her.

'Yes, well, let's just say Frankie wasn't the only one on a hot date last night,' Addison practically sings.

'Erm, hi,' Max says.

Shit, I shouldn't have taken my eyes off the door and, double shit, he just heard Addison saying I was on a date last night. I don't want him thinking I go on dates. It's not that I don't want to seem desirable, obviously I do, but I don't want to seem like I'm dating, I don't want him thinking I have eyes for anyone. Yes, sometimes men want what they can't have, but confusingly they also want what no one else can have either. I need to seem exclusive.

'Hi, hello,' I say, like an absolute loser.

'Wow, you really did spill a drink on your keyboard,' he says, looking down at it.

Suddenly I'm so glad I did. I get that amazing feeling again just from being in his orbit.

'I really did,' I reply.

'And... your tongue is blue?'

'Sucked on my broken pen,' I say, like it's the most normal thing in the world. Smooooth as silk.

Max laughs.

'Anyway, here's your keyboard, and your shirt,' he says.

'Ah, thank you,' I reply. 'You were able to part with it, then?'

'Reluctantly,' he replies. 'My skin hates me. This shirt feels like a cheese grater in comparison. I'm clearly working for the wrong website. Fancy swapping?'

'Oh, absolutely,' I say with an entirely faked sense of confidence. 'I've got a pitch for an article: how to wreck a keyboard in one easy step.'

'It usually takes me two or three steps, so I think the job is probably yours,' he jokes.

I take the keyboard and the shirt from him and place them on Cora's desk, because mine is still covered with coffee. She's pretending to work but she's keeping an eye on us. So is Addison, who has taken a seat at the end of Cora's desk.

'So, you've finally infiltrated *Stylife*,' I say, trying to ignore them watching me. 'Do you think they'll write books about you?'

'Blogs, perhaps,' he replies. 'I think they're expecting me to either not come back, or based off whatever weird fantasies they have built on what they assume is an office full of women, they probably think I'll return gasping for breath, covered in lipstick marks.'

'That can certainly be arranged,' Addison can't resist but chime in. She stands up and walks around to my side of the desk.

'This is Addison, my editor,' I tell him. 'And this is my friend Cora.'

'I did wonder about the audience,' Max jokes. 'It's nice to meet you both.'

'Nice to meet you too,' Addison tells him.

'Well, I'd better get back to work,' Max says. 'Or they'll be sending out a rescue party. See you later, Frankie.'

'Yeah, see you later,' I reply. 'I'll get this keyboard back to you ASAP.'

'No rush,' he calls back as he heads for the door.

When he's finally gone, I turn back to Cora and Addison.

'Okay, Frankie, he's seriously hot,' Cora points out.

'I told you,' I say.

'You didn't tell us he was *that* good-looking,' Addison insists. 'It's a shame he's just some guy from work or I would be telling you to go for it. You seem capable of flirting with him.'

I open my mouth to speak but Addison holds her hand up to stop me.

'You need to take my advice, okay? Stop telling people you sucked a broken pen,' she says. 'Under no circumstances should you tell the truth about something like that. It makes you sound like such a loser, honestly.'

'Got it,' I reply.

'Okay, well, now that the eye candy has gone, I'm going to see about getting you thrown out of a plane,' she says. 'I think we're getting somewhere.'

Once Addison is back in her office, I turn to Cora.

'I'm going to take my lunch now,' I say. 'See if I can get some meet cutes going while I'm out and about. Something, anything, that will seem like a win, so that perhaps she'll forget about this stupid parachute jump.'

'It will have to be something good,' Cora replies. 'She's determined to get you strapped to an army man and flung out into the sky.'

'I'll come up with something,' I insist. 'I feel like my life depends on it.'

12

Flirting, being seductive and oozing confidence all seem to come easily to Addison Anderson. How can I be more like her?

I'm sitting on a bench, watching the world go by, drinking my second iced latte (this one is a decaf, because I don't think being wound up on caffeine will help me be a better version of myself) to hopefully make my blue tongue disappear ASAP.

I suppose I need to be more forward, to assert myself, to command my audience. Then again, Addison told me that my strong suit was to come across as helpless, vulnerable – a woman in need of saving. Saving from what, though? That's the question.

I don't want to do anything too extreme, nothing that feels too manipulative or involves too many props. All I'm doing is trying to meet people in traditional ways, there shouldn't be anything ethically dodgy there, nothing that makes me feel like I'm doing something wrong. Take the incident with the dog in the park. To start with, things felt fine, I was just a girl in the park, looking for a dog. The problem – and the ethical concerns – cropped up when the man who helped me look for this fictional dog presented me with a real one. Desperate as I am to avoid jumping out of a plane, I absolutely don't want to achieve anything by ruining someone else's day. So how do I be helpless in a way that only affects me?

I glance around, looking at all the people passing me by, happily going about their day, whether they're rushing to work or simply enjoying the sunshine, they're not paying me a second thought. I need to catch the attention of someone – a man, obviously – in an absolutely foolproof way.

I can think of tons of bad ideas. Pretending to get mugged would be stupid because if someone called the police (and why wouldn't they?) then I would have to give a statement and a description, and not only is that wasting police time, but knowing my luck, they would probably find some poor innocent man who matched my fictional description. Pretending to lose my keys is stupid too, because how could a stranger even help me with that? The same goes for losing my phone – they would probably offer to call it or let me use their phone to log into the Find My app. Damn, why is this so hard? Come on, Frankie, think!

I stand up to put my drink in the nearest bin. As I do, I lose my footing a little but not so much anyone notices. Publicly stacking it is *just* what I need today. Actually, maybe that really is exactly what I need. If there's anything I'm good at, it's got to be embarrassing myself. Perhaps I can pull this attempt off.

I walk along the pavement until a man, any man, who looks no more than five years either side of thirty and is alone appears. Then, with no real logic or method, I just let myself drop, right in front of him. Thankfully (for the article, and for my body) he catches me, just as I hoped he would. That could have gone so much worse.

'Oh, my goodness, are you okay?' he asks me as he helps me steady myself on my feet. 'Please, sit for a moment.'

There's a bench only a few steps away on the pavement. He ushers me towards it.

Wow, I've hit the jackpot with this one. This man looks and sounds like the actor you cast in an American movie if you want someone to seem so terribly English. A Hugh Grant, Colin Firth, Jude Law type. Loves his mummy, eats crumpets – the works.

'I'm okay,' I reassure him. 'Thank you so much for catching me, you're my hero.'

Am I doing this right? Is this really what men want?

'What happened?' he asks me. 'You didn't appear to fall over anything.'

That's because I didn't.

'Oh, no, I think I just... fainted a little,' I say, because of course I do. What a logical, sensible thing to say.

'You fainted?' he says, sounding concerned.

'Oh, it's okay, nothing to worry about,' I insist. 'It just happens from time to time, I'm fine.'

He narrows his eyes at me.

'Is... is your tongue blue?'

Shit, he noticed the tongue. Addison's voice echoes in my head, reminding me, under no circumstances, to tell the truth about how I got a blue tongue.

'Yes, just a bit,' I say. 'I just... sometimes I wake up with a bit of a blue tongue.'

On what planet is that less weird or less embarrassing than the truth?

The man sits down next to me.

'Has anyone ever mentioned Curt-Adams Syndrome to you?' he asks me.

What the hell?

'Erm, no,' I reply.

'It's a relatively rare condition,' he explains. 'But symptoms include fainting spells and decreased blood flow to the tongue, which presents as a blue tongue, most commonly present upon waking, fading as the day goes on.'

I just stare at him for a moment.

'I'm a doctor,' he tells me. 'Dr Quill. I work at A & E – I'm on my way there now. I think you should get looked at, and we're only five minutes away, walking is the fastest way.'

Shit. Shit, shit, shit.

'Oh, no, honestly, I am absolutely fine,' I reassure him. 'I feel fine, I'm sure I don't have that thing, honestly, I promise.'

'I know you're scared,' he says softly, doing his best to reassure me. 'And you're probably right, I'm sure you don't have it, but it would be remiss of me to leave you here in this state. I promise I'll keep an eye on you, I won't let you faint and hurt yourself.'

I've got to give him ten out of ten for his bedside manner. I just wish I'd picked someone who wasn't a doctor to do this with.

I'm stunned, honestly, this is the last thing I expected to happen. What am I supposed to do? I definitely can't tell the truth now, can I? *Can I*? If I do, he'll probably still insist on taking me to A & E, but to get my head checked instead of my royal-blue tongue.

I just nod helplessly. What else can I do? God knows how I'm going to get myself out of this one.

13

I've always hated hospitals. There's something about them – I want to say it's the smell, the colour of the walls, the atmosphere. It isn't, though, is it? You could fill the place with expensive diffusers, hang luxury wallpaper on the walls, and pump soothing classical music into the air. It wouldn't change a thing. The thing about hospitals that makes them a horrible place to be is because we all know. We know what goes on here. And, while we know we should be focusing on the babies being born and people ringing the cancer-free bell, that isn't what we focus on. Hospitals remind us all of our own mortality, and as scary as they are when you are worried something might be wrong with you, today I am freaking out because I know that nothing is wrong with me. I have to get out of here now.

Dr Quill told me to check in at the desk before getting to work himself, promising to keep an eye on me. Thing is, with the way A & E is laid out, he's basically still in my eyeline, and I am in his. He really can keep an eye on me. So I joined the queue for the desk but then quickly took a seat, hoping he would assume I'd been checked in while he was looking down at notes or chatting to one of the busy nurses. Now I'm sitting here, on an uncomfortable plastic chair, in a room full of people who do genuinely need help, feeling like a prize arsehole, waiting for my moment to do a bunk, when Dr Quill won't be as likely to run after me.

'I'm sure you're going to be fine,' the man sitting next to me tells me.

He looks down at my leg, which I've been jigging nervously, before making eye contact with me again, giving me a reassuring smile.

'I'm Chris,' he says.

'Frankie,' I reply to him.

'We're in this together, Frankie,' he tells me with a smile. 'We'll both be out of here before you know it.'

'Sounds great,' I reply. 'I think I can probably leave right now, to be honest.'

It hasn't escaped my attention that this situation does have all the makings of a meet cute, but I do really, *really* need to get out of here. There's no time for that right now.

'You can't just leave,' Chris says. 'Aren't you waiting for something? There must be a reason you're here? I get that you're worried, so am I.'

'It's nothing to worry about, honestly,' I reassure him. 'Let's just say I had a bit of an accident with a man I don't know and it's left me in this mess.'

Setting him straight – without the embarrassing details – is my only option at this point.

Chris leans in to me, close enough to whisper in my ear.

'I never would have said this, if you weren't so honest,' he starts. 'But that's pretty much why I'm here too. Except with a woman, obviously, but I think we might be here for the same clinic, if you know what I mean.'

I nod slowly as the realisation hits me.

'I just need to go to the loo,' I lie.

'Oh, don't worry, I get it, I totally get it,' he says with a wince.

I doubt my fake smile is hiding my horror. It couldn't possibly.

'Back in a sec,' I say.

I edge away before moving in the direction of the toilets. Once I'm around the corner, I make a dash for the exit.

So, not a meet cute. Not a meet cute at all. Just another total fucking nightmare.

14

'You really don't seem yourself today,' Cora points out over the top of her cup of tea.

'Sorry,' I say, pulling my eyes from my blank screen, to look her in the eye. 'I'm fine.'

'You've not even commented on my T-shirt,' she replies, sticking her chest out.

The bold black text on a white tee reads:

Sorry I'm late, I didn't want to come.

'I genuinely love it,' I tell her. 'Can we get me one for my parachute jump?'

Cora can't hide the look on her face. She feels so sorry for me. I feel kind of pathetic.

'I can't believe Addison managed to get it arranged,' she says. 'How did she even convince someone that it was a good idea?'

'I think, when she eventually realised it was a parachute regiment that she needed, she just called up and said that one of her writers for *Stylife Magazine* was wanting to write a feature about how to get more women into the military,' I explain, my eyes widening at how stupid that sounds.

'Do you really have to do that?' she replies.

'God knows – I hope not,' I say. 'I can't even get people to move their bags off the seat on the bus, no one is going to listen to me telling them they should be signing up to fight for their country.'

'When is it?' she asks.

'Next week,' I reply. 'Do you want to go grab some lunch? I'm starving, and I'm basically in last-meal territory.'

'I would love to, but I've got a meeting in five minutes,' she replies. 'I know it doesn't mean much when you're scared of heights, but they do this type of thing all day, every day, I'm sure it's safe.'

'Thanks,' I say with a smile.

'Could you talk to Addison? Explain just how scared you are?' she suggests.

'She doesn't make anything sound optional,' I reply. 'Everything is a suggestion – unless you're not going to do it, then it's an order.'

'I know what you mean,' Cora says, nibbling her lip, unsure what to say next.

I sigh.

'Well, if it's just me for lunch, I'll pop to the canteen for a sandwich and a breather,' I tell her. 'Addison will be back from lunch soon. I can't face her right now.'

'We could go for a drink after work?' Cora suggests. 'If we put our heads together, I'm sure we can come up with something.'

'Thanks,' I reply. 'Right, time to go raid the baked goods.'

'This meeting is going to be well over an hour, can you bring me a brownie, please?'

'Of course.'

To call the work canteen a canteen is almost offensive. It's a café-meets-restaurant with a bougie menu, artisanal baked goods and overpriced drinks to rival your favourite coffee shop. I'm not complaining, though. How amazing, to have such a thing in the building. It's just a bit like, I don't know, having a McDonald's for a school canteen; an absolute dream to have, but ultimately still full of people you go to school with, and still in school. I do love the food here, and it's a beautiful place, but at the end of the day, I am still in work. It doesn't quite feel like a proper break.

The canteen is always busy – another reason I usually prefer to go out. I shuffle through the motions, grabbing a cheese and chutney sandwich, a bag of chardonnay vinegar crisps, and a bottle of apple juice. I pay for them before aimlessly wandering through the tables, looking for somewhere to sit. I love the seats by the window, because I'm obsessed with the view from this building, but it's always hard to get a window seat. I sigh.

'Oi, Frankie,' I hear a voice call out.

My eyes dart around for a few seconds before I spot him. Max, sitting at a table, eating a sandwich.

'Oh, hi,' I say as I approach him.

'Are you looking for somewhere to sit?' he asks.

'Yes, are you—'

I'm about to ask if he's leaving but Max gets in there first.

'Do you want to sit with me?' he asks.

Is it warm in here or are my cheeks flushing?

'That would be great, thank you,' I reply, as casually as I can, but obviously I'm jumping for joy on the inside. 'How's it going?'

'Ah, you know,' he says with a shrug. I can tell he doesn't quite seem himself, even though I don't really know him all that well.

'I know just how you feel,' I reply as I take a seat opposite him.

'Want to talk about it?' he asks with a smile.

Another reason to like Max. Even when he's clearly having a bad day, he wants to hear about mine.

'It's stupid, really,' I start. 'My editor wants me to do something I'm not comfortable with.'

'I suppose I'm lucky because you don't get that when you write about gadgets,' he replies.

'Yeah, and it's worse than it sounds. She wants me to...' I shouldn't mention the meet cutes, it will make me look crazy, '... write an article, encouraging women to join the military, and for some reason, this is going to involve me being strapped to someone from the parachute regiment, and thrown out of a plane.'

'Wow,' is about all he can say. I can see the disbelief and the pity on his face. 'That's just... wow.'

I raise my eyebrows in acknowledgement. I don't know what it is about Max, but something about him makes me feel like I can be honest.

'I don't know if I've had enough of this job,' I confess. 'Or if I just need a holiday. It's been forever since I went on holiday, or even had a proper break. I'm just always too busy, or everyone else is. Anyway, that's me done complaining for the day, what's going on with you?'

I feel better just for saying it out loud. My appetite is finally back with me, so I open my sandwich and tuck in.

'Well, now you're going to make me look like an arsehole,' he jokes. 'My problem is sort of the opposite of yours.'

'Oh?'

'Yeah, I *am* going on holiday,' he says. 'In a few days, actually.'

Is it pathetic that I feel like I'm going to miss him? Yes. Yes, it is.

'Oh, nice,' I say, putting on a little enthusiasm for him. 'Where are you going?'

'Hawaii,' he replies.

Now I really am jealous.

'The only problem is that my friend has dropped out last minute, he has to work, which means I'm going alone,' he continues. 'And there's a big difference between going on your own and going with a friend.'

'I don't think I'd have the confidence to go on holiday alone,' I admit. 'But I am still really jealous. Jealous that you're going on holiday – and incredibly jealous you're going to Hawaii. I've always wanted to go to Hawaii. Where are you going?'

'A resort in Wailea, Maui, for two weeks,' he replies. 'It's an amazing place. It's got five stars. It's on the beach, it has pools, a golf course, a spa, restaurants – everything you could possibly want.'

I take an almost violently theatrical bite from my sandwich.

'All right, all right, I already told you I was jealous,' I joke. 'I'd much rather be on a plane to Hawaii alone than in a plane above an airfield where I'm going to be promptly yeeted out of the open door against my will.'

Max pulls a face at me.

'What?' I say, starting to feel a little self-conscious. 'Do I have chutney on my face?'

'No, I was just thinking,' he starts, pausing for a moment to gather his thoughts. 'Yeah, no, okay, why don't you come with me?'

'Ha, good one,' I reply before taking a big swig of my drink. I practically spit it at him when I notice the look on his face. 'Are you serious? You're being serious.'

'I'm being serious,' he says with a laugh. 'I know, it sounds crazy, but you need a holiday, I have a holiday. It's free, because it's all already paid for, and you would have your own room, obviously.'

'Oh, so it won't be like the movies, making a little barricade down the centre of the bed, so our arms and legs don't touch,' I joke. I still think there's a chance he's just kidding.

'Your own bed, a whole resort at your disposal, the chance to go to Hawaii,' he says, hyping it up. 'And I don't have to go alone. It's win-win.'

'You really are serious, aren't you?'

'I am, honestly,' he insists with a smile. 'Frankie, person I hardly know, would you do me the honour of coming on holiday with me?'

I cackle, amused, but in total disbelief, and the most excited I have ever been in my life.

'It's only a few days away, it might get you out of your parachute jump,' he points out.

'I'll think about it,' I say. God, imagine, going somewhere as gorgeous as Hawaii, and with Max! But I can't possibly go, can I? Yes, I desperately need a break and, yes, I would do almost anything to get out of this parachute jump. But I hardly know the guy, and I can't just take time off work last minute.

'Let me give you my number,' he says. 'That way, if you decide you want to come, you don't have to go through the switchboard. And maybe you can give me yours – that way, if you don't come, I can send you pictures of my tan to make you jealous.'

His cheeky smile and that twinkle in his eyes when he makes a joke drives me wild.

We swap phones.

'Max Ray,' I say, taking my phone back, looking at his full name.

'Frankie George,' he says back to me. 'I'd better get back to work, but keep me posted, Frankie George.'

'Will do,' I say with a smile.

I let him walk away before I allow my smile to intensify. I can't go on holiday with him, of course I can't, for so many reasons, but he asked me. He asked *me*. I'm going to count that as a victory.

15

I've been trying to get some work done all afternoon, but I just can't get my head in the game. One word: Hawaii.

Yep, even though I obviously can't go on holiday with someone who is pretty much a stranger, that isn't stopping my brain from taking me there, wondering what it would be like, imagining spending time with Max outside of work, the sun kissing my skin as I neck cocktail after cocktail, just spending the days relaxing, taking dips in the pool, breathing in the sea air, visiting the spa, eating all the delicious food. How am I supposed to work under these conditions?

The thing is that, as gutted as I am that I can't go, I think the fact that Max even asked me if *I* wanted to go is huge, and that alone is worth getting excited about. So huge and exciting that I'm struggling to keep it to myself, but Cora had no sooner finished her meeting when Addison called her into her office for a chat. Now I'm just sitting here, practically rocking back and forth in my chair, waiting for her to come out so that I can tell her all about it.

Eventually she emerges. She smiles when she sees me.

'You're never going to guess what happened at lunch,' I say.

'Ooh, what?' Addison asks, hot on Cora's heels. 'Did you finally manage a meet cute that doesn't come with an STD and isn't followed by an arrest?'

I hope she's joking around, but she seems serious.

'Oh, no, it's not work,' I tell her. 'It's just a personal thing.'

'I like to hear those too,' she replies. I'm always suspicious when she paints herself as human.

She sits down in Cora's chair. Cora just hovers behind her awkwardly.

'Erm, okay,' I say, shaking off any worries I have about telling Addison about my personal life. It's bad enough she's so heavily involved in my work. I wouldn't mind her taking a special interest in me and my silly project if it came with the promise of job security. 'I went for lunch in the canteen and I bumped into Max.'

'That's the smoking-hot one from the tech website?' Addison confirms.

'Yes,' I reply, almost uncomfortably, ever so slightly worried she might try to steal him. You never know. 'He asked me if I wanted to eat lunch with him, so I sat down and we got chatting and eventually he tells me that he's going on holiday to Hawaii in a few days.'

'Lucky bastard,' Addison says.

'But, get this,' I start again, pausing for dramatic effect. 'He was going with his friend, but his friend dropped out at the last minute because he has work, and out of nowhere Max asked me if *I* wanted to go with him in his friend's place.'

'What?' they both squeak in unison.

'He invited you on holiday with him?' Cora says in disbelief.

'He invited me to go to *a five-star resort* with him, for two weeks, in *Hawaii,* for *free*,' I clarify, sounding as smug and delighted as I would if I were really going. 'I was banging on about needing a holi-day, he was saying he didn't want to go on his alone, and it was like all the pieces clicked into place and he invited me to take his friend's spot. Obviously I'm not going to go, though.'

'Why ever not?' Addison asks. 'Are you out of your mind?'

'Erm.' I laugh awkwardly. 'Well, it's in a few days, and I have a job, you're my boss, so you expect me to be here, obviously. But also, I don't really know the guy. It would be weird to go on holiday with a stranger, even if he did say I would have my own room.'

'You know everything you need to know about him,' Addison tells me. 'He's one of the hottest men in this building. And, as you know, all employees here are subject to strict checks, so you know he's not an ex-convict or a paedo.'

'The first thing I check for on people's dating profiles,' I joke.

'Also, yes, you have a job, but don't you think this meets the brief of your article?' she says, snapping back into work mode. 'Surely this is the ultimate meet cute? You *have* to go. Readers will love to hear about this. The article is evolving. You need to write about this meet cute specifically – all the others went terribly anyway, bin those off, no one wants to read about your embarrassing stories – people will want to read about whether or not you find love from this.'

'I thought I was jumping out of a plane,' I remind her – why, oh why, do I remind her?

'That was a crap idea,' she says. 'I'll cancel it.'

She pulls herself to her feet.

'No time off needed, this is work, keep your holiday days for later,' she continues. 'I'll have the girls make you up a bag to take with you. Don't take your own things. Perhaps we could see about doing your hair too. Don't leading ladies always get a makeover in these sorts of things? You can't wear things like that.'

I look down at my outfit. A pair of black shorts with a lace overlay and a vintage ACDC T-shirt with the sleeves rolled up.

That's the beauty of working for a women's mag. Fashion and indi-
viduality are encouraged. But not respected, clearly.

'What's wrong with how I dress?' I ask.

'You look like a Year 10 voted "most likely to get pregnant",' she
jokes, rather meanly. 'You need to look like a mature, viable woman.
I'll go make the arrangements.'

Addison disappears into her office and closes the door behind
her before I get a chance to say another word. Cora takes her seat.

'So, it turns out I'm not a viable woman. She's clearly off her
rocker. Obviously I'm not going to Hawaii with a stranger,' I tell her.
'Even if he is a hot one. Addison can't exactly force me to go, can
she?'

'Frankie, Addison is not your friend, she's your boss, remember
that,' Cora tells me seriously.

'Are you okay?' I ask her. I can always tell when she's not right.

'Erm, no,' she replies. 'Addison just fired me.'

She delivers these words so casually it takes an extra couple of
seconds for them to sink in.

'No!' My jaw is on the floor. 'What? Why?'

'She said I'm not pulling my weight,' she replies with a shrug.
'Never mind the fact she kept me busy think-tanking ideas for your
project.'

'I'm so sorry,' I say, making my way around the desk to give her
a hug.

'It's not your fault,' she replies, squeezing me. 'We knew she was
here to do this. But, unless you want to wind up the same, I'd be
going on that holiday.'

'Do you really think so?' I reply.

'Yep. I don't think she's taking no for an answer.'

Shit, am I really doing this? Am I going on holiday with Max?

I grab my phone from my pocket and type a message, keeping

one arm tightly around Cora as I do so. I can't believe Addison has done this to her.

I message Max.

OK, I'm in. Just let me know what I need to do. X

I instantly kick myself. Why did I put a kiss? What on earth was my thinking there?

I receive a reply almost straight away.

Awesome. I'll be in touch. Xx

OK, *two* kisses? Two kisses *and* a free holiday? Is it possible that I've landed on my feet for once? Who knows but, truth be told, I'm actually quite excited.

16

I don't think I've ever been quite so nervous in my life, for more reasons than I can keep track of in my head, which only makes me feel more nervous.

I can't stop thinking about poor Cora being let go like that, seemingly out of the blue, for no reason at all. I've worked across from Cora since we started at *Stylife*, instantly buddying up together as the new girls taking on their first real journalism jobs, and I can honestly say she's always been such a fantastic employee. Better than me, that's for sure. Cora actually likes her job, for one thing.

It just goes to show, our instincts about Addison were right, she should be feared, and any interest she has taken in us has been for work, or for amusement through the workdays, but she doesn't care about any of us, she cares about getting results. If Cora is on the chopping block, then anyone could be. Even me – especially me, given what a terrible job I've been doing with these meet cutes. But I need this job, like it or not, and I really don't want to lose out on the flat of my dreams. So here I am, at the airport, waiting for Max to turn up.

What Addison said, when I told her about the holiday, really made me fear for my job, and as such probably made me agree to all sorts of things I wouldn't usually agree to. For starters, the cute little purple bits in my hair are no more, leaving me with a natural blonde (even if it isn't really natural) do. The girl who did my hair was horrified – but not surprised – to learn I had dyed the purple bits myself. She told me to never do it again before (ironically) sending me away with a bottle of purple shampoo. Next, I was given a suitcase full of everything I could possibly need, courtesy of the swag room at *Stylife* HQ. This could potentially be a great thing – that room is jam-packed with cool designer stuff and luxury make-up brands – and I managed to get Max's favourite Valentino shirt thrown into the mix too.

The only downside is the fact that I haven't seen any of the contents of the suitcase, so I haven't been able to acquaint myself with any of it ahead of time. I am also concerned about what Addison said when she handed it to me. She told me that no one falls in love with the girl in the edgy clothes – they 'bang' her and then settle down with a girl-next-door type. Then she gave me a long floral sundress with some shoes to complement it, to wear on the plane, and scared as I am of losing my job, I took it all without a word. The insult and the outfit.

So I'm worrying about my friend, my job, what the hell is in this suitcase, whether or not I look awful in this outfit – because I feel *so* self-conscious in it, even though it's more subtle than my usual attire, it just doesn't feel like me, so I don't feel like me – but the icing on the cake is that I have no idea where Max is. He hasn't turned up. He told me to meet him in the lounge, but I'm sitting here in the lounge and there's no sign of him, and he's got my ticket, because he sorted the name change.

Obviously I'm too scared to call or text him, because I don't want to look crazy or desperate, which is a concern only women seem to have, because men do so like to interpret healthy interest as

Fatal Attraction. I take my phone from my bag and open our message thread. I check I haven't misunderstood. I haven't, he said to meet him in the lounge, and here I am, in the airport lounge, alone, and somehow putting out a vibe to the people around me that I have been stood up – or at least it feels like I am. We all think we're the main character, don't we? But, in reality, no one is paying any attention to us.

I decide to give my mum a quick ring – you can always rely on your mum to take your call when you need a chat, can't you?

'Hello, darling, is everything okay?' she asks me quickly. Mums can somehow always tell when you call them when you weren't planning to, as well, which is spooky.

'Yes, everything is fine,' I quickly insist. 'I just thought I'd let you know I'm at the airport, I'll be flying soon, so I'll drop you and Dad a text when I land.'

'Have a safe flight, my love. You've just missed your dad, but I'll tell him you called. I'd appreciate a text, but you need to focus on having fun – you and Cora work so hard.'

Yes, I did tell my mum that I was going away with Cora, but only because she would have completely freaked out at the idea of me going on holiday with a man I didn't know, and it doesn't matter that I'm thirty-four because, to my mum, I'll always be her baby. I wonder if that's something people without siblings feel in such force, or if all mums always treat all of their kids like their babies forever. I kind of like it, to be honest. It drove me mad in my late teens, but now there's something so comforting about travelling home to Surrey to stay with her and my dad, getting spoilt rotten, pretending I'm not a grown adult for a while.

'Thanks, Mum,' I reply. I still feel bad for lying to her.

My phone buzzes in my ear. I glance at it quickly and see Max's name.

'Mum, Cora is looking for me, I'd better dash, but I love you loads, Dad too,' I say.

'We love you too, darling, have a wonderful holiday,' she replies.

I open Max's message.

Hey Frankie, are you still coming? Xx

I'm expecting, in a best-case scenario, for him to say why he's running late and, in a worst-case scenario, some bullshit reason why he isn't coming. But it sounds like he thinks I'm not coming, which is odd.

Hi. Yes, I'm here. Where are you? Xx

Now I'm doing two kisses. It's just polite, isn't it, to match the number of kisses of the person messaging you? It maintains equality in the dynamic and stops the other person feeling uncomfortable. I've found, from app dating over the years, that men don't tend to do kisses, whereas I'll use them like they're nothing, like bonus punctuation, an informal sign-off to people I have any level of good feeling towards. Some men always get so funny about stuff like that so it's encouraging to see Max using them without hesitation.

I'm in the lounge. Xx

I look around for him, but I still can't spot him anywhere.

So am I… xx

Why do I feel like I've messed up? Probably because I have. I usually have, if we're being honest.

I think you must be somewhere else. First-class lounge? Xx

Well, I feel like a pleb. I just assumed the lounge was the, you know, the waiting area with the squashy seats as opposed to the plastic ones. Just like a lounge-lounge. I never even considered the idea of a first-class lounge.

Whoops! How do I get there? Xx

Max directs me to where he is and, honestly, I could kick myself. Screw the squashy seats, this place has fancy private booths as well as luxury chairs and sofas.

'Frankie,' Max calls out. I make my way over to him. 'Wow, you changed your hair. You look great.'

'Ah, thank you,' I reply, touching it self-consciously. 'So do you. Sorry, I was in completely the wrong place.'

Was it weird, to return his compliment like that? Probably. It probably sounded insincere, for just being batted back at him. He does look good, though. He always looks good.

'That's okay,' he replies. 'I probably wasn't very clear. I'm terrible for leaving out the details sometimes.'

'Wow, this place is amazing,' I say. 'I can't believe I've been sat out there all this time.'

'I didn't think you were coming,' he replies. 'We probably don't have time for breakfast now but it's okay, we can eat on the plane.'

'Ahh, I'm sorry,' I reply. 'Truthfully, I didn't expect my free ticket to come with access to a room with chandeliers and a fireplace.'

Max laughs.

'Lucky for you my friend had to work, then. Honestly, it's all okay, I'm just glad you're here, I thought you were standing me up,' he admits.

'I thought *you* were standing *me* up,' I reply, almost excitedly.

He smiles.

'We should probably head towards the gate, then,' he says.

I'm very much going to be following Max's lead from now on. He clearly flies way more often than I do.

We make small talk as we go through the motions until eventually it's time to board the plane. Gosh, I feel nervous. I didn't think my fear of heights extended to planes – it didn't used to – but I guess it does now. My legs feel like jelly as I step onto the escalator.

'Excited?' Max asks me.

'Yes,' I reply. 'Nervous too.'

'It's going to be great,' he reassures me. 'Have you flown first before?'

'Have I flow *first* before?' I repeat back to him. 'No, I have not flown *first*. I don't even know to say things like *first*.'

Max smiles at my teasing.

'You'll like it,' he tells me.

I've seen first-class flights in TV shows and movies but, wow, being here in the cabin, I can't believe it's real. What is Max doing that I'm not to be able to afford fancy holidays? I wonder if tech writers get paid more, or if perhaps he's just better at saving up than I am. It has to be said, I'm not great at putting money away. I never struggle to burn through my income each month.

There are just twelve seats here, and each one has its own little private area. The seats don't look like plane seats at all, they look like big luxury armchairs. Also behind our individual privacy screens is a TV, a table, and so much legroom I feel guilty.

'No,' I can't help but blurt, lowering my voice when I remember we're in *first*, with other people who don't want to hear me freaking out with excitement. 'We get pyjamas?'

'We do,' Max replies. 'Nice, soft, fuzzy ones.'

'Oh, my days, I'm in heaven,' I say, sinking into my chair.

'Just wait until they start bringing you booze,' he chuckles before sitting in his own seat, just to the right of mine, but in his own little section. There's a screen between us that pops up and down, in case we want some privacy from one another. He sounds like he's done this before. I really do feel a little *Pretty Woman* now.

I glance around my little pod. I have not one but two windows and a control panel that wouldn't look out of place in the cockpit. Not that I know what any of it does.

Man, this is the life. I've been given a glass of champagne. I'm in my comfy seat. I don't even care that we're about to take off into the sky – the world's highest height, if you know what I mean. Bon voyage, fear of heights.

I grab what looks like a menu. Cheese and port. Soufflé. Mille-feuille. Am I on a plane or in a five-star restaurant? This is unreal. And there's a booklet, with a guide to everything the plane has to offer. Movies, toiletries – this chair even turns into a bed. Honestly, I could live on this plane.

'Ready for take-off?' Max asks me.

'I genuinely can't wait,' I reply.

17

This time last week, if you told me that I would be about to eat dinner in an LA airport, I would have laughed in your face. And with Max too! If you told me I would be eating dinner with an actual man in a McDonald's in London I wouldn't have believed you. But here I am, at LAX, grabbing a bite to eat before our second flight, which will take us to Kahului Airport. Then, apparently, it's just a short drive and we are in paradise. Unbelievable.

Sitting here with Max, eating pizza, drinking my first cocktail in hopefully a long line of many, I can't believe I have the audacity to say this, but it just feels right. I know, me, the dog thief, feeling like I'm getting on with a man.

We have been getting on really well. Once we were up in the air, it was like I left my fear of heights down on the runway. I was too absorbed in everything the plane had to offer. Watching movies, eating cheese, chatting to Max – I even managed to get some sleep, until a few bumps in the flight woke me up, but I was too jazzed to let that bother me.

'I expected such a long flight to feel more draining,' I say between mouthfuls of pizza. 'I swear, the last time I went to Spain, the flight felt more uncomfortable and exhausting. Is that a *first* thing?'

'Look at you, talking like you do this all the time,' he says with a smile.

I watch Max take a swig of his beer before biting into another slice of pizza. Even the way he eats is attractive. Low-key sexy, although I doubt he's doing it on purpose. I think perhaps I've just reached that level of attraction where it doesn't matter what he does, or how he does it, I'm just going to swoon regardless.

'I'll never be able to fly any other way ever again,' I say with a sigh. 'Which is a shame because I highly doubt I'll be able to afford holidays like this anytime soon. I'm almost hoping I have a terrible time, so I'm not devastated when it's over.'

'Frankie, if it helps, I will do everything in my power to make sure you don't enjoy yourself,' he jokes. 'How about that?'

And I bet he'd even look good doing that.

'Thanks,' I reply. 'I still can't believe this isn't costing me a penny. I would have thought I would have had to pay for my flight, at least. Not that I'm complaining because I'll bet that flight alone costs more than most holidays.'

'I guess it's just your lucky day,' he says with a shrug.

It only takes a moment of thought before I narrow my eyes at him.

'I always thought plane tickets weren't transferable,' I say. 'Or is that just something I've picked up from TV and movies that isn't actually true? I assumed, when I sent you all my details, that it must be doable. Gutted for your friend, though, spending this money, not getting to come. I feel guilty.'

Max swallows a mouthful of pizza before taking another swig of beer, keeping eye contact with me the whole time. I can see something in his eyes. A glimmer. A secret he can't contain.

'Okay, you're right, they're not usually transferable,' he admits.

'But we paid extra for insurance, if for some reason either of us couldn't fly, that made the tickets amendable. You sent me everything I needed and luckily it turns out you don't have a criminal record.'

'No, I guess my previous convictions must have expired or something,' I joke. 'That's great about the insurance but I still feel terrible.'

I have no idea how much plane tickets cost, given that I haven't been on holiday in a long time, but first class must be expensive.

'He's just happy it isn't going to waste, and that I'm not going alone,' Max replies. 'You're doing me such a huge favour.'

'Oh, yeah, it feels like it,' I say sarcastically. 'I'm a regular hero.'

I think back to my date with Tom. Not that this is a date, here today, with Max. Then again, neither was the other night with Tom, but my point is that it felt so uncomfortable and forced. We didn't get on at all. Being around Max is easy. It's strange, because I want him to like me, but I don't feel like an awkward mess. I don't think I'm trying too hard. Of course, I'm not exactly pursuing him, and it doesn't feel like he's pursuing me either. Perhaps that's why the pressure is off. Sure, I'm ridiculously attracted to him, but we both know this is just a holiday, and I do really appreciate the break.

'So, what kind of person are you on holiday?' I ask him curiously.

'Depending on the location, obviously. Snowboarding, skiing, surfing, bungee jumping.'

His serious look eventually dissolves into a smile again.

'I'm kidding,' he insists. 'My family always tell me I waste holidays. I would always prefer sitting by a log fire with a book than stacking it down a ski slope. As for Hawaii, my plan is to sit around in the sun, spend time in the pool, drink lots of cocktails, eat too much food. If I'm not bursting out of my trousers by the time we get home...'

I raise my eyebrows.

'From the food,' he insists with a laugh. 'What about you? What are your holiday plans?'

'I just want to be still and warm and relaxed and low-key drunk for large chunks of it,' I tell him. 'Sort of like a last hurrah, in case I'm getting sacked when I get home.'

'Because you took time off?' he asks, concerned this might be something to do with him.

'No, no, definitely not that,' I insist, neglecting to tell him that I'm on the clock just by being here. 'Addison, the woman you met briefly the other day, she's come in to clean house. We're in a sort of trial period where she's figuring out who should stay and who should go. She sacked my best friend. I don't feel like she's far from sacking me.'

'Have you done anything wrong?' he asks.

'Not really,' I reply. 'You know what it's like in this industry, though. If figures are down, they have to blame someone. Changing things makes the higher-ups happy. If you can show them that you got rid of a bunch of dead wood and drafted in some fresh talent, it appeases them.'

'It isn't like that at ByteBanter at all,' Max says. 'Us lowly writers are the only ones who understand what we're writing about. Anyone north of the editor doesn't have a clue. I suppose tech is just constantly evolving. We have nothing to contend with. What sort of things do you write about?'

I choose my words carefully.

'Lifestyle,' I reply.

'Tech is so black and white,' he says. 'It's all science at the end of the day. You can't argue with science – although I'm aware we're living in a world where many people try to. Lifestyle is so vague. You could write the same article twice, for two completely different audiences, and they wouldn't even resemble one another.'

'You're not wrong,' I reply. 'And that's exactly what Addison is doing. Whatever I was writing before, that's not what she wants from me, so I'm having to come up with new things, with completely different angles, to try and impress her.'

'You've got this,' he reassures me. 'Use this break to recharge and reset and then get back to work with a whole new mindset.'

Don't get me wrong, this is a holiday, but how can it not feel like a working one? As much as I want to fully relax and unwind, the fact that Addison is expecting some kind of next-level article from me is hanging over my head like a dark cloud.

'I've always wanted to visit LA,' I confess. 'I'll have to come back sometime, for more than just a flight to somewhere else.'

'My family live here in California,' Max tells me. 'My immediate family. My mum and dad, my brother and, er, his wife.'

'Oh, wow, really?' I reply. 'How come?'

I smile to myself. Asking this question only highlights the fact that I'm going on holiday with a man I hardly know.

'My parents moved here for work,' he explains. 'I lived here, for a while, but moved back to London for uni. Then I moved back here, to be around my family, but I finally settled in London when I got the ByteBanter job.'

'Oh, my goodness, you must really love that job, to leave California for it,' I tell him. 'Surely everything is better here?'

'You'd be surprised,' he says with a laugh. 'London has a lot going for it too.'

Max smiles at me in a way that makes me wonder, just for a second, if he could be talking about me. Of course he isn't. I feel like my own smile drops slightly.

'But Hawaii has them both beat,' he insists. 'I think you're going to love it. It's impossible not to.'

'You've been before?' I say.

'Hawaii is like LA's Blackpool,' he jokes.

'Ahh, I just want to get there,' I say excitedly.

'Well, one more flight to go,' Max says. 'Paradise, here we come.'

First-class flights, a free holiday in Hawaii, Max... Everything seems so perfect. I'd say this were all too good to be true, were it not for the fact that I'm probably going to get sacked when I get home. I'll just have to make the most of it while I can.

18

When you frequently see things and places on TV, online or in books you build up a sort of picture of the place in your head, using all the little fragments you've picked up during the course of your life, and sometimes things aren't as you expected them to be. A good example is the *Mona Lisa*, potentially one of the most recognisable paintings in the world – whether you're into art or not, it's easy to recall the image of Leonardo da Vinci's famous artwork. But, if you go to the Louvre to see it in person, you don't just see that iconic portrait hanging on the wall, it's behind glass, which is roped off, and then the crowd of people trying to get a glimpse will be so deep you'll struggle to see much of it anyway. It's the same with the pyramids – stunning, fascinating, historic... and with a Pizza Hut overlooking them. The Eiffel Tower, the Empire State Building, Buckingham Palace – places we can conjure up an image of in our heads in a heartbeat, but we don't really imagine them with the shoulder-to-shoulder tourists you'll see in real life.

I've seen lots of movies and TV shows set/shot in Hawaii. From the mysterious and creepy beaches and forests of *Lost* to, well, basically every movie Adam Sandler has anything to do with. I know what it looks like in my mind but I have to be realistic, right? Because it can't possibly live up to my expectations.

Wrong! Oh my God. *Oh. My. God.* I have been in Hawaii for, what? An hour maybe, just a bit of time at the airport, and the short drive to the resort, and I can't quite believe it. For starters, I love Kahului Airport. Airports always look and feel like, well, airports, but this one is different. It has a charm to it, in the carpets, in the colours, the loud but beautiful bird-song, the sunshine pouring in from the brilliant blue skies outside.

I love that Kahului Airport is small and bursting with charm. I love that you take the most gorgeous little tram to the car rental place. I also loved how excited Max was, to be getting a car to drive, because he says that one of the things he misses living in London is never driving.

'Mate, you live it up when you're on holiday,' I say, from the comfort of the passenger's seat of the Chevrolet convertible Max has hired for the drive to the resort.

I may not love this sundress that Addison gave me, but it sure is cool when the weather is warm. Hiding behind my aviator sunglasses helps me feel more like myself. Max's shades are mirrored glass, which means that when I look in his eyes, all I see is myself, and boy do I look like a dork around him.

'I just love to drive here,' he replies. I may not be able to see his eyes but his smile is telling me everything I need to know. 'I love that there are no big freeways in Maui.'

Driving from Kahului Airport to Wailea has me convinced that Hawaii is the exception to the rule. Somewhere that lives up to its reputation. A place that is just as beautiful in real life as it is on TV – if not more so, because I can't quite believe that it's real and I'm here. The colours, the scenery, even the smell of the air. I just can't get over it.

'Is there anything you would love to do while you're here?' he asks.

'Anything,' I reply. 'Everything. You've been here before, maybe you can recommend some things?'

'Absolutely,' he replies. 'There's so much to see, on this island alone, but I have a sneaking suspicion you're not going to want to leave the resort.'

The wind feels so good blowing through my freshly coloured and styled hair. I imagine it's going to be all knots by the time we arrive, but it's still fresh from the salon, and feeling silky-smooth. It's hard to care about anything right now.

'I'm tempted to ask more questions but, at the same time, I'm excited to see it all first-hand.'

'Well, you only have to wait another minute or two,' he replies. 'We're almost here.'

Suddenly I feel sick with nerves, like it's my first day at a new job – a thought which makes me feel even worse because that could be on the horizon. I shouldn't look so far ahead, not when there are closer, much more beautiful horizons here. I just need to forget about my real life and snap into holiday mode. If I'm going to get the sack anyway then it makes sense to make the most of it.

Max pulls up outside the Grand Palm Resort, on a short U-shaped road outside the main entrance. I've never seen valet parking in real life. I feel a combination of fancy and guilty.

'Don't worry about our cases,' Max tells me as I make a move towards the boot of the car. 'They'll be in our rooms before we are.'

I smile at him in disbelief. Wow, really?

The lobby is beyond grand. The décor is a mixture of warm creams and brown tones which just scream luxury hotel but, just in case you were in any doubt, pops of colour come in the form of pieces of art and sculptures dotted around the room. We're no sooner through the door than we're almost outside again. Large stretches of lobby are lined with bifold doors, making the outside and the inside one and the same.

As Max heads over to the front desk, I walk over to the nearest open set of doors. I can't help but admire the floor, so shiny I can see my reflection in it, and boy do I have one hell of a smile on my face. I almost don't look like myself, it's like a completely different Frankie is looking back at me, one who has already decided she belongs here. Stepping through the first set of doors takes me onto a small terrace covered with tables and chairs. Beyond that is just... paradise. Everywhere you look is fresh off a postcard. Several post-cards in one. There's grass, the pools, then beach and finally the ocean. It's impossible to look anywhere without seeing palm trees, which I love. Nothing says paradise like palm trees.

'Right, I've got our key cards,' Max announces, pulling me out of my trance.

'I can't believe I'm here,' I blurt. 'Just... unreal.'

'Wait until you see the room,' he replies.

'Let's go,' I say excitedly.

I follow Max through the hotel. He must have been here before because he walks like he knows where he's going. Perhaps I should apply for a job at ByteBanter. I don't know much about tech (although I know not to pour a cold cup of coffee on a keyboard) but I'll learn anything if it means I can afford holidays like this. At present, I can't even afford a bath that I don't have to share with bugs. He must have been saving forever, or live in far worse conditions than I do.

'The suites,' I say in a la-di-da voice, reading it from a sign on the wall.

Max laughs.

'Here we are,' he says.

Max still has the key cards, so he opens the door. What am I even expecting? Why am I wasting my time expecting things? I clearly have no idea about any of this stuff. Still, my jaw drops when I see the suite, because I was not expecting *that*.

The suite is like a house. If it was in London, it would cost *millions*. It's a huge open-plan space with a kitchen area, a large dining table, and then a huge sitting area next to yet another set of bifold doors. I suppose, when your outside is so incredible, why wouldn't you want it to be inside?

'I'm going to get these doors open,' he says. 'Let some air in.'

'I'm going to go check out my room,' I say, like a little kid, as I practically charge towards the stairs. Why, yes, our suite does have stairs. When I get to the top of the stairs there are two doors. My instincts tell me to head through the right one and they are not wrong. A humongous bed sits in the heart of the room. So big I'm tempted to check it isn't two regular big beds pushed together to make one monster bed. Then there are the huge glass windows, which upon closer inspection are also bifold doors, which open up to form a Juliet balcony. I run over to the windows and look out. Our suite must be part of a series of suites, all in one curve-shaped row, overlooking a massive swimming pool surrounded with seating areas, palm trees and even a fountain. This area eventually leads down to a beach. There isn't a soul in sight. Absolutely picture-perfect.

It doesn't matter what the other room looks like because it can't be as perfect as this one. This room has the view. Oh, it *has* to be mine, I am in love. Do you think Max will mind if I take the room with the view?

I turn around and realise our cases are right behind me. Wow, they really did make it here before us. It isn't only my stuff, though, it's Max's stuff too. I suppose, if whoever brought them here had decided to put my stuff in this bedroom and Max's stuff in the other, then perhaps that could be how we decide who gets which room. In which case, I need to drag Max's case to the other room, and fast.

I grab it, dragging it behind me as I make my way back out of one door and through another and... oh. The other door doesn't lead to another bedroom at all. It's the bathroom. It's stunning, don't get me wrong. A bath (that surely must be classed as a small pool), and twin sinks in front of a mirror that covers most of the wall. We have two sinks. Two sinks but one bedroom. This can't be right?

I put Max's case back where I found it and head back downstairs.

'What do you think?' he asks excitedly. He's got that look on his face usually reserved for when you watch people open the present you just gave them. I suppose, if he's been here before, then seeing it through my eyes will give him a hit of that first-time joy. His expression quickly changes when he sees mine.

'You don't like it?' he says.

'There's only one bedroom up there,' I tell him. 'One bedroom, but a bed big enough to chop up and make four small ones.'

I'm about to ask who we complain to when I see it. Something on his face, perhaps, or in his eyes. Something that makes me ask...

'Did you know there was only one bedroom?' I ask him.

'Yes,' he replies simply.

Fuck. I knew this was all too good to be true. That he was too perfect to be real.

'It's not what you think, though,' he quickly explains. 'Look.'

Max heads over to the sofa. He pulls a lever, which lifts the seat of the sofa. A new piece pops out, making a sofa bed.

'This is one of the beds,' he says. 'I thought, if I told you one of the beds was a sofa bed, you wouldn't want to come, or you would insist you slept on it. But you're doing me a huge favour, I want you to take the bedroom. I'm more than happy down here. You see that huge piece of art on the wall?'

I glance over at a framed picture of painted coastline – Hawaiian, of course.

Max points a remote control at it and pushes a button which turns it into a TV. Once he's proved his point, he turns it back to a picture.

'I'm happy sleeping down here with this huge TV, the door open – I love to keep the door open pretty much the whole time I'm here, I could never do that in London – and I'm near the kitchen. Honestly, I'll be in my element.'

I smile because I do believe him.

'That's very kind of you,' I say. 'Thank you. Sorry, I left your case upstairs.'

'I'll go grab it,' he says. 'I need to freshen up, anyway.'

I give Max another smile as he passes me. I feel like a bit of an idiot now, and a total cow for doubting him. Of all the creeps I've met in my adult life (and there have been many), Max hasn't given me any reason to think he is one of them.

I head deeper into the living room, twirling around on the spot now that I'm alone. My instinct, like most millennials, is to grab my phone and start taking photos of everything. I'm also very millennial-esque in that, while I do like to take pictures of everything, I'm low-key embarrassed about it, so I'm keen to do it while Max is upstairs.

I turn around, to take a picture of the place from the bifold doors, keen to get all of the interiors in the shot. I love that everywhere has the same warm tones. It makes me feel so calm.

I take another step backwards, hitting something, which makes me feel a little less chilled for a moment. I'm relieved not to hear anything smash to the floor, but I'm terrified when I hear a man's voice.

'Steady on,' he says.

I jump out of my skin, and out of his arms, and quickly spin around to see a fifty-something couple standing just inside the doors, staring at me, smiling widely.

Do not tell me we've been checked into a suite that already has another couple staying in it! Some luxury five-star resort, if they can't even get something basic like this sorted.

'You must be Fran,' the woman says.

My first reaction, as always, is to privately cringe at being called Fran. It's not a bad name, it just isn't my name, and it's amazing how often people call me it. Of course, that isn't the pressing matter here, is it? Who the hell are they and how do they (almost) know my name?

'Yes,' I reply, sort of weakly.

'Lovely to meet you finally, Fran,' the woman says. 'We're your future in-laws.'

19

I would be lying if I said that I wasn't waiting for the moment when all of this turned out to be too good to be true. That said, I'd also be lying if I didn't admit that, with each step of the way that didn't turn out to be that moment, my confidence grew that this holiday might genuinely be good. Ha! What a moron.

Yes, I was waiting for the moment, and my mind went to some weird and wonderful places wondering what the universe might throw at me, but hats off to it, because *this* (whatever this is) didn't even cross my mind.

'Erm...'

I shift awkwardly on the spot.

'How was the flight?' the woman asks. She has an English accent with sporadic American bursts, as though perhaps she's been living over here for a while.

'Great,' I reply. Oh my God, why am I replying? What the hell is going on?

'Where's Max?' the man asks. His accent is all English. London born and bred. 'He hasn't gone for a snooze already, has he?'

'That's your son,' the woman teases. 'No stamina for long-distance travel.'

I was really hoping for a different explanation but, nope, these are Max's parents. What the hell is going on?

'Sorry, where are our manners?' the woman says as she approaches me. She pulls me close for a hug. The man soon follows and does the same. This is so weird.

'I'm Eva,' she says. 'And this is my husband, Ronnie. I'm sure you knew that.'

She laughs wildly. Eva is beautiful, like a Catherine Zeta-Jones type with a perfect face and long, glossy brown hair. If I had to think of an actor doppelganger for Ronnie, well, he looks and sounds like an older Daniel Craig. Dirty-blonde hair, bright blue eyes, rugged good looks. Max definitely looks more like his mum. Dark features, more on the pretty side than the rugged, a friendly smile that beams reassurance and friendliness in the form of perfect teeth. Perfect for now at least. Just you wait until I get my hands on him.

'Mum, Dad, hi.' I hear Max's voice from behind me. He sounds terrified. Of course he does. He knows that I know. I mean, I don't exactly know what I know yet, not properly, but I know something is going on here.

'Max, darling,' Eva sings as she heads over to give him a kiss on the cheek.

Ronnie offers him a hand to shake before pulling him close for a manly hug. I can't bring myself to look Max in the eye.

'We were just introducing ourselves to your beautiful fiancée,' Eva tells him. She turns to me. 'Honestly, Fran, I can hardly believe you're real.'

God, she doesn't know the half of it. Then again, neither do I, so I do what I always do in tricky situations.

I pat my body up and down, eventually relocating my phone in the pocket of my dress, before looking at the screen and making a face.

'Oh, my goodness, so sorry, it's work,' I tell them. 'I'll just step out and take this.'

'Work, on holiday?' Ronnie says. 'A woman after my own heart.'

'We understand you have an important job, sweetheart, you go ahead,' Eva reassures me.

I smile before heading to the door. As I pass Max, we briefly make eye contact. If looks could kill, he would be on the floor right now. The only look on his face is panic.

'Are you okay, darling?' Eva asks him. 'Are you tired?'

I close the door behind me before running down the hallway. Eventually I reach the lobby where I plonk myself down on one of the sofas. My bum has no sooner touched the seat when I'm calling Addison. Thankfully she answers.

'Frankie?' she says. 'Hello. Did you land safe? What time is it there? How's Hawaii?'

I thought Addison would be angry to hear from me, outside work hours, so soon into my trip, but her friendly small talk says otherwise. Now I'm going to ruin her day.

'Hi, yes, I did land safe. It's half eleven in the morning. Hawaii is lovely but this whole thing is fucked because Max is a sociopath who has totally set me up,' I tell her, without pausing to even take a breath.

'Wow,' she says simply. 'It's half nine in the evening here. Time differences always fascinate me.'

Is she for real?

'Addison, did you hear what I said?' I say, cutting to the chase.

'Go on then, what's so wrong with Mr Perfect on your perfect free holiday?' she asks in a tone that I do not appreciate.

'Well, I've turned up to the hotel, and there's only one bed,' I start.

'Frankie, Max is a fitty, so why on earth is that an issue?' she asks me seriously.

'Erm, because his parents are here, and they think I'm his fiancée, because he's told them I'm his fiancée,' I tell her plainly. Even Addison can't think this is acceptable.

'What?' she replies. There it is. A normal reaction. 'This is fantastic!'

Or maybe not.

'Excuse me?' I say in disbelief. 'Did you just say this was fantastic? Addison, he's clearly deranged.'

'What you're not seeing is how good this is for the feature,' Addison insists. 'The article is evolving. You've had the perfect meet cute with the perfect man. Now what you need to do is write about it – about how badly it's turned out. That's the new story. The desperate lengths men will go to.'

'I need to come home,' I tell her.

'No, you need to stay there and do your job,' she corrects me. 'You need to find out why he's doing this, what his game is, and how it plays out. If you can't do that – your job – then perhaps I seriously need to rethink if it's the right job for you.'

I'm stunned into silence.

'Get me some gold, Frankie,' she eventually says. 'And, for goodness' sake, try to enjoy yourself. You're in Hawaii.'

I still don't know what to say.

'Frankie? Hello? Is it your signal?'

I place my phone on airplane mode, a sure-fire way to make the call seem like your signal has gone, instead of seeming like you've hung up on someone, because hanging up on Addison would be the easiest way to get the sack.

I can't believe she wants me to stay here and write about this. I can't believe I'm going to, but what choice do I have?

I puff air from my cheeks as I slump back on the sofa. Looking out over the resort, down towards the sea, I never imagined my own personal hell to be quite so beautiful. I know, there are worse places to be forced to stay, but I think it's just the fact that I don't feel like I have a choice. Addison will sack me for sure if I abandon the mission and head home. Talk about being trapped between the devil and the deep blue sea.

I feel despondent. Despondent in Hawaii. That would make a great title for something. It certainly feels appropriate for this chapter of my life. Only I could make paradise so shitty.

'Frankie,' I eventually hear Max say, panic in his voice. 'Frankie, I can explain.'

I look up and, for the first time, his easy-going carefree vibe is nowhere to be seen.

He takes a seat next to me.

'That would be great,' I say, extra sarcastically. 'Because, I don't know, it sort of seems like you've brought me on holiday to introduce me as the woman you're marrying to your parents? But that can't be true, because that's insane.'

'I honestly don't know what I was thinking,' he says. 'Well, I sort of do, in places. Every year, my family takes a holiday together. This year, for the first time, I told them that I was coming with my girlfriend, Fran. Fran is a real person – a real person who cheated on me last month. I knew I needed to be honest, because I'm not a total fucking arsehole, I swear, but when I called up... I don't know, I just panicked. Somehow my mum interpreted me saying I had news as me having big, exciting news. She put me on speaker, so my dad, brother and his wife could all hear. I panicked and told them we'd got engaged. I knew, before the words had finished leaving my mouth, that it was a stupid thing to say. I was all set for coming on my own, wondering what kind of excuse I could make that people would buy, for why she suddenly couldn't come after booking the time off work and everything. And then I met you, and your name was so similar, and you needed a holiday, and I never sent anyone a photo of Fran, or told them much about her, because I try not to tell my family much, so it felt like a sign that I should bring you, and I realise how moronic that sounds now, I really do.'

'Wow, there really is no such thing as a free holiday,' I say with a sigh.

'In my head, originally, I thought we could help each other out, and I was going to tell you before we flew, but you didn't show up, and then I got caught up in what a good time we were having, but these are all explanations, not excuses, I should have told you,' he insists. 'It was certainly my plan to tell you before you met my parents. I definitely wasn't expecting you to play along, honestly.'

I finally look at Max. He usually has such a sparkle in his eye but today it's a little harder to see. I do feel sorry for him – of course I do. Getting cheated on is horrendous, and, well, I can't say that if I was in the situation he was, when he called to tell his mum that he and Fran had broken up, I wouldn't have done the same (except I probably would have mucked it up from the get-go).

'Where do we go from here, then?' I ask him.

'I'll tell them the truth,' he says. 'I've made things so much worse, because this is going to be even more mortifying now, but it has to be done. You don't have to go home, though. Stay, enjoy the holiday, I can keep out of your way, you can have the suite, I'll book myself a room in the hotel.'

I think for a moment. Lord knows I've got myself in enough messes like this, okay, perhaps not on this scale, but I did steal a dog, con a doctor and suck down a disturbing amount of blue ink trying to seduce a man who was just trying to do his job. And that was all just last week. Plus, Addison wants me to make this article about Max, and what he's brought me here for. Convincing me to go on holiday with him just to trick his parents into thinking he isn't single is exactly the kind of thing Addison wants me to write about, so staying here might not be so bad for me after all. I've got to keep my eyes on the prize and that prize is my promotion and my new apartment. I just need to focus on that.

'Look, I'm not jazzed about the order of events,' I start. Already I see that sparkle returning to Max's eyes. 'But, okay, I'll stay, and I'll pretend to be your fiancée.'

'Really?' he replies. 'Frankie, you don't have to do that.'

'Yes, really,' I say. 'And we can stick with the original room situation, with me in the bedroom and you on the sofa. It would seem weird if you got a different room.'

'Right, yes,' he replies. 'Sorry, obviously I never do anything like this, so I'm in over my head,'

Oh, Max. I do this sort of thing all the time. Never successfully, but that's beside the point.

'It's fine,' I tell him. 'I'm still mad at you, but I'll help you make this work. This had better be one hell of a holiday, though.'

'Trust me, you can't not have an incredible time, my parents pay for everything, you can have anything you want – they encourage it.'

'I'm not sure how comfortable I feel taking advantage of your parents and spending their money,' I reply.

'A girl after my own heart,' he says. 'But, honestly, it's almost as though they make it their mission to make each family holiday more expensive than the last. You would be doing a favour, giving them something to brag to their friends about. My dad is on the Forbes 400. If I didn't tell you now, don't worry, he'd tell you at some point if he thought there was a chance you didn't know.'

'Who are you?' I ask in disbelief.

Max smiles. 'Come on, I think it's about time I introduced you to the Ray family.'

Now I really am intrigued.

20

It turns out that not only are Max's parents also staying in one of these suites, but pretty much the whole block is booked up for his family members, and the ones that aren't needed are booked anyway, to ensure absolute privacy. Seriously, who are these people?

I quickly tried to google Max Ray while I was freshening up, grabbing the first plain-looking sundress from my case (still too scared to take stock of everything else in there) ahead of meeting his parents properly for lunch (and with a better understanding of the part I'm here to play) but nothing came up. Well, nothing apart from a character from a TV show, *The Centurions*, who was called Max Ray.

We're in Max's parents' suite, sitting at the dining table, waiting for them to come down and join us for lunch. Various hotel employees are fussing around us, laying out a gigantic buffet on the table in front of us. Their suite has the same natural, relaxing décor as ours, except theirs must be four times the size. It's bigger than most people's houses. The fact that it's just the two of them staying in here gives me a glimpse into what I'm working with. I definitely don't belong here.

'My parents never arrive before the food,' Max explains. Sort of. I don't understand why. 'Thank you.'

Max must have thanked me a thousand times. For some reason he needs this, and I mean really needs it. There's a desperation in him that I haven't seen since I went on that date with Tom the mystery diner. Which one of us was desperate? Christ, probably both of us.

'It's fine,' I whisper back.

It occurs to me that I shouldn't be looking up Max on the internet. I should be looking up his dad. Ronnie Ray.

Unlike Max who, if he did have an online presence, didn't show up in search results because he shared a name with a character from a TV show, there is nothing, and I mean absolutely nothing, keeping Ronnie Ray from the top spot.

Ronnie Ray is the founder and CEO of tech giant Optecho. I've heard of them – who hasn't? I've even owned products by them. In fact, my first webcam, when I was a teenager, was made by them, and I spent so much time on MSN I was basically staring at their eye logo the whole time. Lenses are their speciality – it seems like most of the tech they create is some kind of camera.

I take a break from my detective work to look up at Max and give him a reassuring smile. We're not talking much while the servers are laying the table, so I get back to my phone screen.

I click on his Wikipedia page – everyone's initial go-to for research – and sure enough, there is a photo of Ronnie. It's definitely him. Eva Ray is listed as his wife and, when you click her link, there's a photo of her and Ronnie on a red carpet at some big, flashy event. On Eva's page I notice her children. Maximillian Ray. Wow, so that's his real name. No wonder nothing comes up when I search him. He doesn't have a link but his brother, Kingsley 'Lee' Ray, does. It turns out that Kingsley is the COO of Optecho while Max, the eldest son, writes for a tech website thousands of miles away. I wonder why that is? Perhaps that's why he feels so self-conscious about being single, because he wants to impress his family.

Soon enough, it's just me, Max and the buffet to end all buffets. There's a gigantic platter of crudités, an even bigger plate over-flowing with sushi – this is way more than the four of us could eat in a week – along with large pitchers of various cocktails. The smell of the drinks is so good there's a nagging little ache under my tongue, begging me to grab a glass.

A matter of seconds after the staff clear out, Ronnie and Eva descend the stairs with all the swagger and style you would lend to the Oscars. Eva's outfit wouldn't be out of place either. Her sundress makes mine look like a rag. She's wearing a long baby-blue gown-like dress covered with tiny sparkling sequins, making it look like the ocean when the sun hits it just right. Ronnie is more casual, in cargo shorts and a beige short-sleeved shirt.

'Darlings, so happy you could join us,' Eva says. As she approaches us, she kisses us both on the cheek, Max then me.

'We would have been down sooner, but the pillows haven't arrived,' Ronnie tells us. 'So I had to sort that, you know your mum.'

'You don't have any pillows?' I say. A five-star resort like this forgot the pillows? Is that even possible?

'Oh, we do,' Eva says. 'But I always bring my own pillows. I don't like the idea of sleeping on a pillow that someone else has slept on, you know?'

She says this in a way that I think is supposed to come across as relatable, but I can't say I've ever taken my own pillows to a hotel, that's sort of what you expect to be included in the price, second only to the actual bed.

'We don't want to hear about your diva demands,' Ronnie says through a mouthful of sushi. 'We want to learn all about you, Fran.'

'Please, call me Frankie,' I insist. 'Those close to me call me Frankie.'

That ought to make things easier. Well, it is my name, after all.

'Frankie, how lovely,' Eva says. 'Come on then, let's see your engagement ring.'

Eva's eyes narrow when she realises I don't have a ring on. I just had to eat a pastry right as she asked.

'No ring?' she says in disbelief.

'Would you believe it? I took it off to have a shower, before we left for the airport, and I left it in the bathroom,' I lie.

'Oh, that's a shame,' she replies. 'But that just means there's another surprise coming. I have to admit, we were shocked when we learned about the engagement.'

She's not the only one.

'I was more shocked to learn that this one was marrying a spinal surgeon,' Ronnie says with a laugh.

I look at Max and smile with my mouth while I panic with my eyes.

Oh, for God's sake, why did it have to be a spinal surgeon?

'I would love to hear more about that,' Eva says excitedly. 'I don't know the first thing about spinal surgery.'

Once more, with feeling this time: she's not the only one!

'Oh, bones are really quite boring,' I say with a dismissive bat of my hand. 'Nowhere near as interesting as what you guys do, I'm sure.'

'And yet this one still won't work with us,' Ronnie says as he points an extra-long raw carrot baton at his son.

I relax in my chair as he changes the subject.

'I did try it,' Max reminds him. 'It wasn't for me.'

'And yet you had the audacity to give our bodycams a three-star review,' Ronnie says.

'Are we really doing this now?' Max asks with a laugh. 'Come on, Dad, it's supposed to be a holiday.'

'We always work on holiday, you know that,' a man's voice says.

A couple walk in through the open bifold doors. The man has to be Max's brother because he looks just like him, only somehow like a far more serious version. The woman on his arm, bizarrely, is a similar type to me, but I'm probably a Poundshop version of her. Her blonde hair is brighter, her cheeks are chiselled, and she's much smaller than me. I imagine, if I were to go to a cosmetic surgeon, this is how they would propose making me look, not that they could physically make me about half a foot shorter, and not that I would ever even consider changing the way I looked at the suggestion of someone who said they could make me perfect.

'Here he is,' Eva says as she jumps to her feet. 'And my darling daughter-in-law, hello.'

They both get two kisses. Kissing is clearly very much a thing in this family.

'Frankie, sweetheart, this is my youngest, Kingsley, and his wife, Paige,' Eva tells me.

'Lovely to meet you both,' I tell them.

'Call me Lee,' he insists with a smile. He pats Max on the back. 'Hello, bro.'

'Hi,' Paige says as she sits down opposite me. She has an East Coast American accent and, I don't know what it is, but I feel like she hates me already and, sure, there are plenty of reasons to hate me, but none that Paige could possibly know of yet.

'So, this is the missus?' Lee asks Max.

'Yeah, this is Frankie,' he replies.

I only hold Lee's attention for a moment.

'Dad, I hate to do this to you, but I've got Kidman on hold in my suite,' Lee tells him.

'Can't it wait?' Ronnie asks, gesturing at his lunch.

'Not with the time difference,' Lee replies. 'And Mum, I spotted Uncle Albert in the lobby, I'm guessing he just sailed in. Looked like he was more concerned with finding a drink than checking in.'

'Well, that's brothers for you,' Eva says with a smile. 'I suppose, if the boys are going for a meeting, I should go and welcome him.'

'So, we're abandoning lunch?' Max confirms. It isn't quite in disbelief, it's more like he disapproves.

'There will be plenty of time for lunches,' Eva reminds him. 'I'll send someone in to clear it out. Unless, by all means, if you, Frankie and Paige want to help yourselves, be my guest.'

'I think I'll come with you,' Paige says quickly. 'I need to stretch my legs.'

'Of course,' Eva says with a knowing smile – God, I hate that it feels like everyone knows something I don't.

Ronnie and Lee leave the room out of the bifold doors while Eva and Paige leave via the main door. Then it's just me, Max, and enough food to feed about thirty people.

'Erm...' I say before I just laugh.

'Yep, welcome to my family,' Max replies. 'You might as well tuck in. They really will have all this food thrown away, and then probably prepared again in about forty-five minutes when they realise they're still hungry.'

He doesn't sound impressed by their antics.

'Your mum and dad seem really nice,' I tell him. 'Lee too.'

'Yeah, they're all right,' Max replies as he loads up his plate. 'I suppose, in the interest of honesty, I should fill you in on my situation with Lee.'

I raise my eyebrows expectantly. I could tell things were oddly cold between them.

'We were both working for the company,' he tells me. 'Paige is an executive assistant now but, back then, she was just my girl-friend. I got her the job at the company, which was probably my first mistake. We broke up and at first I thought perhaps she had just used me to get the job, but then she ended up with Lee really soon after the split. I always suspected some, shall we say, overlap. Anyway, I didn't want to be around them, so I quit the company and moved back to London, and they're married now, so all is well that ends well.'

Suddenly it all makes sense. Oh my God, I can't believe she was with Max before she was with Lee. That's got to be an awkward Christmas dinner.

'Is that why you didn't want to turn up single?' I ask him.

'That is why I didn't want to turn up single or alone,' he replies. 'I'm over it, it's not like I still have feelings for her, and I was the best man at their wedding, so...'

Max laughs to himself for a second.

'Yes, I'm aware how tragic this all makes me look,' he says.

'It doesn't make you look tragic,' I insist honestly.

It does make me feel incredibly sorry for him, though. Imagine getting dumped by someone who then goes on to marry your sibling, and having to be around them all the time. Absolutely brutal.

Max shrugs.

'Well, I'm not actively involved in the company any more,' he says, shuffling in his seat. 'And I'm usually thousands of miles from them, so it's not a problem.'

The idea of Addison wanting me to strip this poor man's private life for parts, to use in my article, showing the lengths men will go to, well, that didn't exactly sit right with me before, but now it definitely doesn't. I can't do that to Max, not after everything he's been through. I'll just have to get back on with the meet cutes and try and salvage the original idea. If I can do a good job with it then maybe that will be good enough for Addison and I won't have to throw Max under the bus. I won't tell her any of this. I'll say I was mistaken or that it was a prank or something. Anyway, perhaps I'll have more luck with the meet cutes on holiday. I've seen enough destination romcoms. Perhaps this is the key to making it work.

It has to be.

21

With a moment to myself, finally, I'm walking around the resort, taking it all in. Not just the scenery and the facilities, but also scoping out potential meet cutes. I can't stop thinking about Max, and how unlucky in love he has been. I'm unlucky in love, but in a different way, because I can't ever find any. I thought I did, once, and he cheated on me, so I understand how that feels, how much it hurts every inch of your body. Since then, I struggle to get so much as a second date. Max, on the other hand, just seems to keep getting his heart broken. It's amazing he even gives love another go.

Don't think this is me going soft, because it isn't. I am so mad at Max for getting me here like this, for throwing me in at the deep end, giving me no time to even prep, and for landing me with the responsibility of not only pretending I'm in a relationship with him but that I'm a bloody spinal surgeon! This has certainly taken the shine off Max for me, the googly eyes have been knocked clean off my face.

The sun here is glorious. I'd stay outside all day if I could. After making my way through the gardens, where the grass is so perfect it almost looks like carpet, past one of the enormous fountains which, frankly, I kind of want to crawl into just to feel the cool water on my warm skin, I happen upon one of the pool areas that is surrounded by cabanas. They're big enough for two but I, as always, am just me on my own. I plonk myself down, only to realise there is some kind of lizard sitting next to me. Okay, that I'm used to. It quickly scurries off when it notices me lie down next to it. I'm used to that too. This pool has a really natural look to it. It's an irregular shape with large, real rocks along the edges and through the centre, forming barriers that section off different parts of the pool. Everything here looks perfect. Even as I look out to sea, and see the formation of the clouds sitting on top of the horizon, piled up like mountains, it looks so good it appears almost fake.

Wait, that might be another island I can see in the distance. Wow. I've never seen another island, with my own eyes, from the one I was standing on. Not unless Hope Island in Yorkshire counts, but even then the causeway was open, so it didn't even look like an island. I'm not sure tidal islands count. I pull myself back up, deciding to walk down to the beach for a closer look. I follow a narrow, winding stone path lined with neat little hedges, until I reach a sign warning me that I am technically leaving resort property and entering a public beach with strong waves and tides. I don't know why but the idea of leaving the resort, even if it's just by stepping over an invisible line, both appeals to me and terrifies me. It's scary because it makes me think I'm out on my own in a country I've never visited before, but it does feel like a good place to get a breather from the mess I've landed myself in.

As beaches go, this is definitely the kind you see on the postcards. Stunning golden sands, beautiful blue waters, and sunshine that you just don't get back home in the UK. The water is close, leaving quite a small sandy area, but it isn't too busy down here. I slip off my sandals and take my first steps onto the sand. You can't beat that feeling, can you? Warm, silky-smooth sand between your toes, the kind that doesn't stick to your skin, it just falls away. I dig my toes into the ground, burying my feet a little, before pulling them back out again. Heavenly. This time yesterday, I was in the office, and look at me now. I told Max that I wouldn't be long, that I would meet him by the pool after I got some fresh air. He explained to me that, after travelling from the UK to Hawaii, you can pretty much write off your first day as your body adjusts to the new time zone.

I do feel quite tired, so I'm going to head back to the suite and try to sleep. Hopefully, if I can wake up at a good time, my body will adjust. I'm hoping everything will feel better in the morning. I certainly can't wait to see more of the resort, and even the island, if I'm allowed to leave. I'm hoping that fiancée duties are light. I still can't believe I agreed to it.

I grab my sandals before I make my way back towards the resort, this time heading up the steps instead of walking back up the winding path. You would think this route would be better but, as I take a step up, I catch a toe on it, clipping the step and losing my footing. It feels like I'm falling for ages, as though it's happening in slow motion, as I wildly flap my arms in an attempt to grab something. My flapping only sends me sideways, into the bushes that run alongside the steps, and I feel myself make contact, but it's so light, as though there's a force pulling me back to my feet. I suddenly feel more present, now that the fall is over, but it's only over because someone has saved me. A man has grabbed me by the belt of my sundress and now he's got me almost suspended in the air. Once he has control of the situation, he pulls me up, taking my hand as he helps me back to my feet.

'Thank you,' I say breathlessly. 'Oh my God, that was so embarrassing. I hope no one else saw.'

'I hope they did,' he replies through a laugh. 'I don't think I could do that again if I tried.'

'That was, honestly, I don't even know, amazing, I don't know how you managed to save me,' I babble. 'Sorry, I still feel a bit shaken up. I don't think jet lag suits me.'

'You get used to it,' he says with a shrug.

Now that I've got my wits about me a little more, it suddenly occurs to me that the man is English. He's probably around my age, tall, with golden-blonde hair, and blue eyes, and a neat beard that is so short I think it's technically stubble. It looks intentional, though. Like it's all part of the look.

'Ah, well, I am not used to it,' I confess.

'I hate to break it to you, but it's worse on the way home,' he tells me. 'Flying east shortens the days.'

'Well, London is notoriously flat,' I reply. 'So hopefully there won't be any steps for me to fall up before I recover.'

'I'm from London too,' he says, smiling to have found someone from home. 'Kensington. Where are you?'

I manage to find a way to scoff inside my head. Christ, not bloody Kensington. This resort is definitely too fancy for the likes of me because everyone here is clearly so very rich.

'Soho,' I lie. Well, sort of. I work there and I do want to live there. I'm trying to live there. To some well-to-do types, supposedly anything south of the river is wasteland.

'Oh, nice,' he replies. 'I love the vibe in Soho. Though, I must admit, I don't know it as well as other areas. I need someone who knows the place inside and out to show me the sights.'

'I could show you the sights,' I joke. 'For a hero like you, who saved me from injuring myself on the first day of the first holiday I've had in years, I'd show you... anything.'

I don't know where I was going with that sentence, or why I thought 'anything' was the right word to end it on. I think I was trying for a joke. Instead, it's come across like a proposition. Why do I always lose my cool around people when I feel attracted to them?

Still, the man seems charmed by it.

'You show me yours, I'll show you mine,' he replies through a cheeky smile. 'There are places in Kensington you only get to know when you live there for a while. I could show you a good time.'

'Well, they do say blondes have more fun,' I point out, nodding towards his hair.

'They do indeed,' he replies. 'I've been here a few times now. Perhaps I can show you the sights here? Tomorrow, of course, when I won't need to carry you.'

'That would be lovely,' I reply with a smile.

'I'll be hanging around the bar, just up there, at midday,' he tells me. 'If you fancy a drink, you should drop by.'

'I'll do that, thank you,' I say with a smile. 'I'm Frankie, by the way.'

'Albi,' he replies. 'Nice to meet you, Frankie.'

I go to pick up my sandals and realise there's only one there. Shit, where is the other one? I guess it is possible for a grown woman to lose just one shoe.

Albi realises I'm looking for my other sandal, given that I've only got one in my hand.

'It's in the bushes,' he says, spotting it behind me. 'I'll reach it for you.'

He leans forward and grabs it.

'Here you are.'

'Thanks,' I reply.

'I'll walk you back up the steps, make sure you get there safely,' he tells me with a smile.

'Thank you. Well, I'd better go, try and get some sleep,' I say once we reach the top. 'Or I'll be sleeping through our date tomorrow.'

The word catches on my tongue. Date. Why the fuck did I say date?

'Not date as in date-date,' I babble. 'A date like a diary date. Like a date with a thing. Uh...'

I just said date far too many times.

Luckily, he laughs.

'I know what you mean,' he insists. 'See you tomorrow for the non-date-date diary date.'

I've always loved it when men tease me, which is fortunate, because I say the wrong fucking thing *all the time*.

'See you then,' I tell him.

Albi heads back down the steps, towards the beach, which I suppose is where he was originally headed. Wow, was that an actual meet cute? One that I didn't do on purpose, that actually went well? Incredible. As I turn around, I'm confronted with Max and he does not look happy. My own smile falls.

'What are you doing talking to him?' he asks me, a little on the angry side.

'Erm, talking,' I say, obviously. 'Actually, I fell, and he caught me.'

Max eyeballs Albi as he's walking away. Honestly, he looks like he hates him.

'You do know we're not really engaged, and I can talk to who I want, right?' I remind him. 'What's the problem, do you know the man or something?'

'He's my uncle,' Max tells me simply.

I laugh. Then I realise he isn't kidding.

'What?' I squeak. 'Albi isn't your uncle. He's, like, the same age as you.'

'Actually, he's three months younger,' Max replies, like it's the most usual thing in the world.

'Your uncle is three months younger than you?' I repeat back to him, because I must be misunderstanding the situation.

'Yep,' he replies. 'My gran was pretty young when she had my dad and then, I suppose, quite a bit older when she had Albi, so she was pregnant at the same time as my mum. I really don't like to think about the ins and outs of it. And I'm dying inside because I said "ins and outs of it" so can we not talk about it, please?'

'That's absolutely incredible,' I tell him. 'I can't even begin to imagine having an auntie or an uncle my age. Or a pregnant grandma! So, when Lee mentioned Uncle Albert...'

'Yes, that's Albi,' he replies. 'We call him Uncle Albert because, well, Albert is his name. He always turns up to these things on a yacht, and pretends he sailed here himself, when the truth is that he lands in Honolulu and has staff sail him the rest of the way. It's sort of an *Only Fools and Horses* reference. Look, can we not talk about it, please? Albi is a bit of a dick, I don't get on with him at all.'

'Okay, fine, sure,' I reply. 'Let's head back to the suite. I'm definitely ready for bed now I've filled my lungs with sea air.'

It's probably for the best that I don't tell Max about the plans I just made with Albi. To be honest, given what I'm here to do, it's probably for the best that I don't go at all. It isn't exactly a good look, being here as Max's fiancée, and then flirting up a storm with his fit uncle. God, that sounds weird.

As we head back in the direction of the suite, my legs still feel a little like jelly, but it's reassuring knowing there's someone around to catch me, even if I do absolutely need to stay away from him. I'm going to land myself in big trouble if I don't.

22

I am up and at 'em, out and about, feeling fresh, ready for the first proper day of my holiday and, most importantly of all, ready to work.

My day didn't get off to the best start. When Addison said they were going to pack me a case full of swag to enjoy while I was here, perhaps stupidly, I only saw the positives. Free clothes, cosmetics and toiletries – and all high end too – what's not to love? What I didn't consider was that, when this selection of holiday supplies was being prepared for me, it wasn't done by someone who had me in mind. I thought yesterday's sundress was just something flowery and floaty that Addison thought I should wear on the plane, to look like I was in full holiday mode, but given the fact that Cora once described my style as 'a fourteen-year-old at a house party while her parents were out of town' (which I took to mean I wore whatever I wanted but also things that would make parents of daughters panic), flowery and floaty isn't exactly my bag. Unfortunately, this entire bag isn't my bag. It's more befitting of a spinal surgeon, so that's a stroke of luck, but it isn't just not right for my taste, it isn't right for my body either. It's all my size, that's what the tags say, but some of it is just a serious no-no.

When did swimwear become so obscene? Genuinely, the first one-piece I pulled out was cut so high above the leg, it barely covered my downstairs, and with my stomach not exactly being flat, it sort of poked out of the sides, before sitting next to my thigh-brows. There are a bunch of bikinis, which I'm even more scared to wear, so I've chosen the one-piece that provides the most coverage, although it does have slashes across the front, which I'm going to need to watch. One wrong movement and I'm worried a chunk of tummy – or, even worse, an entire boob – might just find a way out. There is one problem with every single item of swimwear in this case, though, something that I didn't really think was a trend, something I wrongly assumed only existed among the perfectly toned bodies on *Love Island* but, nope, it's real, it's a thing, and it's all I've got to work with.

Every single item of swimwear, to put it frankly, goes up your arse. There just isn't a bum part in any of them, just a thong back – is that even allowed in real life? On *Love Island*, sure, everyone is perfect on paper and shagging in a room with a camera, no one is worried about their cellulite or having their cheeks out in front of kids and old people, but here… I don't know, man. I'm not comfortable with it at all. Luckily there's a teeny tiny sarong that, if worn at the right angle, just about covers my bum. I'm only thirty-four, so it's rare that I feel old, but today I definitely do. No one thinks they're going to get old. We think we'll always be cool and in touch, with our fingers firmly on the pulse, but then it starts happening. You hate modern fashion, contemporary music sounds like noise, teenagers annoy you just by having fun within proximity of you, and all the men you used to lust after in romcoms are suddenly silver foxes, exclusively cast as dad characters. I live in fear of the day Freddie Prinze Jr is cast as a granddad.

Max was up and out before me today. He left me a note saying he was going to see his parents, and that I should explore the resort, so I'm currently walking the pool area, looking for potential meet cutes.

I'm in Maui, in a luxury resort, so I'll hazard a guess most of the people around me are here for a holiday, and often single people are looking for a holiday romance, right? It's just about working out who the eligible bachelors are then making my move, or starting to at least, because I obviously don't want any of these meet cutes to actually go anywhere. I sort of did with Max, until he lied to me, and it turned out he had a lot going on, and, to be honest, I kind of fancy his hot uncle, but obviously that's not going to go anywhere either. If not for the obvious reason, then because I look ridiculous in this swimsuit (although, let it be said, it doesn't look ridiculous because I don't have a rock-hard body, it's because I feel so awkward in it, walking around like a crab).

There's a large pool with a fountain at the heart of it, so my dream of climbing in one of the fountains can become a reality. It's been a long time since I took a dip in a pool – and even longer since I did so somewhere warm and outdoors – so I decide to step inside. Perhaps I'll be able to think more clearly, in the cool water. I bet it would be even easier with a cocktail. I could certainly get used to these working conditions. It's not quite midday, so I hold off on the drink, even if I am on holiday. However, without a lot to drink, there's no way I could even consider removing my sarong, so I'm just going to keep it on, to protect my modesty. The thought of getting my arse out in front of all these people genuinely terrifies me. I'd rather keep my sarong on and look a bit weird.

I wade through the water. Man, it really does feel good. You can't top that feeling of nice cool water on a hot day somewhere warm and sunny. Now I just need to find someone to try to have a meet cute with. I suppose I am a little excited about it again, if excited is even the right word. I think, after so many misses back home, the idea of being able to start from scratch – somewhere I can leave, where I don't have to worry about seeing anyone ever again – appeals to me. Don't get me wrong, though, I am still feeling the pressure – my job (and now Max's pride) depends on it.

I spot a young couple playing together in the water, so I rule them out. The same goes for the family, the elderly lady, and the man swimming intense widths in the deep end. So far, he's the only potentially eligible bachelor, but I really don't think he would appreciate me interrupting him, plus that kind of seems like an accident waiting to happen.

Hmm, an accident, that's it. Not a real one, of course. But the idea has flagged someone I am completely overlooking, someone who could be perfect: the lifeguard. I look up at him, sitting on a tall chair, in his Baywatch red shorts. He's wearing sunglasses, has a whistle around his neck, and gives off that cool, calm, chill vibe like so many lifeguards do. I suppose that's what you want from the person who is supposed to save your life. Someone calm who knows what to do, not an anxious worrier who will panic and possibly do the wrong thing.

I can swim. I wouldn't say I was especially good at it, but I can. If I found myself unexpectedly in water, I wouldn't have a problem swimming to safety, but I'm not going to be competing in any races anytime soon. What I could do is swim to where the water is a little deeper and then try and seem like I'm struggling. That way the life-guard will help me – that has to be in meet cute territory, right?

I swim until I'm in the deeper water and then I start struggling a little, flapping my arms, dipping my head under. I don't usually like to go under the water, not without holding my nose, so I don't quite go all that deep at all. I compensate with extra flapping.

'Ma'am,' he calls out. I have his attention. 'Ma'am. If you're struggling, that part of the pool is only four feet deep, just stand up.'

I allow my feet to feel for the floor of the pool and, sure enough, there it is.

'Oh, thank you,' I call back. Mortifying.

I shuffle back towards the pool steps and pull myself out. Okay, I don't care what time it is, now I need a drink.

Never one to be beaten, when I spy three men in their thirties/forties sitting together at the bar, chatting, I decide that this could be my shot to try a different approach. In need of help, but not helpless.

I straighten up my soaking wet sarong, making sure the knot is still nice and tight, because now that it's wet it feels like gravity might pull it clean off me. It still seems to be firmly on, so I take a seat at the bar, just one space away from the men on my right. I'm hoping being wet will make me look sexy, but I suspect I look like a drowned rat.

I glance over the menu, gently running a finger up and down the page, trying to remember what Addison told me about being seductive.

'What can I get you?' the twenty-something man working behind the bar asks me.

'Ooh, I would love a Pacific Pear Maui Martini, please,' I say.

'Coming right up,' he replies.

I wait a second or two before…

'Oh, gosh, sorry, I've left my purse, my key card, my phone – everything in my suite,' I tell him.

I can see in my peripheral vision that one of the men is raising his hand to get the bartender's attention. Is he going to offer to pay for my drink? Am I finally having some luck?

'You're in one of the suites?' the barman asks.

'Yes,' I confirm.

'Oh, so you're part of the Ray family,' he says with a smile. 'In that case, just take the drink. It's not a problem.'

'I need to pay for it,' I insist.

'No, you don't,' the bartender replies. 'The Ray family means a lot to the Grand Palm Resort. We're here to take care of you.'

He hands me my drink. I smell it before I see it and, genuinely, I don't think I've ever smelled a fresher, fruitier cocktail in my life.

'Thank you,' I reply, trying to mask my disappointment, because obviously I should be grateful to the man.

I take my first sip and it is heavenly. The texture, the taste – it doesn't even taste like it has alcohol in it, which is dangerous, because it means I could easily sink these bad boys all day long.

Feeling a little awkward, having failed at my mission, I turn around to skulk off with my drink, only to – in perfectly on-brand Frankie style – smash into the person behind me. I really need to start paying better attention to what I'm doing.

The sort of good news is that this time I've spilled my drink on a shirtless man. The ultimately bad, embarrassing news is that the man in question is hot Uncle Albi.

Albi swipes one of his fingers across one of his pecs before placing it in his mouth. He makes an approving face.

'Two more of these please, buddy,' he tells the barman.

'Right away, Mr Ray,' he replies.

I shoot Albi a look. The barman knows his name?

'I was here yesterday,' he tells me. 'For, er, quite a while.'

'Nice,' I reply with a smile.

Albi takes our cocktails and hands me mine.

'Were you starting without me?' he teases.

'Oh, no, well, about that,' I waffle as I find the right words.

'Are we related?' he asks next. 'I just overheard the barman said you were in the Ray family.'

'That's what I need to talk to you about,' I reply.

'You're soaking wet,' he points out.

'Yeah, I was just in the pool,' I explain, as though it isn't obvious.

'This pool?' he asks.

I nod.

'We have our own private pool,' he tells me. 'The one by the suites. Are you really here with my family?'

'I am,' I say. 'I'm staying in one of the suites, I just didn't realise that was a private pool next to them.'

I suppose it makes sense, that the pool is just for the suites, but I needed a pool full of potential meet cutes anyway, and definitely not people who are related to Max, for obvious reasons.

'Well, why don't we go there now, take a dip, and while we're walking, you can break my heart by explaining to me exactly how we're related,' he suggests.

'Sounds good,' I say with a laugh. 'We're not actually related, though.'

'Oh, no, who are you here with?' he asks, sounding almost playfully disappointed.

'Max,' I tell him.

'Shit,' he says, stopping in his tracks for a second. 'You're Max's mysterious fiancée?'

I reluctantly nod my head.

'I was so sure you were made up,' he tells me as we start moving again.

'Nope, I'm here, I'm real,' I insist. 'He saw us chatting yesterday. When he told me you were his uncle, I couldn't get my head around it.'

'Max *hates* that I'm his uncle,' Albi explains – he looks quite amused by it. 'Especially because I'm a bit younger. We went to school together, you know? Same year and everything, but we weren't friends.'

'Is that weird?' I ask.

'We're completely different people,' he replies before sipping his drink. 'Always have been. Do you think it's weird that he pretends he isn't loaded?'

'Each to their own,' I say with a shrug and a smile. 'Do you work for the company?'

'Not exactly,' he replies. 'I have shares, and a seat on the board – we're a family-run business. But I would be lying if I said I did much.'

'Sounds great,' I reply.

'What do you do?' he asks curiously.

'I'm a j... a, erm, a spinal surgeon,' I say with not all that much conviction.

'Wow, that's a real job,' he says. 'Impressive. I take my hat off to you. I had an ex who fractured her L5 while we were skiing – at least I think that's what it was, does that sound right? She crashed into a tree, it was awful.'

'Sounds horrible,' I reply. I have no idea what an L5 is, but it can't be good if she crashed into a tree. 'How is she doing now?'

'Oh, I don't know,' he replies. 'We didn't stay in touch. I think she's all right, though. Right, here we go, the private pool.'

It's quiet here, at the pool behind the suites. There's no sign of anyone, not a sound to be heard apart from the roar of the sea at the bottom of the garden.

There are tables built into the pool, with underwater chairs. Albi places his drink down on a table before jumping in.

'The water is so much better when you don't have to share it,' he insists.

I begin walking into the water – no jumping for me, thanks – pausing part of the way in to turn around and place my drink on the table next to Albi's. As I reach out to put it down, my soggy sarong finally gives way and falls into the water below.

'Frankie!' Albi exclaims. 'You're killing me. Are you sure you're marrying my nephew?'

'That's what I'm told,' I joke, mostly for my own amusement, and to hide my embarrassment, of course. I'm just relieved it only came off in front of one person, and not in the public pool, in front of all the families.

'It must take a long time, to become a surgeon,' Albi thinks out loud.

'Yeah,' I reply. I have no idea how long it takes, or what to say next. 'It's worth it, though.'

'When did you decide you wanted to cut people up?' he asks.

Hmm, around the time Max landed me in this situation, I'd say.

'I always knew I wanted to help people,' I tell him, because that's true. It's just worked out that I help them with their hearts, instead of their bones. Well, I try to. I'm not exactly leading by example, am I? 'What did you want to be when you grew up?' I ask.

Albi smiles as he pedals water. 'This, I suppose.'

'What's this? An international playboy?' I joke.

'Play your cards right and I'll show you my yacht,' he replies with a wink.

'I'll bet you say that to all the girls,' I say.

I turn around to sip my drink.

'Right,' Albi shouts playfully. 'That's it.'

I feel one of his arms hook around my waist, pulling me away from my drink, deeper into the pool. I'm so caught up in having fun that it takes me a moment to notice Max, sitting at a table just outside our suite. I don't think he was there when we got here, there wasn't a soul in sight. I wonder how long he's been watching us? Thankfully, I think he's too far away to hear us properly.

Albi just follows my gaze.

'Oh, the future hubby doesn't look too happy,' he says. 'Better go do some damage control. Anything he's angry about, you can blame on me.'

'You're a true gent,' I tell him sarcastically. 'I'll see you later.'

I make my way back towards the edge of the pool. I go to pick up my sarong but leaving it damp, on the floor, has made it look kind of gross. As I walk over to Max, I use my index fingers to try and free my costume from my bum, for all the good it does.

'You two look like you're having fun,' Max says.

'Albi was just showing me the private pool, I was in one of the public ones,' I tell him. 'Are you okay?'

I pretty much shut down the idea of Max being remotely interested in me romantically when it turned out he'd got me here under false pretences, so I got any ideas of any romantic feelings I may have had for him out of my head, lest I embarrass myself. Again. Seeing him, the way he is right now... he's not jealous, is he?

'It's my dad,' he replies.

Oh, right, okay, so not jealous at all. Thank God I didn't ask him.

'Is he okay?' I ask, taking a seat, keeping my nearly bare bottom facing whichever way Max isn't.

'He's fine, I think,' he replies. 'I was just chatting with Mum. She says Dad is planning to retire soon. I never thought he'd retire.'

'Perhaps he just fancies taking it easier?' I reply. 'I'm sure he's okay.'

'Yeah.' Max thinks for a moment. 'I suppose Lee will take over. I think Dad always wanted it to be me, as the eldest, but then I left the company...'

'Is that okay with you?' I ask.

'Yeah,' he says quickly. 'Well, I was sort of forced out, I suppose. It was more the country I wanted to leave than the job. Eventually we wound up with a London office, but that's your new best friend's playground.'

Max nods towards Albi. I look over and see him floating on his back, his drink somehow carefully balanced on his stomach. I can't help but laugh.

'Is he being okay with you?' Max asks me, sort of vaguely.

'Erm, yes,' I reply. 'Why?'

'He's just a bit of dick sometimes,' he says, before changing the subject. 'Can I borrow your iPhone charger, please? I think mine must have a loose wire, it won't work.'

'Yes, of course,' I say. 'It's just on the chest of drawers, in the bedroom.'

'Don't worry, I can get it,' he tells me. 'You can get back to your pool.'

Max gets a twenty-second head start on me before I remember what I left lying on my bed. Shit.

I jump up and follow him, as fast as my feet will allow. You see, earlier, when I was unpacking my case – the one Addison packed for me – along with the revealing swimwear and outfits, she decided to throw in some lingerie. Not just knickers and bras, though. What I can only describe as sex lingerie, the kind you would only wear if you were in bed with someone, and even then, you wouldn't keep it on very long.

By the time I get to the bedroom, Max is sort of frozen in time, staring at it. Stupidly, when I realised it was there, I laid it out on the bed, to send a photo to Cora, to try and make her feel better that she doesn't have to do what Addison the psycho tells her to do, because God knows what her thinking was behind sending me away with this. It's some kind of bodice, not that there's much to it. A combination of red semi-sheer mesh and PU panelling, but any sort of material is in short supply, because it has fully open cups (only three strips of thin material frame each boob) and, as for the crotch, well, a shiny gold zip runs from the front right up the back. I quickly hurry in front of him and grab it, for all the good it's done, he's definitely already had a good look at it. Then I realise that, by diving in front of him, I've pretty much just treated him to a... whatever it is you call a full-frontal, but from the back.

'It's not mine,' I insist.

'It's definitely not mine,' he replies.

'My boss packed me a bag,' I try to explain. 'More from the freebie room.'

'And she thought you'd need this?' he says in disbelief.

'I suppose she just wanted me to have all bases covered,' I reply with a casual shrug, trying to style it out.

'That's definitely crotchless,' he says, nodding towards the offending item in my hand. He seems quite amused by it now. 'It's not going to cover any bases.'

I can feel my cheeks flushing redder than the bodice, so I throw it out of the open window behind me.

'Okay, I get it, you think this is hilarious, can we just leave it, please?'

'Sorry,' he says, removing the smile from his face, but I can see the corners of his mouth still twitching ever so slightly. 'I'm going to put my phone on charge then have a shower, if that's okay?'

'Yeah, it's fine,' I say plainly, walking past him, heading back downstairs. God, that was embarrassing. I can't believe I left it on the bed, I should have known someone would see it. Do you know where else I should have known someone would spot it? On the bloody floor outside our bloody suite.

'Yours?' Albi asks me, swinging the bodice in his hand.

I am mortified but, I have to admit, I do see the funny side now. I nod.

'Thanks,' I say, after he tosses it to me. 'Wouldn't want to lose this.'

'Perhaps you shouldn't be throwing it out of the window for me, then, should you?'

'Thanks again,' I say, not rising to his teasing, turning to head back inside.

'It looked really good on the floor,' he calls after me.

I raise a hand to wave to him, behind my back, as I keep walking.

Oh, Uncle Albi. Why did I have to meet you here and now?

23

After an afternoon of awkwardly hiding in my room, waiting for my face to stop resembling the colour of the bodice that got me into this mess in the first place, Max knocked on my bedroom door. When I said he could come in, he playfully averted his eyes the whole time, which made things feel a lot easier between us again. The reason for his appearance was to invite me for dinner with him, his parents, his brother Lee, and his sister-in-law/ex-girlfriend Paige. It was an invitation, and not a summons, but as optional as it sounded, given the part I'm here to play, I had no choice but to say yes, right? Plus, I was starving when he asked me, so he caught me when I was weak.

So here I am, once again, sitting at a table with Max's parents, as well as Lee and Paige. Thankfully, we're in one of the hotel's restaurants this time, and not their suite, so I don't feel quite so cornered.

'I know we still need to plan you an engagement party, but what are you thinking for the wedding?' Eva asks me.

Scrap what I said about not feeling cornered. I'm on the spot now.

'Errrrm,' I say, stalling.

'We've not really thought about it yet,' Max says tactfully.

You would think that would be the end of that, but it isn't.

'Darling, you might not have thought about it, but I'll bet Frankie has been thinking about it ever since she was a little girl,' Eva corrects him.

All eyes are on me now.

'Errrm,' I stall again. 'I've never really been that sort of girl.'

'Bullshit,' Paige chimes in. 'Anyway, what's wrong with *that sort of girl*?'

She makes a poor attempt at my accent on those last few words.

'Oh, nothing,' I insist. 'Nothing at all. I've just never really thought about it. I imagine I'm just too pessimistic to plan ahead like that.'

I garner a few polite laughs.

'I've always known exactly what I wanted my wedding to be like,' Paige says, smugly, as though that makes her better than me.

Now it's my turn to call bullshit. She didn't even know which Ray brother she wanted to marry. I don't say that, though. I just smile.

'To be honest, if I were to give it a little thought, I imagine I'd go for somewhere like here,' I say. 'I love the idea of a beach wedding, somewhere warm and sunny, and everything I've seen here so far – wow, I'm really falling in love with the place.'

'Here as in Hawaii, Maui, or this resort?' Ronnie asks through a mouthful of Wagyu.

'Well, all of the above,' I reply. It wasn't an overly detailed vision, just an idea. I don't want to sound like I think there are better resorts than this one, given the fact that this is where they always come.

'Why don't you get married now?' Ronnie suggests, like it's the most casual thing in the world. 'While we're here.'

'Don't be silly, Ron,' Eva tells him off.

'We're already here,' he reminds me.

Shit. Fuck. No, no way. I'm all for committing to the bit, but I'm obviously not going to marry the man.

'Don't be stupid,' Eva says. 'Frankie will want her family to be at her wedding too.'

'I'll fly them out,' Ronnie says, once again, like it's such a normal thing to say. 'I'll be paying for the damn thing anyway. May as well do it while we're here.'

'Aren't you two getting married?' Lee reminds them.

'Never again,' Ronnie practically laughs.

'Exactly,' Eva says. 'Thank you, darling. Your dad has clearly forgotten about our *vow renewal*.'

'I haven't forgotten,' Ronnie says. 'You mention it every bloody day.'

'Oh, you're renewing your vows?' I say, eager to change the subject.

'Yes,' Eva tells me. 'Maximillian, didn't you tell her?'

It's strange, hearing him called that. I know, it's not like I've known him a long time, but he definitely kept that one quiet. I'm not surprised he and Kingsley go by Max and Lee. It's like their parents wanted them to sound rich.

'I must not have,' he replies with a shrug.

'This family hasn't had a good knees-up since our wedding,' Lee tells him.

'Apart from every time we've got together since,' Max points out. 'This family never has its knees down.'

'He's got a point,' Ronnie laughs. 'Speaking of which.'

Ronnie flags down a waiter before ordering another round of drinks.

I'm loving eating outside. I'm also really enjoying my fish and fries, which is a delicious Hawaiian take on fish and chips. Beer battered 'fish of the day', shoestring fries and tartar sauce. The vibe here is so nice. Under more normal circumstances, I would be in heaven. I really could see myself getting married somewhere like this – well, I could, if I could actually see myself getting married generally.

'Lee and I have a lot of work to do, before we can think about vow renewals,' Ronnie announces. 'Interested in knowing how it's going, son?'

Max realises he's talking to him.

'Good, I imagine, given that we're here and not in Brighton,' Max replies.

'There's nothing wrong with Brighton,' I remind him.

'Oh, I'm not saying there is,' Max says. 'But this lot would never go there. Their passports read like a Beach Boys song.'

I snort at his 'Kokomo' reference. No one else seems to get it or, if they do, they don't find it very funny.

'The English coast isn't for everyone,' Eva says, as politely as possible.

'We're future planning,' Ronnie tells Max, even though he didn't show much interest. 'I'm practically a dinosaur now, it's all about the new blood, who will take over when I step down.'

'That won't be for a while, will it?' Paige says. I get the feeling it's of more interest to her than just curiosity.

'You never know,' Ronnie says. 'But, when I do, I'm looking for a forward thinker to take over. What I need right now is new ideas.'

'I'm working on it, Dad,' Lee reminds him.

'I know, son, I know,' Ronnie replies. 'Max, anything for me?'

Anyone can see that Ronnie is actively trying to get Max to engage with him about the family business. Max hardly seems interested.

'He never had any good ideas,' Lee butts in, only semi-playfully. 'That's why he writes for a living. Hiding behind his desk in London, giving our products bad reviews.'

Max shrugs.

'I'm not saying Dad is old, or that he should retire, but if forward thinking is what you're trying to do, that's a good shout, that's why I give you average reviews sometimes,' Max says. 'You're still one of the big boys, but it's a fast-moving industry, and if you don't try to be more innovative – like you used to be – then you're going to be overtaken.'

'Shut up,' Lee says, like a moody teenager.

'He could be right,' Ronnie says.

'He doesn't know what he's talking about,' Lee insists.

'Well, let's make it interesting, then,' Ronnie continues. There's a twinkle in his eye when he's talking about work. It genuinely excites him, unlike the vow renewal he had forgotten all about. 'How about the two of you come up with a pitch for me, for something new, and I'll choose the best one.'

'I'm just here for the holiday,' Max reminds them. 'And the vow renewal.'

'Sounds like you're scared of the competition,' Paige points out, standing by her man. Her *second* man.

'You never know, this might be how your dad chooses his successor,' Eva points out encouragingly.

'Seems like you're just after cheap labour,' Max says. 'Which I'm pretty sure you've already been in trouble for.'

'Unsubstantiated claims,' Ronnie says, like he's probably said it a million times before. 'Think about it.'

'If the boys are playing with their toys, perhaps Paige and I could help you with some wedding plans,' Eva suggests excitedly. I suddenly feel bad, that she's so enthusiastic about a wedding that is never going to happen.

'That would be great,' I lie, because what else can I say?

'Let's see if we can't get you acting like you do want to get married,' Paige says, through a smile that I don't have a whole lot of faith in.

'Sure,' I reply.

I feel bad, but I promised Max I would help him out, so I'll go along with it. To a degree, at least. I draw the line at actually marrying him. I'd say hopefully it won't come to that but, with this family, I feel like you never really know...

24

Things are still a little bit weird between me and Max. We have an understanding now but, somewhere inside it, we've misplaced that fun friendship we shared. We are coexisting in our suite but keeping very much apart where we can. With the lounge being Max's bedroom, I tend to stay out of it, and he keeps clear of my bedroom, lest he find any more of Ann Summers' finest.

I have to admit, I'm kind of disappointed, because I felt like we had really hit it off, and now we're uncomfortable around each other, but we're going to be spending time together today, so hopefully we can find our way back to friendship.

That said, we'll be spending time together today as a couple, for what Max is calling the 'forced fun' day with his family. Yep, the Rays schedule their fun. I don't know if it's because they all work so much, that they feel like they need to designate time to spend together, but (to an outsider at least) it looks like their entire life is just endless fun anyway. It's certainly endless food, endless drinks, endless holidays. Their money seems endless. It's interesting that Max doesn't seem to want any of the family fortune. He mentioned that the holiday and flights were paid for but, otherwise, he prefers to make his own money and live within his means. I do respect that, because if my parents were loaded, I wouldn't take much convincing to sack off my job and live the life of Albi. I'm dying to ask Max more about why he feels that way, but we'd probably need to be on more normal speaking terms for that.

So far, 'forced fun' isn't as bad as it sounded initially. There are a few more Ray family members here today. Max ran me through their names, as he pointed them out, but told me not to worry about remembering them. He said that, unless I wanted to pretend I was royalty, or Bill Gates' daughter, that I probably wouldn't hear much from any of them. They all seem nice enough, in a bourgeois sort of way. I definitely feel like the odd one out, especially when people start chatting about where they holiday, or who they're hiring for their annual house redecoration. I just heard one of the cousins talking about the two different marbles they were deciding between for their kitchen refurb and the price made me throw up in my mouth a little.

Here's me, scrimping and saving, trying to afford the deposit and rent on a flat of my own, and here's them, paying more for marble than several months of my rent. Don't get me wrong, I know that I'm not exactly in a position of poverty, I know that there are people much, much worse off than I am, but there's a different between 'I can just about afford to rent in the capital' and 'my 2022 kitchen costs more than five times what the average person in the UK makes in annual mortgage payments'. I don't feel like I fit in at all here. This is an annual thing for the rest of them. For me, it's a once-in-a-lifetime freebie, with a suitcase full of stuff from a cupboard at work. Speaking of which, another day, another arseless swimming costume. I'm trying my best to either be in the pool, with the water up above my waist, or keep a towel around me at all times.

I really, really don't like having my bum out around my fake fiancé's family.

Other than just generally feeling self-conscious about how exposed and relatively poor I am, I am enjoying myself, drinking lunchtime cocktails, playing games, and it's a great scenario for people watching, that's for sure.

Lee sourced a basketball hoop for the pool, so that we could shoot some hoops from the water. Max whispered to me that, at school, Lee was on the basketball team, so that's why he wanted to play it. Max didn't want to join in. I was forced to play a ton of netball when I was at school, so I hopefully held my own, which Lee didn't seem to like.

Next up was the game where you work in pairs, in the pool, with one person on top of the other's shoulders, while you wrestle the opposition, to try to knock them off. I politely declined this in a heartbeat, because not only would that have made a spectacle of my exposed bum, but it seemed like a sure-fire way to accidentally pop a D-cup out in front of everyone. If I so much as sleep in a vest with a skinny strap, I usually wake up with at least one boob out. I definitely don't need one wiggling free in front of all these people. In the end, it was Paige and Lee versus Albi and one of the other, more distant cousins – I think her name is Jenna – fighting it out. It was Lee and Paige who were victorious. It's almost as though the more Lee wins, the more games he wants to play. It's as though it's the victory that powers him, gives him his energy, makes him feel alive.

Now we're sitting by the pool, having more drinks, chatting in small clusters. Ronnie is engrossed in his phone, something Eva routinely tells him off for, but he pays no attention.

'Frankie, you're so lucky that Max has no real ambition,' Paige tells me, rather rudely.

Max frowns at her.

'Don't give me that face,' she tells him. 'I just mean that, with you not wanting anything to do with the company, you're not constantly working, always looking at your phone. Honestly, Frankie, I envy you. And, Max, I have a lot of respect for you, for living a simple life.'

'You know I'm not on a farm, only eating what I grow, getting by without electricity, don't you?' he says.

'You may as well be, bro,' Lee jokes. 'Dressing in Primark and drinking Prosecco.'

Lee visibly shudders at the concept.

'Leave your brother alone,' Eva ticks him off, kind of half-heartedly. 'Max, if you're happy, I'm happy. I do think you should take part in your dad's little challenge, just as a fun little holiday activity, but there's nothing wrong with how you choose to live your life.'

'He's just too scared to compete with me,' Lee says through a smug smile. 'He knows he can't compete with me.'

'Frankie will be making more than Max,' Ronnie pipes up, still not taking his eyes from his phone. 'A surgeon probably makes four or five times what a journalist does.'

I feel like this lot judge a person's worth on how much money they make.

'That's a good point,' Lee says, delighted at the fact.

'If I wanted to live off someone else's money and hard work, I would have stayed here, like you lot did,' Max replies. It doesn't appear to be getting to him. Then again, I don't really make more than him. In fact, although we have a really similar job, I wouldn't be surprised if I made less than him, either because I'm a woman, or because I write for a women's publication, at least. Obviously there is going to be more money in tech.

'Are you his sugar momma?' Paige asks me through a grin.

'Ignore her,' Max tells me.

It's such a strange conversation to be a part of – or a spectator of, at least.

Max pushes his sunglasses further up his nose before making himself more comfortable on his sunlounger. He's acting like it's all water off a duck's back. I wonder if that's really how he feels, or whether their sniping gets to him. Lee and Paige seem to always be on his case. I wonder if it's just their history. Lee will always know that his brother was with his wife before him. Paige will always have to live her life with her ex-boyfriend popping up at family events. Max obviously has it worse than both of them, for the same reasons, just flipped around. Although, while he might not act like it gets to him, the very fact that I'm here, playing the role of Fran, proves that it must.

'Come on, let's play another game,' Lee says. 'We haven't played Convince Me in forever. Teams of two, let's do this.'

'I've never played Convince Me,' I admit.

'I've never known anyone outside this family play it,' Max tells me. 'But lying is one of the main rules of the game, so obviously this family thrives at it.'

'It makes sense that you two team up,' Lee tells us. 'Max can explain it to you as we go. Paige and I will be a team and... Albi, Jenna, come on, time to win your self-respect back, if you can.'

Lee's yelling attracts the attention of Albi and Jenna, who get up from where they are sitting to come over and see what's going on.

'We're playing Convince Me,' Lee tells them. 'Mum, Dad, are you playing?'

Eva says yes at the same time as Ronnie says no.

'Never mind, then,' Eva says. 'Maybe next time.'

'I'm not really bothered for playing,' Jenna says. 'I'd rather top up my tan. Eva, you can play with Albi if you like.'

'The brother-sister dream team,' Albi says, sitting down next to Eva, who I still can't believe is his sister. 'Let's do this.'

Lee dashes off before returning with two pieces of card and a pen. I watch as he writes something on each one.

'So, the aim of the game, if you can even call it that,' Max starts, sitting up again, leaning closer to me. 'Those two pieces of paper say "true" or "false" on them. The game is played in rounds. One person from each team choses one of the two cards at random, and it's their job to share a fact that they know, or an anecdote about themselves, or someone they know – but it has to be something that is unbelievable, otherwise it would be too easy. If they choose the true card, then they tell a true story. If they choose the false card, then they have to make something up on the spot and tell it to the group. The team whose turn it is to guess then say "convince me" and try to work out if what you're saying is true or false. They can ask you questions but no phones and no conferring.'

'Wow, that sounds like a lot of fun,' I say. It really does. 'Although I'm not sure how good at lying I am.'

I do hear the irony in what I – the fake fiancée – am saying. But I'm generally not all that successful when it comes to deception. Not that I'm a deceitful person, I'm talking about what I do for work, obviously. Either way, I'm crap at it.

'Well, for this lot, telling the truth isn't something that comes naturally,' Max points out. 'So you should be fairly well matched.'

'I know you're not talking about your mum,' Eva ticks him off.

'Everyone apart from you, Mum,' Max tells her.

'Now you're the one who's lying,' Ronnie quips, his eyes still firmly fixed on his iPhone screen. Forced fun must not apply to the head of the family.

Eva rolls her eyes.

'Right, on with the game, shall we?' she says. 'I'll go first. Paige, you're guessing.'

'Ready when you are,' she says, making herself a little more comfortable.

'Okay.' Eva takes a deep breath. 'I lost my virginity to Simon Le Bon.'

Noises of sheer horror come from the male participants of the game, which is no surprise, given that they are Eva's sons and brother. Ronnie just chuckles.

Paige just pulls a face.

'Who?'

'Simon Le Bon from Duran Duran?' Max asks in disbelief.

'Yes,' Eva replies. 'But you know the rules, if it's not your turn, you're not allowed to speak.'

'This is why we used to have that rule where you had to drop a ten on the table if you spoke,' Albi says. 'At least then the winners made some money.'

A ten? What's that? Ten pence, ten pounds, more? Nothing would surprise me. Actually, scratch that, if it's true that Eva lost her virginity to *Simon Le Bon from Duran Duran*, that would surprise me.

'Sorry, I forgot to mention that rule,' Max tells me. 'No talking when it's not your turn.'

I nod in silent acknowledgement.

'Well, okay, convince me,' Paige says, getting the first round well on the way.

'I was the biggest Duran Duran fan when I was a teenager,' Eva explains. 'I followed them around the country. Simon was always my favourite. I met him a few times, before we did the deed. Normally what happens on tour stays on tour, but for the purpose of the game...'

'What year was this?' Paige asks.

'It would have been 1982,' Eva says confidently. 'The Rio tour.'

I glance at Max. I can only describe the look on his face as pure horror, as he battles with the image of his teenage mum being a groupie for Duran Duran.

'I think I'm going to need a little more convincing than that,' Paige says, before turning to Lee. 'Unfortunately.'

Lee turns to Max and gestures with his hands. He shows ten fingers, then five. Fifteen. Max's eyes widen as he catches on. Lee is highlighting that, in 1982, Eva would have been fifteen. I wonder if it's true. I think back to when I was fifteen. Busted were my Duran Duran. But if they had invited fifteen-year-old me onto their tour bus, and one of them had made a move on me, would I have slept with one of them? Oh my God, maybe it is true! That said, fifteen-year-old me was an awkward weirdo who thought safety pins were a must-wear accessory. I had a chubby baby face and I was so shy, I never went near a tour bus, it didn't seem worth my time. Eva looks like a supermodel, though, so I fancy her chances more than mine.

'Security was never as good as it is now,' Eva explains. 'My friend Elizabeth and I snuck on to their bus. They thought it was funny and asked us if we wanted to have a drink with them. We told them we were eighteen, only to look cool, though, I don't suppose people paid much attention to ages back then. It was a different time.'

'Then what happened?' Paige persists.

Lee grunts, unhappy with what he's hearing from his mum.

'Pretty much that,' Eva says, referencing Lee's grunt that, now that I think about it, did sound kind of sexual. 'Elizabeth's parents were picking us up, so I had her tell them that my mum came for me early, because I wasn't feeling well. I was supposed to be staying at her house. Instead, I stayed on the bus.'

Paige thinks for a moment. She narrows her eyes at Eva while she deliberates.

'I'm going to say that you are... telling the truth,' Paige says.

'Well, you would be...' Eva pauses for effect, '...wrong! Of course that isn't true. I was only fifteen. I did try to break into their tour bus with my friend Elizabeth, but security stopped us. Anyway, I'm more of a John Taylor kind of girl.'

'Okay, we are allowed to talk between rounds, and I can't believe this rule doesn't exist, but no one is allowed to talk about sex if they're playing with someone related to them. Sound good?' Lee says, without taking a breath.

'Seconded,' Max replies.

'That's me with nothing to talk about,' Albi jokes.

It's always so funny, watching other people's families. It doesn't matter whether you're rich or poor, families are families. No amount of money can offset petty squabbles or embarrassing parents. Suddenly, I don't feel quite so much like the odd one out.

Next up is Albi, presenting a true or false story for Max.

'Just before the yacht docked on this island, we stopped offshore for some lunch and a swim, and a turtle swam right up to me,' he says.

'Of course he mentions the yacht,' Max practically moans.

I so want this to be true. I love the idea that turtles swim up to you here, like friendly dogs in the park. Unfortunately, it turns out to be made-up, and probably just a way for him to mention the yacht.

We play a few more rounds. It's a very fun game. You need a wild imagination, of course, if you draw the false card, but this entire holiday is basically about me pretending things are true anyway.

Eventually it's Lee's turn to tell a tale and my turn to work out if he's fibbing or not. When it's my turn to guess, the storyteller has a huge advantage, because I don't know as much about this family as everyone else, so they have a lot more to work with.

'Okay, Frankie, let's do this,' Lee says, wiggling in his seat, making himself more comfortable. 'So, when Max was at school, kids used to call him Maxi Pad.'

I snort. Max gives nothing away with his face, not to me at least, but does appear to be exchanging some sort of silent sibling glance with Lee. It's as though they're having a whole conversation no one else can interpret.

'Erm, you're going to have to convince me,' I tell him.

'Max, Albi and I all went to the same school,' Lee starts. 'Like all kids that age, at that time, we were obsessed with wrestling – the American kind they showed on TV, more about the storyline than the actual sport. Anyway, there are a several belts in wrestling, but the Hardcore belt was the one we "had" at school. We didn't have an actual belt, our Hardcore belt was more of a state of mind. The deal with the Hardcore championship was that it could be challenged anywhere, anytime. So you would be watching it on TV and the person with the belt would just be set about while they were sleeping. This meant that our version could too. So, for a while, break times involved the defending champ trying to protect their title, and everyone else trying to take it from them.'

'Wow,' I blurt. 'That's absolutely crazy. So how did the nickname come about?'

'Max was involved in one of these play-fights, but even though they were just for fun, kids would still get hurt. One day, Max took a rogue trainer to the face. It burst his nose, which bled all over his white school shirt. One of the kids, naturally, called him Maxi Pad, and it stuck.'

'If this is true, honestly, kids are just as awful as I remember them being,' I say. 'I always tell myself school wasn't as bad as I remember it being, but I could be wrong. I don't want it to be true...'

I really don't. To teenage boys, a name like that probably carried a lot of weight. However, my faith in humanity is telling me that it probably is.

'True?' I say, a wobble of uncertainty in my voice.

'It is true,' Lee says through a huge grin. 'Isn't it, Maxi Pad?'

'Thank you so much for bringing up such a horrible memory,' Max says sarcastically. 'Really appreciate it.'

'What?' Lee laughs. 'It's funny now, no? You don't think you're still that loser, do you? Losing out on all sorts.'

Lee places an arm around Paige and pulls her close. Is he taunting Max? It sort of seems like his is.

'Is that why you don't want to compete with me, with the challenge Dad set?' Lee persists. 'Because you know I'll win?'

This catches Ronnie's attention. He looks over, waiting for an answer.

'You know what, fine,' Max says. 'I'll rise to it. May the best man win.'

'Now we're talking,' Ronnie says. 'My sons, both working together.'

I wouldn't exactly say pitting them against each other is the same as them working together.

'Max, I need to charge my phone,' I lie. 'Can you help me find the charger, please? I couldn't find it earlier.'

'You're not on call here, are you?' Paige laughs.

I ignore her, taking hold of Max's arm as we head to our suite.

'Your brother is a bit of a dick,' I say. I feel like I can say that, even based off the little information I have.

'I know,' Max replies. 'I meant what I said, though, I want to do it, I want to show him that I've still got it in me, and, if Dad is retiring, I don't want him handing things over to Lee, he'll only make a mess of things. I'm going to go for it.'

'Wow, okay,' I blurt. 'That's amazing. Do you have an idea?'

'I had an idea the second Dad mentioned it,' Max says through a smile. 'What do you think, do you fancy helping me?'

I smile too.

'I would love to,' I say. 'Let's wipe the smirks off their faces.'

'As fake fiancées go, you're a pretty great one,' Max tells me. 'Fancy having dinner with me later? I can tell you all about it.'

'Sounds great,' I reply.

It genuinely does. Somewhere, in all of this, the Max who caught my attention at work seems to be showing his face again. And I can't wait to hear what he's thinking.

25

'I'm sorry things are so weird,' Max says as we stroll through the resort gardens.

It's after 7 p.m. now so the sky is getting quite dark here but the gardens are bursting with beautiful lights everywhere. Little lights on the floor that line the pathways, inside the plants to illuminate them, and even bursts of overhead twinkling light curtains that sort of look like stars. Max and I are headed for dinner – a working dinner, of course – but we're taking the long way, because we've got a little time to kill before our reservation.

'I accidentally stole a dog last week,' I blurt.

'Erm, what?' he asks with a laugh, stopping in his tracks.

'You said you're sorry things are weird,' I remind him. 'I'm showing you that, despite your best efforts, my life was already pretty weird.'

'I appreciate that,' he says sincerely. 'But I'm going to need to hear the story about the dog, please.'

'It was a stupid misunderstanding, really,' I insist. 'While talking to a random man in the park, he thought I'd lost my dog, and then he dashed off and found one, and brought it to me. I was too embarrassed to say it wasn't mine. I found the owner not too far away and reunited them a few minutes after.'

'That doesn't make a lot of sense,' Max replies as we start moving again.

I don't suppose it does, without the full story.

'Clearly I'm not very good at lying,' I say. 'Today's game proved that.'

When I pulled the false card, and wound up having to try to convince Albi that I once spent a party locked in a shower cubicle, he saw straight through me. I wouldn't mind, but I had a strategy and everything. It was really my housemate Marcus' then-boyfriend who locked himself in the shower, right after offering to share his drugs with me, although he couldn't promise me what it was because he couldn't remember if he'd picked up his coke or his ket. I've never been one for doing drugs at house parties but even I know that drugs are dangerous enough, without the lucky dip element. I still don't know what he took – whichever one makes you crawl into a shower cubicle before accidentally pulling the handle off, locking yourself in. I left the part about the drugs out of the story, obviously, instead saying that I was having a shower, because that's what it's for. Thinking about this only reminds me how much I want to get my own place.

'You're doing a good job of pretending to be my fiancée,' he says. 'No one suspects a thing. I know I've said this a few times now, but I really can't thank you enough for playing along. Lee and Paige are so difficult to be around. It's like Lee is always competing with me, trying to prove that he's the upgrade, and Paige does that thing: show your ex you're living your best life without them.'

'I probably shouldn't be saying this, because they're your family, but the two of them aren't very nice to you,' I point out.

'I'm used to it,' he says. 'I usually ignore it, but today it was like a switch flipped inside my head, and I decided that this might be a battle that's worth fighting. It might be because you're here.'

I laugh.

'I'm serious,' he insists. 'I don't know if it's because I want to look cool, or I feel like I have an ally. I just want to make the right moves, do the right things. Lee is ruthless, which can be a good quality in business, but he takes it too far. That's why, if Dad is stepping down, it can't be Lee who takes over.'

'So, what's this big idea that's going to knock Lee off the top spot?' I ask.

'Well.' As Max starts talking about it, he lights up. You can tell he's passionate about these things, and that he isn't just doing it to get one over on his brother, but because he really does have an idea that he believes in. 'I've worked for the company but I've also worked as a reviewer. I've seen both sides of things. Multiple perspectives are important in business. Coincidentally, my idea is for a new sort of multiple-perspectives camera.'

'Why do I get the feeling this is going to be something I couldn't possibly understand?' I say with a sigh.

Max laughs.

'It's simple, I promise,' he reassures me. 'I shoot review videos for ByteBanter, usually a mixture of talking to the camera, showing the product, showing my reaction as I'm using it, and if it involves a screen then showing the screen too. Usually, each part of this process requires its own camera, lots of changing angles, editing the footage, repeating actions to get the different shots. What I want to develop is one camera, multiple lenses, different perspectives, in a position that can catch them all in one go, and I want it to be something that anyone with a YouTube channel can get.'

'Wow,' I blurt. 'That's actually brilliant. And even I know it's brilliant.'

'Thanks,' he replies. 'I need to figure a few things out and put a pitch together.'

'Well, I'm your girl for that,' I say. 'I started out as a copywriter. I think about making the change back to it all the time, but you know what it's like, when all your experience eggs are in the one basket.'

Maybe he knows that, maybe he doesn't, because even though I'm sure Max fully deserved his position at ByteBanter (he certainly seems like he's good at his job and incredibly knowledgeable), being a part of the Ray family can't have hurt. If I turned up at a digital agency or something, looking for a copywriting gig, there would be so many people up for the same role who had more experience that I did. I wouldn't stand a chance.

'I would really appreciate your help,' he says. 'If you help, how about I give you a reference or, better still, I'll get my dad to.'

'I don't know if you're kidding, but you really don't know what that would mean to me,' I reply.

Just thinking that I have some kind of backup plan, if Addison does send me packing, really takes the pressure off.

'You do have to do a good job, though,' he says in a playfully strict way.

'Oh, of course, boss,' I reply with an army salute.

'Well, let's chat more about it over dinner,' he says. 'The Ray family love to have meetings over dinner.'

'Oh, well, I feel like one of you already,' I reply. 'Not that I think we're really getting married, I've not gone crazy.'

Max just laughs. It's nice to see the Max I fell in like at first sight with making a return with his cheeky smile.

'Come on, we'd better hurry, or we'll miss our reservation,' he says.

'Erm, I'm pretty sure you could burn down the restaurant here and, if you mentioned your surname, they would fall over themselves asking if it was cooked just right for you,' I joke, but it's probably true.

'I prefer the food,' he says simply.

I don't want to get ahead of myself, but the idea of working on something with Max really excites me. I want to be involved. Let's just hope I know what I'm doing, because it already feels like I'm in over my head.

26

The thing that I can't quite wrap my head around with these Ray family holidays is the jarring mix between business and pleasure. Obviously they *are* on holiday. Everyone calls it a holiday – their annual family holiday, no less. And yet, everyone is always working, business never sleeps. Even when they take time out from work to eat or play games by the pool, they're still on with it, thinking about it, looking at their phones, talking about it. Even Max, now that he's here, is caught up in it too. I suppose it's in his DNA.

'Where are your family?' Eva asks me.

I'm currently sitting, eating breakfast with Eva and Paige, which I'm not jazzed about. Eva seems nice. It is possible to be so loaded that you're out of touch, with zero ability to read the room, but to be a lovely person at the same time. Paige, on the other hand, is a bit of a cow. I don't know if it's because she thinks I'm her ex's current, or because she just finds something unlikeable about me, but she can't really hide it. Eva is lovely, don't get me wrong, but there's no way she isn't detecting the tone Paige uses with me. That's another thing I've noticed about this lot. They let each other get away with almost anything. Consequences don't exist. Do what you want, sleep with who you want, marry who you want. Everyone in this family has so much, it's as though they have nothing to lose, no one thing that could ruin their lives. I wouldn't dare marry my sister's ex. I can't even imagine what that would do to my family. Here it's just business as usual.

'My family are all in Surrey,' I say.

'Oh, how lovely,' Eva says. 'That's where we're from. We still have a house in Cobham, not that we get there much. It made sense to move the family – and the business – to Silicon Valley. We've got a stunning place in Palo Alto, you must visit. Where in Surrey are your family?'

'Guildford,' I reply.

'Ah,' she says. Perhaps it's not posh enough for her there. Imagine if she knew my mum and dad lived in a semi! 'Lovely. I imagine they've met Max, being so close to London compared to us?'

See, this is where problems arise, because Max is in our suite, working on his idea for the pitch. I got pulled for this breakfast with the girls. The problem is that, when Max isn't here, I don't know how to answer questions like this. We need to sing from the same hymn sheet. If I say one thing, and he says another later, this whole operation comes crashing down.

'We did really want to introduce everyone at the same time,' I say, implying they have met, but in no way committing.

'That's okay, we understand,' she insists. 'I imagine you'll continue to live in London, for work, but do you ever think you would move?'

'Erm...'

'It was pretty much Max who convinced me to move to Palo Alto,' Paige tells me. 'But then he left me, so be careful with that one, okay?'

She says this in a sort of jokey way. Eva pulls a bit of a face but doesn't really react.

'It was after you had broken up, darling,' Eva reminds her. 'Anyway, I thought, if it's just us ladies for the day, perhaps we can do a little wedding planning, while the men are hard at work?'

'Not all the men are at work,' Albi says as he approaches us.

We're sitting at a table outside Eva and Ronnie's suite. It was laid out with food when we got here – always too much food. I'd be lying if I said I wasn't loving all the luxury, but it can be excessive. They must throw so much away, when they lay out these lavish buffets.

'Are you ever working, darling?' Eva asks him.

'We're supposed to be on holiday,' he says, taking a pastry from the table. 'Anyway, I'm not here to distract you from hardly working while the menfolk are working hard, I'm here to steal this one.'

I realise he's pointing at me.

'What do you want with her?' Paige asks with a level of disbelief that is frankly offensive.

'I promised Frankie I'd take her snorkelling,' Albi tells them. 'She really wants to try it, I love it, so we made a plan.'

We absolutely didn't, but I'm so interested to see where this is going.

'Then I guess wedding planning will have to wait,' Eva says.

'Come on,' Albi says to me, gesturing away from the table with his head.

'Oh, are we going now?' I say. 'Am I okay like this?'

I've got my usual cheek-strangling swimwear on (this time, one of the bikinis) under a peachy pink sundress. It isn't really a sundress, it's an oversized T-shirt, but I'm honestly so sick of wearing things that are not me that I took a pair of scissors to the neckline and turned it into an off-the-shoulder dress. It's strange, how feeling myself makes me feel more confident.

'Yeah, that's fine,' he says. 'Come on, we'll be late.'

'I'll see you ladies later,' I tell them. 'I really don't want to miss snorkelling.'

'Can't wait to hear all about it,' Eva says politely. 'Take care of her, Albert.'

Eva says this in a sort of stern way, but it's so non-committal, like she's warning Albi to behave, just in case, but either she doesn't think there's anything to worry about, or we're back to no consequences being very much a thing. I'm sure it's the former. He is supposedly going to be my uncle-in-law, after all.

We walk a little, until we're out of earshot, before Albi says a word.

'Morning,' he says.

'Morning,' I reply through a grin. 'What's happening?'

'I know what that lot are like,' he says. 'I just thought you might want a break from Ray family bullshit.'

'Oh, well, thank you,' I tell him.

'You're welcome,' he replies. 'Do you want to see my place?'

'Aren't you staying here?' I ask.

'Nope,' he replies mysteriously. 'Come on, I'll show you.'

I pause for a second.

'Come on,' he says again, laughing to himself. 'You'll love it.'

Curiosity firmly takes a hold of me.

'Okay,' I say nervously.

This should be interesting…

27

It turns out Albi isn't staying at the resort – he isn't even technically staying on the island, either.

After a trip to the bar to return the bartender's badge that Albi explained he was wearing last night, after his favourite bartender let him hop behind the bar to prepare the drinks he was buying, we headed along the coast a little on a golf cart. This seemed slightly strange... stranger still when we pulled up to a speedboat.

'You're sleeping on a boat?' I asked in disbelief.

'Yes,' he replied. 'But not this one.'

I hopped on board with him, to take the short journey to where he's staying: on board a superyacht. We're just pulling up next to it now, in water the likes of which I have never seen in my life, it's so clean and inviting. And I'm sure it goes without saying, but I've never been on a yacht before. Not a regular yacht, nor a superyacht. My God, am I excited. I'm so glad I brought my phone, because I am going to Instagram my hand off.

'It almost sounds like a stupid question, but why do you stay on here instead of at the resort, with your family?' I ask.

'Because it's awesome,' he replies. 'Because my family drive me crazy if I'm around them too long, hence me saving you today. Also, I love being in big trouble.'

I raise an eyebrow at him.

'That's the name of the yacht,' he says. '*Big Trouble.*'

'Nice,' I reply.

Finally on board, Albi directs me to a small cupboard where we can leave our shoes, before slipping on pairs of – what? Boat-safe shoes? – that are waiting for us. Our next port of call, just a few steps away, is a young woman holding up a tray. She has two cocktails.

'Here you go,' Albi says, handing me one of the drinks.

'It's morning,' I say with a laugh.

'It's mostly fruit,' he replies through a smile. 'Cheers.'

Well, I am on holiday, after all.

'Cheers,' I reply.

'So, I'm thinking a quick tour, then we can head back up to the deck, then maybe I have a surprise for you,' he teases.

'A man with a plan,' I say.

'No plan,' he insists. 'Just showing you around my home for the summer and then, okay, maybe one technically planned thing. But I was doing it anyway.'

'Why am I scared?' I laugh nervously.

'Nothing scary,' he says.

Albi first leads me into a large living room. It's strange because you could almost forget you were on a boat at all, it doesn't feel like one, it just looks like a fancy apartment. There's a large corner sofa facing a TV on one of the walls. The place has such a modern finish, with cool colours and contemporary artwork everywhere. A room divider leads to a dining table, big enough for at least eight people.

'No one really spends that much time here,' he explains. 'The lounge is good for chilling, but we only use this table if the weather is really bad, then it's better to eat here, but generally this room gets ignored.'

'If this is the worst room on the yacht then I dread to think what else you're going to show me,' I reply.

Going through the next set of doors takes us to two staircases, with one leading upstairs and one that goes down.

'Downstairs first,' Albi says.

I follow his lead. This place is seriously amazing. I can't get over how big it is. I suppose I've only ever been on a narrowboat. This yacht couldn't be any less Rosie and Jim if it tried.

'There are four en suite bedrooms down here,' Albi tells me. 'So, if you find yourself wanting to escape...'

'Four!' I squeak.

I peer inside the room Albi is standing outside of, too scared to step inside for some reason. A large bed sits in front of an enormous leather floor-to-ceiling headboard. Albi's bloody boat bedroom is bigger than my bedroom at home! There's another massive TV, more contemporary artwork, and I can see the door to the en suite reflected in a full-length mirror. The bathroom might even be bigger than my bedroom at home.

'Seen enough of this?' he says. 'Okay, back up the stairs.'

As we head upstairs, a large open window slowly reveals itself to us. The view stretches across the water to where the island is. Wow. I know this sounds stupid, but it looks so perfect it could be a desktop background.

'Not a bad view to see first thing in the morning every day,' he says. 'Or at night. You'll have to come back one night and see all the lights.'

'I'm honestly just stunned,' I tell him. 'I've seen yachts on TV but... in person... wow.'

Wow is pretty much all I can think right now. I'm practically speechless.

'This is the master suite,' he says as we continue.

'Wait, that wasn't your bedroom downstairs?' I say.

'No,' he replies. 'Do you really think I wouldn't have tried to keep you down there a little longer if it were?'

Albi has a very cheeky sense of humour. It feels harmless, though. It's just charming, rather than sleazy.

I just shake my head in disbelief.

'So, we've got the study first, not that I ever use it,' he continues. 'This is the walk-in wardrobe.'

Okay, this is definitely bigger than my bedroom at home. I'm starting to feel a bit sick now.

'And this is the bedroom.'

The master bedroom is like one of the bedrooms downstairs, only much bigger, and with huge floor-to-ceiling windows on two sides.

There's another big TV on the wall opposite the bed with a door either side of it.

'His and hers bathrooms,' Albi says. 'Two showers, two sinks, two toilets. Not that I've got a her though, so I just alternate between them for fun.'

I laugh.

'My God, how the other half live,' I say with a sigh.

'It should be how your other half lives,' Albi points out. 'He just chooses not to.'

'I think Max enjoys working too much,' I tell him.

'Not to get all socialist on you,' Albi starts. 'But no one should enjoy working. Selling your time isn't right. Life is short.'

I smile. No one on this planet would describe Albi as a socialist. A socialite, maybe.

'Okay, last part,' he says. 'The best part for sure. The bridge.'

Upstairs is another lounge, although this one is almost entirely surrounded by glass, providing a view from almost every angle.

Another huge corner sofa, yet another TV (this one the biggest of all). Finally, the doors that lead out to the deck.

'This is the bridge deck,' Albi announces as he escorts me outside.

There's a barbeque, a dining table and a huge U-shaped sofa.

'Please, take a seat,' he says.

I do as instructed, twisting and turning like a fidgety child, but only because I want to take in every inch of the view. The stunning sunshine bouncing off the clear water, panoramic views of our island, other islands, out to sea where the water just disappears into the horizon.

'Albi, it's stunning,' I tell him. 'Just... unbelievable.'

'I'm glad you approve,' he says. 'This is just more my style than a busy resort, even if they do have a private pool.'

'This is much better than snorkelling,' I admit.

'Oh, we're still snorkelling,' he replies casually.

'We're...'

'We can snorkel here,' he says. 'Off the yacht.'

'I'd be lying if I said I wasn't terrified now,' I admit. 'But... I'm willing to give it a go... I think...'

'Yeah?' he says excitedly. 'You want another drink first or...?'

'No, I'm good, thanks, I don't want to lose my nerve,' I reply quickly.

'Okay, let's do it,' he says, springing to his feet.

Albi takes me to a part of the yacht where you can access the water.

'You can swim, right?' he double-checks.

'Yes...'

I sound about as confident as I swim.

'Here, take this.'

Albi hands me a large version of one of those foam boards they give you at school when you're learning to swim.

'Just lie on it,' he says. 'It will make you feel more secure. I'll stick close by anyway, but you can just put your face in the water and look down, that way I don't need to teach you how to breathe underwater.'

'Thanks,' I reply. 'I feel like a big baby.'

Albi pulls his T-shirt over his head and drops it on the deck. I do the same with my dress, even though I don't have the impressive abs he boasts.

'Frankie!' he starts.

'What?' I ask quickly, worried about doing something dangerous.

'What is that bikini?' he says.

'Oh, God, sorry,' I apologise – why am I apologising? 'I was doing that thing you do on holiday where you wear a bikini as underwear.'

'You don't have to apologise,' he insists. 'I love it. It's probably not usual snorkel attire, but it will give the fish something to look back at.'

'Mr Ray,' a member of the boat crew interrupts us. 'The captain would like to see you for a moment.'

'Back in a sec,' Albi tells me.

'Hi,' I say to the young man who, for some reason, has stayed with me. He's probably in his late twenties. He's dressed smart, in a shirt and tie, which I imagine is a requirement for the job, which must suck in heat like this.

'Hello,' he replies. 'Is there anything I can get you?'

I hug my body awkwardly before mentally telling myself off, reminding myself to own it. I loosen up.

'I'm fine, thank you,' I reply. 'Oh, actually, do you have any sunscreen? I didn't realise I was doing this today, I didn't put any on before I left my hotel.'

'Of course, ma'am,' he replies. 'Let me get that for you.'

He's no sooner gone when he's back again, a bottle of sunscreen on a small silver tray.

'Thanks so much,' I say as I take it from him.

'You're welcome,' he replies.

I notice him look me up and down. Is he checking me out or just being nosy? I'm as bad at telling when people are attracted to me as I am at orchestrating meeting new people, clearly. Which only reminds me that I am trying and failing miserably with the meet cutes. I need to up my game, if I'm going to save my job and get away without hanging Max out to dry in my article. I should try to flirt with him, right?

I open my mouth to speak but he gets there first.

He says something so quietly I can hardly hear him. I lean in closely to try and make out what he's trying to say.

'What's that?' I ask, just inches away from him now.

The man looks down at my bikini. I follow his gaze down to my chest where, oh my God, one of my boobs has popped out of my bikini slightly. I'm as mortified as he is but, so that I don't make him feel bad for alerting me, I quickly reach down and just casually pop it back in. Of course, any embarrassment this saves us is quickly undone when I hear Albi clear his throat. The crew member quickly scarpers. He definitely saw that, didn't he?

'Did you just flash the crew?' Albi asks through an amused grin.

'I, erm...'

I have no idea what to say. I stall for time by squirting sun cream into my hand before trying to rub it into my shoulders.

Albi takes the bottle from me before massaging some into my back where I can't quite reach.

'You're a bad girl, Frankie,' Albi whispers into my ear. 'I'm going to have to keep my eye on you.'

Wow, he's genuinely impressed. That is... that's something. I get that he's a bit of a bad boy, so I probably wasn't doing anything he wouldn't do, but I thought he would be furious at the idea of me doing something like that behind his nephew's back, not think I'm cool.

'Come on then, let's snorkel,' he says.

Albi helps me into the water and onto my float. I copy what he does, pulling my goggles over my eyes and placing my snorkel in my mouth.

I watch Albi dip his face under the water a few times before giving it a try myself. Here goes nothing.

I don't know why I'm surprised that the water is so clear. It's a definite shade of blue, but so easy to see. I can see so many fish – not that I'm knowledgeable to identify any of them, of course, but, wow, it's fascinating to see, and so surreal seeing them up close and in their natural habitat like this. I pop back up again when I feel Albi tapping my arm.

'Follow me,' Albi says. 'We don't have to go far to get to shallow water, where you'll see a lot more.'

I do as I'm told – I'm too scared not to. Albi taps me before pointing something out under the water. Oh, my goodness, is that a sea turtle? I can see it, not too far away, just happily drifting through the water. It's beautiful.

For something that seemed so scary, I can't quite believe how relaxed I feel right now. It's the feel of the water, the motion of bobbing gently on top of it, the sun on my back, the beautiful colours and patterns under the water. I don't want to go home. I wonder, if I asked Albi if I could just forget my life and live on the yacht with him forever, if he might say yes. I'm sure he would, until he got bored of me in, I don't know, a week? Two, tops. As much as I'd love to stay on holiday forever, I can't forget about my real life back in London. I desperately need to get something together for this article. But not right now, though, right now I'm just enjoying the ocean. Real life is a problem for future Frankie.

28

Max's brilliant idea is really starting to take shape. He's managed to get hold of enough bits and pieces of existing Optecho tech to make himself a sort of prototype. Nothing like how the real thing will work, but something that will simulate it. He has everything set up in our living room – his bedroom – but he's clearly loving it. He has everything connected to the large TV, which means he's working with a seriously big screen. I've been watching him and it's fascinating. I'm starting to get a better idea of how it's going to work – I really do feel like I'm learning things along the way. Watching the creation process is just what I need, though, to help Max write his pitch, making sure he says the right words to make his idea shine. It doesn't matter how good your idea is if you don't do a good job of selling it.

After working late last night we inevitably slept in – in our separate beds, of course – this morning. I was a little taken aback, when Max said that he had a surprise for me, and that I should get dressed and accompany him *somewhere*. I excitedly did as I was told before Max led us to the hotel lobby, where we collected his rental car and then hit the road.

'When do I get to find out where we're going?' I ask him.

'When we're too far for you to jump out of the car and run back to the resort,' he jokes.

'Oh, God, you're not taking me to that zip-lining place you were telling me about last night, are you?' I ask him.

We may have stayed up late working last night, but we were chatting too. Max has been here on holiday so many times he's practically a tour guide.

'Well, I'm fully aware of the fact you hate heights,' he reminds me. 'So swimming with sharks is higher up the to-do list.'

'I'm pretty sure I'm scared of those too,' I reply. 'I've just never had to think about encountering them before now.'

'No heights, no sharks,' he reassures me. 'I really appreciate everything you're doing for me, Frankie. Pretending to be my fiancée, helping me with my pitch, being nice to my crazy family. You're doing all of that and I've finally remembered why you're here in the first place: because you need a holiday.'

That's not strictly true but, sure, why not, we'll go with that.

'So today I am giving you a holiday,' he continues. 'I'm going to show you some of the sights outside the resort.'

'That sounds amazing,' I reply. 'I can't wait.'

'We're heading south right now,' he says. 'It really isn't far at all. It doesn't take much more than an hour to walk, but then what was this cool car for?'

I laugh.

'An excellent point,' I reply.

Eventually we stop, abandoning the car before continuing on foot.

'This way,' he says as we approach a small gap in a gorgeous stone wall. It's an intentional opening, but only about the size of a door. There's a small blue sign about beach access, but otherwise no indication that we are anywhere in particular.

'Okay, come on, where are we going?' I ask eagerly.

'Secret Cove,' he replies.

'*Secret* Cove?' I repeat back to him excitably.

'Yep,' he replies. 'So, it's not as secret as it used to be, but it's still incredible, look...'

At the bottom of the path, as we step out from under the canopy of the leafy green trees above us, Secret Cove is in front of us. A crescent of sand sits in front of rocks and then the ocean with views to die for.

'This is... wow,' I blurt.

'Just let me step into tour guide mode,' Max says, shaking his body out.

I laugh.

'So... these rocks are lava rocks,' he explains. 'As beautiful as they look, be careful walking on them.'

The rocks are so dark and textured. As the water gently hits the edges, it couldn't look more blue in comparison. It's one of the most picturesque beaches I've ever seen. Nothing like the one at the resort, which I thought was gorgeous, but this one is just so untouched. So perfect. I can't see any sign of anything. No shops, no bars, not so much as a portable toilet. There's nothing but nature here.

'That, over there, is Molokini, a crescent-shaped, partially submerged volcanic crater,' he says as he points it out. 'It's uninhabited but you can go scuba diving there and things. That over there is Kahoolawe, another volcanic island. And this beautiful sand right here is where you're going to sit and chill with me.'

'Sounds great,' I say with a sigh.

I decided yesterday that while the swimwear I have with me may not be the kind I would have chosen for myself, I shouldn't worry about how I look in it, or what people think. I'm on holiday. I whip off my custom-made sundress to reveal the black bikini I wore yesterday. I imagine it's some kind of faux pas to wear the same thing two days in a row, but yesterday was the most comfortable I've felt the whole time I've been here. I turn around just as Max is taking off his shirt.

'What?' I can't help but squeak.

'What?' he replies, dusting himself off, checking he isn't being attacked by some kind of creature.

'No, sorry, it's nothing,' I say quickly. I didn't mean to freak him out. 'Sorry, erm... I was just surprised.'

Max looks behind him, then at me again, waiting for some kind of explanation. Shit, I guess I just have to be honest because you can guarantee, if I try to blag my way out of this situation, I'll only make things worse.

'I mean this in the nicest possible way,' I start, but from the look on Max's face, it's like he's bracing for something that is going to upset him. 'I just didn't expect you to have all of that going on. You look incredible – in a work-of-art kind of way.'

Max looks at his body and laughs.

I hadn't really thought about it, because I've been forcefully booting all ideas of anything close to feelings for Max firmly out of my head, so I guess it hadn't occurred to me that I haven't seen him without a shirt on. I don't know what I expected. I suppose I didn't expect anything. I certainly hadn't entertained the idea of him having rippling abs, plump pecs, and bulging biceps.

'Nerds *are* allowed in the gym,' he tells me.

'I clearly missed that memo,' I reply.

I sit down on the sand, lean back on my hands and dig my toes into the deliciously warm, silky-smooth sand. Secret Cove is no longer a total secret, there are a handful of other people here, but it doesn't compare to the well-trodden sands at the resort. Here, because it's such a quiet spot, and because it's still early in the day,

I'm sitting on fresh, untouched sand. It was perfect until I got here, which is an ongoing theme, I suppose.

'While we're being inappropriate,' Max jokes, sitting down next to me, 'you're wearing the hell out of that bikini.'

'Ha! Thank you,' I reply, a little awkwardly. 'My boss didn't pack me anything with a bum. Or maybe she did but it's all intended for a much smaller bum than mine.'

Max laughs.

'No, I like it,' he insists. 'Do you know how white my bum is whenever I get back from holiday? If I had a pair of those, I'd be sorted.'

'Perhaps we can sneak behind an especially big chunk of lava rock and swap?' I suggest playfully.

'Surely doing it in the sea would be expert level?' he replies. 'With the waves, the way the water is moving, I don't fancy your chances getting those pants off.'

'Perhaps you would have more luck,' I can't resist saying cheekily.

I don't know if it's because I'm over the shock of how we wound up where we are, or because we've been working so closely together, as well as a big dose of the overwhelming attraction I felt towards Max when we first met, but flirting with him just comes so naturally. I've been trying not to think of him that way, I really have, I swear, because it seems like he's had his heart broken, and he's in a fragile place, but these feelings I have, lurking in the back of my brain, just will not clear off, no matter how many meet cutes I attempt or sexy uncles I meet.

Max purses his lips and raises his eyebrows. Have I just managed to make him speechless?

'Thanks for helping me,' he says, changing the subject. 'With work and with... *other*. Yes, I know I keep saying it.'

'Well, I'll keep saying you're welcome,' I tell him. 'You know, if you'd told me that you wanted me to come on holiday with you and pretend to be your fiancée, I probably would have said yes.'

'To be honest, as unbelievable as this is going to sound, it was never really my intention,' he says. 'I could've asked anyone to do that. I was all set for heading off on this holiday alone, with a bunch of different excuses lined up. But then I met you and you seemed like the break would do you good – and your name being so similar seemed like a sign. I called up my mum's PA, said the ticket had accidentally been booked in the wrong name, got another one booked in your name. I thought maybe, if we arrived together, and I wasn't alone with… things, for lack of a better term, it might actually be an all right trip. I just didn't get chance to tell you, or my family, before they walked in. I know it all sounds like shit. I wasn't even going to waste my time explaining. But, I knew, when I met you, that there was just something about you that I liked, that I wanted to keep around me. Being in a room with you gave me this high, this feeling, this energy I started feeding off, one that I didn't want to give up.'

Max sighs. He almost looks as though he regrets saying it. I lightly place my hand on top of his.

'I'm not saying you didn't handle this kind of terribly,' I tell him. 'But it is possible I overreacted, ever so slightly, because I'm just so used to men being absolute freak shows.'

'Is it really as bad as everyone says?' Max asks, wincing slightly. 'I know there are a lot of horrible people out there. Perhaps ignorantly so, I think men tend to think if it's not them doing the bad things, it's not a problem. I try to check myself, and my mates. I think that's why I felt so ashamed, seeing your face, when you realised my family were here. I never ever wanted to put you in an uncomfortable position.'

I do genuinely believe every word he's saying. Now I feel bad for making him feel like a bad guy, even though I know it's not really my fault.

'I've app dated,' I tell him, pulling a face. 'How about I tell you some of the nightmare dates I've had, just to make you feel better about yourself? You can realise that there are so many men, so much worse than you, and you can have a bit of a laugh at my expense.'

'Oh, God, go on,' he says, preparing himself.

'Well, my very first Matcher date was with a guy called Smithy,' I start. 'The name should have been an instant red flag – who introduces themselves to a girl with the name their football friends call them? Anyway, we met up on Oxford Street, for a walk around the shops because it was just before Christmas so I thought it might be nice. Right from the get-go all he was talking about was sex. "I shagged this person, this is why sex is better without a condom, you're wearing red lipstick, did you think we were going to fuck today?" Seriously all just... beyond gross.'

'What did you do?' Max asks.

'I did what any sensible, mature woman would do in my situation,' I reply. 'I suggested we go for a walk in the Winter Wonderland, gave him the slip and then blocked his number.'

'Nice,' Max replies.

'One guy turned up and hardly said a word to me the whole time, which was really weird, and there was another who seemed okay, until he told me that he was visiting from Manchester, and was only looking for a hook-up,' I continue.

'Not a lot of second dates, then,' Max says.

I realise my hand is still on his. It probably doesn't need to be, but I don't want to move it.

'No,' I reply. 'Even the ones that did... there was one guy. He was doctor, a little bit older than me, charming, good-looking – all things that make you trust a person, even though you shouldn't. On our first date, we went for a drink together, it was going great, we were talking about our jobs and getting on really well. I promise you this is relevant but when I was in primary school, one of my friends stabbed me with a freshly sharpened pencil and the tip snapped off inside my finger. I remember my mum trying to get it out at the time, squeezing it, trying to work it out with a needle, and me being a big baby, crying, asking her to stop, so she did. Anyway, it's still there to this day, so I have this tiny piece of pencil in my finger forever. I remember showing it to the guy. He took my hand in his and had a look at it. He told me he could cut it out for me, if I wanted him to, but that the scar would look worse than the little black dot did.'

It's my other hand, so I hold it out to show Max the small mark on the index finger. I suppose it's officially a part of me now. It's been in my body for longer than it hasn't. I was genuinely quite relieved, though, when he told me I didn't have to worry about it.

'Wow, that's kind of cool,' he says. 'Almost like a tattoo.'

'I later found out they're called trauma tattoos, which sounds way cooler than it is. Anyway, once he had my hand in his, things got a bit weirder,' I continue. 'He kept my hand. I thought he was holding it, but then he started sort of admiring it. Eventually he said he was looking at my veins, working out what size cannula he'd use on me.'

I glance at Max. His eyes widen.

'Wow,' is about all he can say.

'It was one of those things that, it's so weird, you think it's a joke,' I continue. 'I mean, it probably was a joke. He never actually performed any medical procedures on me, obviously. But we did stay together long enough to get intimate and... I don't know. I wish we hadn't. I should have known he was a weirdo, from everything I just said, but you really can never, ever tell.'

'What happened?' Max asks. 'You don't have to talk about it if you don't want to.'

'It's not a big deal,' I tell him. 'Or maybe it is. I don't know. Things aren't as black and white as people used to think they were – if you know what I mean. I wanted to be with him at the time... it just felt a bit weird and, after, I realised I was covered in scratches, bruises, love bites. You give your consent, thinking it's going to be something and, when it's not what you expected, well, you agreed to it, right? To something... I remember looking at my body in the mirror after, wondering how someone I was dating, who seemed so nice and charming and was an actual doctor – someone who was supposed to help people – could leave me such a wreck.'

Max, reading the room perfectly, hardly moves a muscle. Instead, he follows my lead, wiggling his fingers slightly so that they entwine a little tighter with mine, my hand still on his. It's just the right amount of comfort I need.

'That's horrendous,' he says. 'What a bastard. Frankie, I'm so sorry.'

'The best part of the story is that, afterwards, I never heard from him again,' I say. 'I wondered if this was just what he did, lulled women into a false sense of security, had weird sex with them, and then never called them again, or if he was ashamed of how he treated me, because he got carried away, and so he just couldn't face me any more. I imagine the reality was something in the middle.'

'It's so hard to trust again, after something hurts you,' Max replies.

'Tell me about it,' I say. 'He's the last person I was with-with. My last proper boyfriend before that cheated on me. I don't need to tell you about that, though, do I?'

'Seeing as we're in a sharing mood,' he says. 'If you've bared your soul, then so can I. My last two serious girlfriends have cheated on me – I suppose I thought the relationships were more serious than they did. At this point, I'm starting to think it might be me who is the problem. With Fran, it was pretty standard stuff. I was suspicious, I watched her a little closer, I saw the signs, the dodgy behaviour, hiding her phone while she was in the shower kind of thing. So I confronted her, she admitted it, and that was that. With Paige...'

Max's voice tapers off. He doesn't say anything for a few seconds.

'I thought being cheated on once was bad, but twice,' I say, filling the silence with sympathy. 'I honestly don't think I could stand trying again if it was me. Sometimes I wonder whether that's why I'm so cautious, because I need the next time I fall in love to be a love that lasts forever. I know, that sounds kind of corny, but another heartbreak would be another failure, another reason to give up altogether. I'm starting to think that's why I tank my chances with anyone I meet. I'm scared everyone is going to hurt me.'

I wonder, just to myself, of course, whether that's why I'm so keen to stay single, and why I'm always too willing to try out things for the articles, because I know that nothing real can ever come from them. I get to have a love life, of sorts, without running the risk of being intimate with someone again, only for them to hurt me one way or another.

'I can't even imagine what it must be like for you,' I continue. 'Paige being with your brother, the two of them being married, having to see them together all the time.'

Max chews his lip thoughtfully.

'Can I tell you something?' he eventually asks. 'It's something I've never told anyone before.'

'Of course,' I insist. 'I've never told anyone what I just told you, so you know your secret is safe with me.'

'Paige is with Lee now, and I do honestly believe they're happy together, and right for each other, but Paige hasn't always known what she wanted,' he explains. 'Or who. Can I interest you in a little childhood trauma to frame what happened between us?'

'Of course,' I say with a jokey enthusiasm. 'I've offloaded my baggage on to you. Please, feel free to do the same.'

'Albi and I were in the same year at school,' Max explains. 'The same class, we even hung around in the same friendship group. Albi realised, pretty early on, that he could... I don't know, leverage the fact he was my uncle, to gain street cred. He thought it was hilarious. So did everyone else, to be honest, it's an impossible thing for kids to wrap their heads around. He used to say he had authority over me, as my uncle, and that I had to do whatever he said. I was his little punching bag, the butt of all his jokes, the person he made look small to try and make himself look big. That story Lee told when we were playing Convince Me. *Albi* was the one who made my face bleed when we were all wrestling – absolutely on purpose, it wasn't a rogue trainer, it was the one on his foot – and *he* was the one who started the godawful Maxi Pad nickname that followed me all the way through my A levels. As we got older, Albi couldn't stand to see me with anything he didn't have. Better grades, cooler clothes, girls. He stole my girlfriend a week before our prom, just to show me that he could, I suppose, and then he dumped her a few days after. I hadn't been with her long, and I was a teenager, so I got over it, obviously. But then, with Paige... I suppose she was what you would call a bit of a social climber back then.'

Max takes a breath. I'm tempted to tell him to leave it there. That he shouldn't dwell on the past. But honestly, I feel so much lighter for sharing what I carry around with him. I think telling someone is something I've needed to do for a long time.

'It's awful when someone cheats on you, of course it is,' he continues. 'The hurt, the betrayal, all the questions. The only thing that makes it worse, as if it could be, is when you catch that person cheating on you. When you walk in on them in bed with someone else, you see them so wrapped up in this other person, so lost in the moment, yourself so far from their thoughts until their eyes accidentally meet yours. That's how I found out Paige was cheating on me. Albi was the person I caught her with.'

'No!' I blurt.

I knew Albi was a bit of a playboy, but I honestly thought he might be all talk, to a degree. Lee might be the kind of guy to marry his brother's ex, but for Albi, his uncle, to sleep with his girlfriend! When will I learn that just because people are nice, good-looking, funny and charming, that none of that speaks to their character at all?

'I'm not making excuses for anyone, but she knew I was wondering about my role in the company, I wonder if I wasn't serving as the right kind of step for her any more,' he says. 'Albi probably seemed like a more viable option but, as I said before, he would want what I had, take it and then quickly discard it. Lee doesn't know any of this. Neither does anyone else in the family. I don't think Paige is the same person she was back then. Maybe she accidentally genuinely fell in love with Lee or maybe she decided to change. No one ever needs to know. And look, I know we're not really engaged, but Albi doesn't, so maybe watch yourself around him, I know it's been a while, but I wouldn't put anything past him.'

'Thanks,' I say softly. 'He paints himself as such a charmer. I've chatted to him a few times... He told me about his girlfriend, who broke her back skiing.'

I don't tell him about us going snorkelling together because I don't want him worrying about the two of us hanging out.

'Well, I wouldn't have ever called her his girlfriend in the first place, more just the girl he brought on one of the family skiing holidays, and even if that weren't the case, she definitely wasn't his girlfriend after she had to *obviously* cut the holiday short, so he never contacted her again.'

Wow, what a prick.

'I do wonder if it's me,' Max continues. 'Whether I'm just so damn easy to cheat on for some reason. I don't know. Maybe I should give up, but I suppose I'm a tragic romantic at heart.'

He laughs his way through the second half of his sentence. Then we fall silent for a second.

'Well, we're ruining Secret Cove,' I eventually say.

'We really are,' he replies. 'What a couple of losers. Who is sad in Maui?'

I laugh as the mood lightens again.

'I really don't want the memory of here to be me spilling my guts on the beach,' I say.

'Oh, I've done that before in Maui,' he says. 'Come on holiday with us a few more times. Spilling your guts on the beach on holiday is one of the great British pastimes.'

'You know, an actual Secret Cove sounds like a great place to bury all this rubbish,' I say. 'We could leave it here, so to speak.'

'Okay, deal,' he says. 'I'll let go of it if you will.'

I dig a small hole in the golden sand, pretend to fill it with *something*, and then fill it back in. I do all of this with my free hand because I desperately don't want to break contact with him.

'Well, now that's out of the way, fancy a dip in the sea?' Max suggests.

'Now that's a memory for the day I'll be happy with,' I tell him.

'As nice as that would be, don't get ahead of yourself,' he warns me. 'We're going somewhere else later that might just top it.'

I smile. Max really is going all out today, to give me a day that resembles a normal holiday, and I couldn't be more grateful. Screw the meet cutes. Even if it is just for a day.

29

Have you ever found yourself in a moment that is just perfect?

After spending time at Secret Cove, and visiting one of the most popular beachfront diners on the island, Max has brought me to Haleakala National Park to see the sunset. It's taken us a while to drive the twenty miles up the winding road that takes you up 10,000 feet, but Max promised me it was worth all the potential car sickness, and a brief break from the hot sunny weather up at the top. It was worth it for the car trip alone. We've been chatting the whole way up here, about anything and everything, laughing, joking, getting on like a house on fire again.

'People make reservations way in advance and get up early to see the sunrise here,' he tells me. 'Not everyone realises that the sunset is just as beautiful.'

'The beginning is usually more beautiful than the end, I suppose,' I reply. 'But this... this is... thank you so much for bringing me here. Why do I want to cry?'

Max takes his AirPods from his pocket. He puts the left one in his ear and the right one in mine. He places an arm around me and pulls me close as he messes with his phone.

'I once came here on my own and I listened to this James Bay album as I watched the sun set,' he explains as he searches for what he's looking for. 'And as I did, I decided what I wanted to do with my life, and that was to move back to the UK and take the job at ByteBanter.'

'What a place to do it,' I reply.

'Somehow, as I watched the sky and listened to the music, everything fell into place. I figured out exactly what I wanted. Here, try it.'

Max gives his phone one final tap, and the music starts playing.

As though it weren't beautiful enough up here before sunset, looking out across the island from above the clouds, now, watching the day turn into night, it's really a sight to behold. As the sun reaches the carpet of clouds, it sinks into a bright yellowy-orange sky, taking every last bit of warmth with it, so Max holds me closer still, and as 'Let It Go' fades into 'If You Ever Want to Be in Love', I finally feel that wave of clarity Max felt before he moved to London. I know exactly what I want. It's him. It's Max.

In a moment that is so unlike me, I turn to Max to kiss him. In an even less likely event, considering this is my life we're talking about, Max's lips are already on the way to find mine, and as the last part of the sun finally disappears, we share our first kiss, 10,000 feet in the air, thousands of miles from the real world, and I couldn't think of a more perfect way to describe how it feels. Like he's the missing piece of the puzzle. The broken bit of something that, when it comes together with the pieces of me, makes something fixed. Something whole. This is the last thing I expected to happen today, but it's the best too. I don't ever want to come back down.

30

After a day like yesterday, and the sunset that followed, I couldn't have imagined anything that could possibly ruin something so perfect. What about the fact that it's the next morning and Max is acting like it didn't happen? That really takes the shine off things.

I'm not mentioning it either, of course. Well, if he isn't going to, then neither am I. Two can play at that game... it's just a shame, because I thought my days of playing games might finally be over.

Eva came over relatively early, to see if Max wanted to play tennis with her. She invited me too, but I said I had work to do. This made her laugh, because she couldn't imagine how a spinal surgeon could possibly work from a hotel room on holiday, but she didn't question me on what it was. I suppose I could always claim patient-doctor confidentiality if she did.

I'm out and about, in the resort, trying to trigger some meet cutes, because reality is coming for me any day now. I'll be back home before I know it, fighting for my job, desperately searching for somewhere I can afford to live, while still being stuck somewhere that has bugs in the bath and Stuart's latest fella trapped in the shower.

I've tried angling for men to buy me drinks at the bar again, except it's the same bloody barman (Ori, who is genuinely a really nice man) so he keeps just giving me free drinks and telling me to pass my regards on to the rest of the Rays. I didn't waste my time trying to drown myself in the baby end of the pool, I'll keep that ace up my sleeve for when I have no other options. Now I'm walking through the gardens, where I've just spotted a marquee full of people. It looks like a party. Now that's a great place to meet people.

I sneak up to the entrance to the marquee before slinking my way inside. I weave in and out of people, until I'm more in the centre of the crowd, trying to blend in a little more.

I find myself next to a table where a forty-something man is eating a very colourful piece of cake.

'That looks delicious,' I say, breaking the ice.

'It's not bad for a kids' cake,' he replies. He has an American accent that I can't place and I'm also very much aware of the fact that he said it was a kids' cake. I glance around the room. Colourful balloons, a clown, a piñata – yep, this is totally a kids' birthday party. 'Where's yours?'

'Oh, I'm not having any,' I reply.

'Huh?' he says, confused.

'I'm not having any cake,' I say.

'I mean your kids,' he says with a laugh.

'Ohhhh.' I chuckle awkwardly. 'I don't have any kids.'

'You want some?' he jokes, gesturing at the crowd of screaming children behind him, all yelling at the birthday boy, who is smacking the piñata with a scary amount of strength.

'Hey, buy me dinner first,' I joke – imagining that's what Addison would say if she were in my shoes (or what she would tell me to say now if she were watching), because I have to keep my mind on my job, even if I really don't want to. 'Calm down, mister.'

Oh, God, he does not look impressed with that.

'It's my son's birthday,' he reminds me. 'If you're not one of the moms, who are you?'

'Oh, is that the time?' I say, looking at my watch, except I decided not to wear it today because I'm starting to get a huge white patch on my wrist where the sun hasn't managed to tan. 'I'd better go take my medicine.'

I stand up and hurry my way out of the marquee, heading back in the direction of the suites. It's no use. I officially suck at meet cutes. And it's not like a romantic encounter is just going to drop from the sky and fall at my feet, is it?

Right on cue, a balled-up piece of paper lands on the floor in front of me. I pick it up and straighten it out. It reads:

I love you.

I quickly glance around and eventually spot Ronnie Ray, sitting at a table alone, with a pen, a pad, and enough screwed-up paper to explain a missing rainforest.

'Frankie, sorry,' he says. 'I didn't mean to throw that at you, I just lost my temper.'

'That's okay,' I say as I return the piece of paper to him. I set it down on the table, message side up, so he knows that I've seen it. 'Is everything okay?'

'Between you and me, not really, no,' he replies. 'It's this stupid vow renewal tomorrow. Not that the renewal is stupid, it's just the vows, I can't write a thing to save my life.'

I take a seat at the table next to him.

'Perhaps I can help you,' I suggest. 'I'm pretty good at this stuff.'

I am a writer, after all – not that I can tell Ronnie that.

'You're welcome to try,' he says. 'But I've got nothing. Nothing but I love you.'

'That might sound bad when you say it like that, but if we put the right spin on it, we can use it,' I tell him. He raises a curious eyebrow. 'Why don't you try and tell me why you love Eva, or why you think you're still together, after all these years.'

'Well, she was with me before I was a billionaire,' he starts off, rather unromantically. 'And all my friends, they've all got girlfriends on the side, one, two, sometimes even three. But not me. Never have, never will.'

I didn't think Ronnie could get any less romantic than 'she's not a gold digger' but he proved me wrong with 'I don't cheat on her like all my friends do with their wives'. Impressive.

'Okay, so not traditionally things you would say at a vow renewal,' I say, allowing myself a slight chuckle. 'But, what about this: Eva, you've stood by me since the day we met, through the ups and the downs.'

Ronnie's eyes widen.

'Hang on, let me write this down,' he says eagerly. 'Okay, what else?'

'Next...' I think about his not-cheating line. 'In all the time we've been together, I can honestly say I've never even looked at another woman, no one has ever come close. No one can compete. No one could have given me such endless support, such a beautiful family...'

Ronnie laps up every word I say. It's as though he can't believe his luck.

'Anything else?' he asks.

'To finish, I'm thinking...' I think for a moment. I don't just want to write any old romantic mush, he could have searched for that on the internet, Eva would spot it a mile off. 'Of all the things I have to say, the only thing that matters is this... I love you.'

'Fucking beautiful,' he tells me. 'Honestly, absolutely perfect. And you're a doctor? You should be a writer!'

'It's been said before,' I joke, entirely for my own amusement.

Ronnie has no sooner raised his hand than a waitress is standing alongside him.

'Yes, Mr Ray?' she says.

'A bottle of champagne, please, for me and my daughter-in-law-to-be,' he says. 'The most expensive one you have.'

'Oh, you don't have to do that for me,' I insist.

'After what you did for me?' he replies. 'We're going to have a drink, I'm going to take a breather from work – because I gave myself two hours, to try and write this bloody thing – and instead I'm going to get to know you a little better. It's been a long time since I've heard my son talk about a girl the way he talks about you.'

I smile.

'That's real love, that is, believe me. I've been with Eva more than two decades, I know what real love looks like,' he insists.

'Real love?' I repeat back to him.

'Of course,' he says. 'You are getting married, you know? You do love each other, right?'

Ronnie laughs, as though I may have forgotten. Obviously I had.

'Of course I love him,' I reply and, as the words leave my lips, I can't help but wonder... do I love him? Do I actually love Max? Is that what's going on here? Oh, brilliant, that's just what I need. Only I could fall in love with my fake fiancé. I've really excelled myself this time.

31

'Oh, Max,' I blurt as I find him in the living room of our suite. He's on the sofa, messing with his camera parts. 'You're back.'

'I am,' he replies. 'Should I not be?'

'No, no,' I insist. 'I just... I guess I lost track of time. What are you up to?'

'You know when I talk about the spec and you stare at me blankly?' he says with a smile.

'Got it,' I reply. 'Well, the good news is that before I went for a walk, I finished up the keynote for the presentation. Here, have a peep.'

I grab the laptop from the coffee table and fire it up, proudly brandishing it for Max to see. It's a good job I finished it earlier, because, honestly, I swear I'm a little tipsy from drinking champagne with Ronnie.

Max flicks through the slides, reading what I've written based on what he told me. Hopefully I've managed to capture exactly what Max wants to say about the camera he's created, and why.

'Frankie, this is brilliant,' he says. 'I swear, I didn't say half of this, but I was definitely thinking it.'

'Thanks,' I say, edging into shy territory, because for some reason a compliment from Max is too much to take right now. 'I really do fancy making the shift back to copywriting, if I can.'

'I haven't read any of your articles,' he says. 'But if you're this good at copy, and that's what you want to do, I say go for it. Is that what you thought about, when we were watching the sunset?'

'Oh yeah, sure,' I reply. 'That and wanting to give you that kiss that we're apparently not mentioning.'

Okay, that was definitely the champagne talking.

'Erm... sorry, I wasn't expecting you to say that,' Max says.

'I bet you didn't,' I say with a confidence I don't usually have. 'So, are we just not mentioning it, or...?

'Are you okay?' he asks me.

'Yes.' I sigh. 'Sorry, this probably isn't coming out right, I've been drinking champagne with your dad.'

'What?' he asks with a laugh. 'You and Dad?'

'Yep,' I reply. 'Don't tell your mum but he was struggling with his vows, so I helped him. It was all his own thoughts and feelings. I just helped him get them into words you can say at a vow renewal. The champagne was because he was really happy with them.'

'My dad doesn't hang out with anyone,' Max muses. 'He measures his time in terms of money. He must really like you.'

'Yeah, I'm really likeable,' I insist with a smile.

'Look, about the kiss,' Max starts, getting the conversation back on track. 'I only didn't mention it because you didn't. I thought perhaps you were regretting it.'

'I thought you were regretting it,' I reply. 'And I wasn't mentioning it because you weren't.'

'It's a good job you were day drinking with my dad,' he points out. 'Or we would have both politely never mentioned it again.'

'Good old day drinking,' I say, leaning back on the sofa.

Max's camera is plugged into the TV but it's pointing at his face.

This means that I can look at him without actually looking at him. I can see the look on his face, his eyes moving as he thinks, the corners of his mouth twitching as he goes to speak but then backtracks.

'Okay, we've been doing this all wrong,' he eventually says. 'We met, I invited you on holiday, we're pretending we're engaged – none of that shit is usual.'

'I can't say I've had much experience recently,' I reply. 'But, no, I don't suppose it is.'

'Frankie.' Max pauses to push his sketches out of the way, so that he can kneel down on the floor in front of me. He tries to keep a straight face, but I can see a smile fighting to break its way out. I've never felt more alive. 'Would you like to go on a date with me?'

'Ha!' I practically cackle. 'Sorry, that got me. Yes, yes, I would love to go on a date with you. Do you not need to work on your pitch for the morning?'

'There's one small thing I need to figure out with the camera,' he says. 'But I'm doing that now. Otherwise, I think we've done everything we can, all that's left is to do it. We deserve the night off.'

'Okay then,' I say, trying not to sound as enthusiastic as I feel, lest I look like a total dork.

'Okay, great,' he replies. 'I'd say pick you up at seven, but we're kind of living together right now. See what I mean, all in the wrong order.'

I smile. It quickly falls.

'What's wrong?' he asks.

'Ah, it's nothing,' I say. 'It's stupid, it's just that I pretty much hate everything my boss packed for me. It's just a shame that I'm going on my first real date in ages and I don't have anything "me" to wear.'

'You know there's a boutique here, right?' Max says.

I stare at him.

'Does this look like the face of a girl who knows there's a

boutique here?' I reply, pointing at myself. Okay, I seriously need to get some coffee in me, because this can't be charming.

Max just laughs.

'And a spa,' he adds. 'I've got some work to finish up on this. Your part is all done. Why don't you go treat yourself?'

'Because I saw a nineteen-dollar bag of crisps at the bar,' I reply.

'Yes, but what you're forgetting is that you have a keycard to a room paid for by Ronnie Ray,' he reminds me. 'And you can use that keycard in any of the shops and in the spa.'

'As heavenly as that sounds, I cannot possibly use your dad's money to buy clothes,' I tell him.

'Frankie, honestly, there isn't anything you could buy that would make our room charges higher than anyone else's, I promise you,' he insists. 'I'd be amazed if my dad hadn't mentioned that he was a billionaire by now.'

'Oh, he has,' I say with a laugh.

'I promise you, it feels like you're taking the piss, but you're not, that's what this holiday is for,' he says. 'It's my parents spoiling everyone rotten. Go get spoiled.'

'Sorry, this just sounds so fake,' I reply. 'But, okay, sure, why not, I'll go buy something to wear on our actual date.'

'Great,' he replies. 'And if you see a Valentino shirt, grab it for me.'

He's definitely joking, however...

'Oh, I totally have your Valentino shirt in my case,' I tell him. 'The one you borrowed. I brought it for you. It's been washed, it's good as new again.'

'Well, I know what I'm wearing tonight then,' he replies with a smile. 'Thank you.'

'Right, okay, well, I'm about to go live out my *Pretty Woman* fantasy,' I tell him. 'Have you seen that film?'

Max shakes his head.

'You're just going to have to take my word for it that what I just said isn't as bad as it sounds,' I insist. 'See you in a bit, don't work too hard.'

I practically sing those last few words at him but, my God, I am so happy right now. I have a date. A date-date. A date-date with Max! I need a dress, maybe I'll see if I can get a blow-dry and, most importantly of all, I need to find a buttload of coffee, because I definitely drank too much champagne with Ronnie. Still, it gave me the confidence to get what I wanted, and to clear up my misunderstanding with Max. Perhaps good things can finally start happening now, and it's all kicking off tonight. Tonight on my *date*!

32

'I'll never understand why pineapple and cheese, as a pairing, is so divisive,' I say as I finish up the last of my Hawaiian nachos. 'What a dream team.'

'I'm with you on that one,' Max replies.

I shuffle in my seat.

'I could eat those again but I won't, because every bit of media I've ever consumed has warned of the terrible consequences of overeating in front of a man on a first date,' I joke. 'Plus, I'm leaving room for dessert.'

'That's more like it,' he replies.

Dinner with Max has been so far so amazing. He picked me up right on time, and I was ready bang on seven. I mean, yes, okay, we are staying in the same suite, but I could have made him wait. There's a lot written about 'making them wait' for basically everything. Dates, replies to messages, kisses, sex. Relying on a manipulative system to try to control the narrative of a relationship is a terrible idea – no one has ever let me put that in an article, though. That definitely wouldn't make it to print. I'm supposed to tell people to wait this long for this, don't do that if you want that to happen, blah blah blah.

I assumed we would be going to the restaurant, but Max had something better planned. Our own private table down on the beach, surrounded by tiki torches, with nothing but the roar of the sea to keep us company.

Max did wear the Valentino shirt, which I really like, because it reminds me of the first time we hung out together. He looked so good in it then and he looks even better in it now – especially against his suntanned skin. Of course, I know what's going on underneath it now, that's a hard sight to forget. But let the record show that I was massively attracted to Max long before I realised he has the body of an Avenger. As for me, well, after a trip to the boutique here at the Grand Palm Resort, let's just say I found a dress that has me written all over it. Not literally, obviously, it doesn't have anything written all over it, just Alexander McQueen written inside it. It's a black square-neck minidress with a box-pleat skirt and silver zip all the way up the front. It's short and full of attitude. Kind of like me.

It's amazing how just wearing my own clothes – or clothes that I picked out, at least – is making me feel more myself. I feel more confident, I feel sexier and, bizarrely, I actually feel like I'm on a proper date.

'You look unbelievable in that dress,' he tells me. 'I like the zip, although I have to admit, it kinds of reminds me of that thing I accidentally found in your room.'

'Which...? Oh, that thing,' I reply.

'Yeah,' he laughs. 'That thing was interesting.'

'It certainly was,' I reply. 'So... dessert?'

The reason I'm changing the subject is because – don't laugh – I've totally got the bodice on under my dress. I know, it sounds... presumptuous, but that wasn't what I was going for. Or maybe it was, I don't know. I kind of thought it would be funny, to tell him I had it on, but that was probably just because they gave me more champagne at the spa. I'd be lying if I said I didn't want to pounce on Max but, give me a break, it's been a while since I felt so comfortable thinking about a man like that. Still, no matter what the reason is for me wearing it, the reason for me taking it off when we get back to the suite will probably be because it's so uncomfortable. How on earth can anyone feel sexy in this?

'Yes, dessert,' Max replies, clearing his throat. 'Obviously it's got to be the vanilla-bean crème brûlée or the chocolate macadamia nut tart.'

'That was exactly my thinking,' I reply.

'Well, then, let's order both and share,' Max replies with a smile.

Eventually our desserts arrive. Usually, if I agree to share two desserts with someone, there will always be one that I like the most, that I wish I had ordered for myself, but not today. Both are absolutely stunning.

'How does this first date measure up then?' Max asks curiously.

'I mean, you haven't tried to perform any medical procedures on me, and I haven't taken you into the gardens to try and give you the slip, so that's at least a six out of ten,' I joke.

'My highest score yet,' he replies.

Max notices a little chocolate on the side of his index finger so he brings it up to his mouth and sucks it lightly. Now that I'm focusing on his mouth, all I can think about is how much I want to kiss him again. That kiss last night was really something. It wasn't even just a quick kiss in the moment – once we started, neither of us wanted to stop. If it hadn't been so cold up there once the sun was fully down, we might still be there now.

'Do you want another drink or a coffee?' Max asks. 'Or do you want to go for a walk?'

'A walk would be lovely,' I reply.

'Okay, let's do it,' he says.

As we walk from the beach, back into the heart of the resort which is alive with music, families and couples, chatting as we go, we somehow just naturally gravitate out of the noise again, towards our suite. It's strange, because neither of us leads the way, it's just where we end up. Once there, we head inside.

'It's warm in here,' Max says as he partially opens the bifold doors.

'I'll grab us some drinks,' I say as I head for the fridge.

Eventually I join Max on the sofa, taking a seat next to him, our legs just inches apart. I stare down at the gap between us, willing myself to move into it, but being too nervous to do it.

'Do you—' Max says.

'Did you—' I say at the same time.

'Sorry,' Max quickly apologises. 'You go first.'

'I was just going to say, did you work out that problem you were having with your camera earlier?' I ask him.

'Oh, yes,' he says. 'Look.'

Max messes with the TV remote before the camera on the table in front of us switches on. On the screen there's a perfect image of us. It's strange, kind of like watching yourself on *Gogglebox*.

'So, obviously this monstrosity I've constructed is made up of several existing pieces of Optecho tech,' he says. 'The finished product will look sort of like it does in those drawings. But I've swapped the camera on us for one that is able to follow you around so, if you move out of shot, see...'

Max leans away from me. Sure enough, the camera does its thing and the image on the TV widens.

'And if we get closer together,' he continues.

He slides back over towards me. Now our thighs are touching. The camera zooms in closer on us.

'That really is amazing,' I say, placing my hand on his leg. 'You've absolutely smashed it.'

'*We've* smashed it,' Max replies.

I keep my eyes on the TV, looking at my own hand on Max's leg. My heart is pounding in my chest. My breathing feels heavy. I wiggle in my seat awkwardly.

'Are you okay?' Max asks me. 'You've seemed a little... I don't know... uncomfortable all night. If you want to walk things back a little, or—'

'Oh, God, no, it's not that,' I quickly insist. 'It's nothing like that. It's my dress. Well, it's what's under it, to be honest. I don't think it's designed for sitting down to dinner.'

'Er... what's...' I detect the slight wobble in Max's voice. 'What do you mean by what's under it?' he dares to ask.

I wish I could be as brave in showing him. I have an idea. Something that might make this a little easier. I keep my eyes forward, on the TV, and slowly pull down the zip on the front of my dress, allowing it to fall open slightly at the front. God, those fully open cups are really, well, open. The open pieces at the front of my dress are just about covering my nipples still, but not by much.

'You're wearing it,' Max says before puffing air from his cheeks.

'Mhmm,' I reply.

'Does that dress unzip all the way?' Max asks, his eyes fixed firmly on the TV.

I decide to show him, rather than tell him, which I probably only feel brave enough to do because I've kept a slow, steady drip of alcohol into my body all day, but I'm glad because the sexual tension in this room is practically suffocating.

Max takes his eyes off the TV to lean over and kiss my neck. It's kind of sexy, watching him on the 80" TV in front of us, in a way that it absolutely wouldn't be if we recorded it and watched it back. Seeing yourself like that can be awful and embarrassing, apart from when you're in the moment, like we are now. I'm too wrapped up in Max to care.

I finally turn to Max and remove his shirt. As I mess with his belt, he leans me back on the sofa, pressing his body down on top of mine. Finally, we're kissing again and this time we don't have to stop for anything.

Max kisses his way down my body. I turn to look at the TV, but I'm quickly distracted by the reflection on the partially open doors. Okay, we don't have to stop, perhaps just a brief pause though.

'Wait, wait a second,' I giggle, pulling him back up to eye level. 'We should go upstairs. If anyone is out there, they'll be getting a major peep show, if they can see the TV.'

'You're right,' Max says. He kisses me for another ten seconds before jumping to his feet, helping me to mine and then leading me up the stairs.

Once we're in the bedroom, the door safely closed behind us, I push Max back onto the bed before finally removing my dress (which I'm surprised is still hanging on to me at this point) and climbing on top of him.

As we start kissing again, upstairs, safely out of the way of the camera, I finally relax. It surges through my body like a wave. Suddenly nothing matters. I don't care where I live, I don't care if I'm going to lose my job – forget them, there are other apartments, other jobs. Right now, all I care about is Max, and he has my full, undivided attention.

33

Today marks my sixth day of waking up in Hawaii, and while each night's sleep has been better than the last, today has them all beat by a mile. For the first time, I am in actual paradise, lying here in bed with Max, my head on his chest. I could honestly lie here forever but that's not an option, especially not today, because we've got one hell of a day ahead of us.

'Are you ready for your pitch?' I ask him as I play with the hairs on his chest.

'I am, thanks to you,' he replies. He leans forward to kiss me on the forehead.

'And then the vow renewal?' I continue.

'More Ray family forced fun and intimacy,' he says with a laugh. 'It will be fine. It might even be fun, now I've got my fiancée with me. Hmm, is it weird calling you that, now that we're kind of a something?'

'I'm used to it now,' I say with a smile.

'You've just reminded me of something,' he says. 'Back in a sec.'

Max jumps out of bed, grabbing his boxer shorts before disappearing down the stairs. Eventually he returns with a small green box wrapped in a white bow.

'I was going to give you this last night,' he starts. 'But then... er...'

'...you gave me something else,' I joke.

'Well, yeah,' he laughs. 'So, I thought I'd give you it now and, let me start by saying, it's not as weird as it seems.'

I open the box. Inside, there's a white-gold ring with a small diamond held firmly in the centre.

'Let me get the disclaimers out, quickly,' he says as I take it from its box. 'It's not an expensive ring, at all, and it's not any kind of ring, I bought it as a small thank you, for everything you've been doing for me. It's not for *that* finger. And, to be honest, it's making me feel bad that you're my fake fiancée and you're not even getting a ring out of it.'

He's obviously kidding about that last part but it's cute.

'Max, honestly, I love it,' I say. I slip it on *that* finger but only for, you know, continuity. I can move it over to the other hand once we're headed home. 'It's stunning.'

I practically lunge at him, wrapping my arms around his neck and my legs around his waist, pulling him back down to the bed with me.

He's into it for a minute, before he quickly stands up.

'Okay, as much as I want to, we've got a pre-vow-renewal business meeting to attend,' he says. He offers me a hand, to pull me up. 'Do you know what you're wearing?'

'I definitely bought two dresses last night,' I confess. 'Don't worry, the one I'm wearing today isn't as sexy, it's very family-friendly.'

'Oh, damn,' he jokes. 'Well, the idea is to get ready now, then pop over and pitch to Dad over breakfast, then it's off to the beach for the vows and the rest of the day will pretty much just be one big party. Sound good?'

'Sounds great,' I reply. 'Come on, let's do this.'

Max and I both get ready, finally able to share the bedroom and the bathroom, as though we were a normal couple. I don't know what we are, to be honest, but right now I don't mind. I'm happy. What else matters?

All dressed up and with somewhere to go, we head downstairs to gather the things we need.

'I can't find my... oh, there it is,' Max says, picking up a pile of papers from the floor. 'We must have knocked these over last night. We left the door open, too.'

'Well, we were busy,' I remind him.

'We were indeed,' he says. 'It's a good job this thing doesn't record.'

With everything we need for the pitch, we head over to Ronnie and Eva's suite where – of course – a breakfast for 5,000 people is waiting. I'm starting to think I'm going to miss it when I'm back home, with little more choice than deliberating between two boxes of cereal, and if they might taste okay with water because someone has finished off the milk.

Lee and Paige are already here. It's such a shame Max's relationship with his brother is so broken. I don't suppose they ever get the chance to work on it, living so far apart. I don't think he holds much against his brother, it's more just that it's an awkward situation, but there's no love lost between him and Paige, and he certainly isn't his uncle's biggest fan. What was it Max said to me last night, while we were chatting over dinner? Something about how families just have toxic parts sometimes, and that it's just about loving the ones you love, dealing with the ones you don't, and keeping yourself sane in the process. I think that's a really healthy way to handle it. None of us owe people love, just because we share a family tree, do we?

As we walk into the room, it's Paige who spots us first. She looks us up and down, grinning like the cat that got the cream. Well, she hasn't got it yet. She needs to wind her neck in. There's no way Lee's idea can top Max's. Not unless he's invented a camera that can read minds.

'Right, let's get this done,' Ronnie announces. 'The sooner we're done, the sooner we can drink.'

Today might be the first day – okay, after this first bout of work-related chat is out of the way – that Ronnie takes almost a whole day off Optecho business. Imagine that.

'I'll go first,' Lee insists.

Obviously the men are all in their suits, ready for the vow renewal, but it does lend a certain level of serious business to what is supposed to be an informal pitching breakfast – whatever the hell that is.

Lee connects his laptop to the TV. He doesn't have anything physical to show, just a presentation, although it sounds like his job is more about the business than it is the tech behind the products.

Ronnie and Eva take a seat on the sofa. Max sits down next to them. I hang back, out of the way, but close enough to see and hear. Paige saunters over to stand next to me.

'Working from home is more common than ever,' Lee starts. He places a slide on the screen, showing some stats about how many people are now working from home instead of from an office. 'But, as we all know, the problem with working from home is ensuring a high level of productivity. So, I bring you...'

The slide changes to a sketch of, well, basically the exact thing Max came up with. Max turns around and stares at me in absolute disbelief.

'That's *my* sketch,' he mouths at me silently before turning back.

'But how do you know your employees are actually working?'

Lee says. 'With my device you can watch your employee, their desk in front of them, and their screen all at the same time, to ensure that your workers are doing their jobs.'

As Lee begins to talk about the manufacturing process, the potential global reach, shipping, things like that, I try to get my head around what the hell is going on. Okay, has he actually invented a camera that can read people's minds?

'Honestly, it was like Amsterdam walking around the pool last night,' Paige whispers to me quietly.

'What do you mean?' I ask her.

'Seriously, Frankie, you need to be more careful,' she replies. 'Your little porno caught my eye while I was out getting some fresh air. And you left your door open. Anyone could have just wandered in and stolen your phone, your jewellery, papers from the coffee table...'

I glance at her. Is she saying what I think she's saying? She is, I can see it in her eyes. Wow, Paige has gone full Lady Macbeth. I could almost be impressed, if I weren't so devastated for Max, he's worked so hard on this.

'Max has told me all about you, you know,' I reply, packing as much disgust as I can into a loud whisper.

Paige just bats her hand dismissively.

'What did he say, that I could have been his aunt?' she practically laughs.

'Almost,' I reply. 'You got one letter wrong.'

Okay, so taking petty swipes at Paige isn't going to change anything, but it certainly makes me feel a bit better.

'That was great, son,' Ronnie tells Lee once he's done. 'Max, you're up.'

Max takes to his feet and heads over to plug his laptop in.

'Good luck, bro,' Lee says, patting him on the back.

I can tell, just by looking at Max's body language, that he thinks he's beaten. Well, how can he top his own idea? If Lee has stolen the show with it, then Max's idea can only seem like a copy.

'My idea is... well... for the same device,' Max says. 'But the intention behind it isn't for corporate spying. My goal is to make an accessible, affordable must-have tool for vloggers and content creators all over the world, getting Optecho into even more homes, establishing a new product in a rapidly expanding industry that people can get excited about.'

Max's belief in his idea recharges his batteries. He stands taller, says his words with more confidence. Suddenly he's in work mode. He doesn't care if his brother stole his idea and pitched it first. All Lee was able to copy from Max's sketches was the tech – not the heart behind the concept.

I beam with pride as I watch Max absolutely killing it with his pitch. Not just because he's amazing and I'm proud of him, but because I'm proud of my work too. I've honestly really enjoyed it – more than I have failing at meet cutes, that's for sure.

'Fantastic, son,' Ronnie tells him when he's finished. 'Right, let's get to the beach, the ceremony will be starting soon.'

'Wait a minute, Dad,' Lee says. 'Aren't you going to tell us who is taking over when you retire?'

'Well, why would I do that?' Ronnie replies. 'It will be a long time before I retire.'

'I thought you were retiring soon and this was all about picking your replacement?' Lee persists.

'Where would you get an idea like that?' Ronnie asks him.

Both Lee and Max look over at their mum. She's applying lipstick in front of a compact mirror. She doesn't let her face slip for a second.

'At least tell us who won,' Lee pushes him.

'Okay, fine,' Ronnie says. 'Max.'

'What?' the two brothers both say in disbelief.

'But we pitched the same thing,' Lee says.

'You pitched the same device in two completely different ways,' Ronnie points out. 'Max had the best idea. Not only that but, come on, Kingsley, you think I don't recognise my own son's sketching? Max clearly came up with this idea.'

Lee doesn't know what to say. He looks over at Paige. She looks upset that her idea didn't pan out. Now I couldn't care less that she's seen me basically topless because she looks far more mortified than I ever could.

'Max, the company needs you,' Ronnie tells him. 'Somewhere near the top, running the show.'

'Erm, I'm COO,' Lee reminds him. 'What, you're sacking me for him?'

'I need you both,' Ronnie insists. 'Max has his finger on the pulse, he knows what people want and how to make it happen. Lee, you're a whizz with the business side of things and, to be honest, you're a ruthless motherfucker, selling out your own brother. Like I said, I need you both, in some kind of collaborative position. Anyway, something to think about, let's get to this ceremony so we can get it out of the way and then we can all get drunk.'

Ronnie pats Max on the back as he passes him. Everyone heads for the door.

I slink up to Max and kiss him on the cheek.

'You smashed it,' I whisper to him. 'And you got a job offer!'

'Yeah,' he replies, still a little stunned. 'I wasn't expecting that. It's one hell of an offer but, I don't know, leaving my life in London to move back here, starting all over again. Well, sort of. Something to think about, hmm?'

'Exactly,' I say enthusiastically, although now I suddenly feel like I've no sooner got my hands on him, I'm now encouraging him to leave me.

I make my way down to the beach with the rest of the family. It's strange, I almost feel like I'm one of them now, just, you know, a comparably poor version who isn't really a part of the family at all. Still on a high from last night (and this morning), I'm not going to worry about it now. I'm going to party, Ray style, and make the most of my time with Max.

I've already seen how the copy I wrote for him went down. Let's see how Ronnie's vows do with Eva...

34

The hotel marquee looks so different without all the balloons, clowns and kids. Today is positively sophisticated, with lilac and silver décor, a wedding-style table layout, there's a dance floor and a DJ set-up, as well as an enormous bar that has been constructed in the centre of the marquee, one that is capable of catering for the Rays, their nearest and dearest, and a whole bunch of other people.

After a delicious lunch, hilarious speeches and even a bizarre tossing of Eva's bouquet, as the day is turning into evening, the vibe is shifting more into that of a party. I've stuck to Max like glue all day until just now, when Ronnie asked if he could talk to him, so I'm using the opportunity to nip to the loos and the bar.

'Can I get a mai tai, please?' I ask the barman. It's Ori again. He's mixed me so many amazing cocktails this holiday, he probably knows what I'm having before I do.

'Sure,' he replies.

'...so this bloody chihuahua runs up to him, tries to bite him, and he drops his iPhone, shatters the screen. I said to him, that's the most expensive shag of your life, pal. You're lucky you've still got your knob.'

I catch the tail end (no pun intended) on an anecdote told by a familiar voice. It's Albi. He's the last person I want to bump into, especially alone, without Max flanking me. It was cool, seeing his yacht, snorkelling, but I don't know, now that I have more context from Max, I'm starting to wonder, did Albi have an agenda? Were his flirty remarks harmless or charged with intent? I had to cut the trip short, before lunch, because Max called me to see about working on the pitch together, so I said I had to go. Albi seemed annoyed. This is the first time I've seen him since.

I quickly turn away, facing in the opposite direction while I wait for my drink. Unfortunately, just because I can't see him doesn't mean he can't see me.

'Oi, Frankie,' he says as he approaches me. 'Where have you been hiding, huh?'

'Ahh, you found me,' I joke awkwardly.

'I thought we said we'd pick up where we left off?' he replies.

Obviously when we had a conversation along those lines, it was about lunch. You know, food, eating, one of my favourite things to do. Mostly it was just one of those things you say when you feel bad about bailing on something, like, so sorry, we'll do this again sometime.

'Sorry, I've just been so busy,' I explain. 'Max took me out for the day, and then we were busy with his work, today is the first time I've had a spare minute in days. If I haven't been helping Max, I've been helping Ronnie. You know how it is.'

He probably doesn't.

Albi ushers me around the side of the bar, into the corner where staff walk in and out, steering me before I have a chance to make a beeline for anywhere else.

'I heard the two of you are sleeping in separate beds,' he says.

'Me and Ronnie?' I reply, playing dumb.

'You and Max,' he says. 'Obviously.'

'Who told you that?' I ask with a scoff. Obviously there's some truth in it, so I'm curious to know how he knows.

'Those suites are like 30 per cent glass,' he reminds me.

'Well, whoever you're getting your information from, they're wrong,' I tell him. 'Why don't you go and ask Paige if that's true? She was walking past our suite last night. Let's just say we gave her one hell of a show.'

In an attempt to lay on super thick just how sexually active Max and I are (to dispel any separate-beds rumours), I potentially come across a little too strongly, causing Albi to misread the signals. Before I know it, his arms are slithering around my waist, yanking my body into his. As he tries to kiss my neck, I pull back, dropping my drink in the process. Nothing attracts a crowd like a glass smashing at a party. A few people shout 'wahey', which quickly identifies all the Brits in the room. Here in a flash there's Max and Ronnie, quickly followed by Eva, Lee and Paige.

'Get off her,' Max tells him, pushing his way between us, giving me some much-needed space.

'Albi, what are you doing?' Eva asks him under her breath. 'As charmed as we all are by your antics, can you please cut this shit out for one day?'

'*I'm* the one who is in trouble?' he says, sounding like a ticked-off teenager. 'She's just as bad as me. She encouraged me. She's been flirting with me all week. She wanted me too.'

'Come on, that's not true,' I insist.

'I've seen her flirting with every man who has sat at the bar,' Ori offers up from behind his post. Well, of course he's coming to Albi's rescue, because Albi has been giving him thousands all week. Annoyingly, though, he's not wrong, but it's not what it sounds like, is it?

'I've seen her doing it too,' a woman chimes in.

'Sorry, who are you?' I ask angrily. I'm starting to feel a little ganged up on.

'I'm the events coordinator,' she tells me. 'I was at the children's party yesterday. You were flirting with the birthday boy's dad.'

'And, when you were on the yacht with me, you were flirting with one of the staff, you flashed him a boob,' Albi says, quite casually, given what he's saying I did. 'You were flirting me too. You wanted it.'

'Okay, I'm starting to get the feeling every girl who steps foot on that yacht "wanted it",' I point out angrily.

'You were on his yacht?' Max asks me.

Of everything that has been said so far, this is the thing that upsets him the most. I don't know why I didn't tell him about it. I really wish I had now, because it was nothing to me. Just something to do. I suppose I worried he wouldn't have liked me hanging out with his uncle, and it's not like anything was going on with me and Max at that point, so I didn't think it would matter.

'She was,' Albi tells him. 'We hung out the other day while you were working.'

'You said you were going snorkelling,' Eva points out.

'So *that's* what the kids are calling it,' Paige joins in smugly, laughing to herself.

'All right, you're one to talk,' I reply, but then I remember that Max said he didn't want anyone to know, so I try to get things back on track. 'Albi asked if I wanted to see his yacht, I said yes, it's not a big deal, is it?'

'Except you didn't tell me,' Max points out.

'I am genuinely quite concerned,' Eva joins in. 'Frankie, have you really spent this entire holiday on the pull behind my son's back with... well, with everyone?'

I sigh. It's time to come clean. I can't let Max's family think his fiancée is on a mission to cheat on him. That really would make him look bad, especially after what happened before. I need to own up about my job, maybe I can style out that I lied to Max about that, because I guess I did, but the lies are so messy now.

'Look, okay, no, I haven't been on the pull,' I tell them. 'I'm a journalist. I'm not a doctor. I'm currently working on an article about meeting men the old-fashioned way so I'm basically just setting up ridiculous scenarios and seeing how they play out. Yes, I think it's dumb too, but that's another story.'

'You're not a real doctor?' Eva says, stunned, then relieved. 'Thank God I never asked you for advice on... that thing I was going to ask you for advice on.'

My goodness, I am so, so glad she didn't ask.

'You couldn't take a week off for a holiday?' Ronnie asks in disbelief. 'Why ruin our holiday with it? Why not just be honest?'

'My bloody editor made me come on this holiday,' I blurt, because I really don't like being cornered. 'She made it pretty clear that, if I didn't come, I was going to lose my job, in fact I probably still will, because she isn't interested in all my failed meetings, she wants me to write about Max.'

'Wait, I'm a work project?' Max asks me. 'You're here messing with me for some kind of social experiment for your magazine?'

'No, not exactly,' I insist. 'I can explain better under less weird circumstances.'

'Why did you tell us you were marrying a doctor?' Lee asks. 'If she's saying she's a journalist? Did you know?'

'Yes, I knew,' Max says. He puffs air from his cheeks. 'She's not the real Fran.'

Oh, God, it's all coming out now. I was hoping we wouldn't have to admit this part yet, but Max is clearly so upset that I didn't tell him about my project, and I'm not surprised. I'll try and explain it to him when we're alone so he knows that there is no way in hell I am using him for an article.

'She's just some girl I invited on holiday with me who, it turns out, is using me for an article,' he continues. 'Telling me all sorts, getting me to open up, to write about, take the piss out of me, all for strangers to read.'

'Okay, wait a second, that's not true,' I insist.

'I'm not doing this now,' Max says before he storms off.

I go to follow him, but Eva takes my arm and pulls me in the other direction.

'A word,' she says. 'Just before you go.'

'Eva, I promise you, all of this sounds bad, but it isn't,' I say. 'What may have started as Max inviting me on this holiday with him has turned into something so much more.'

'Max has been hurt before,' she tells me.

'I know, he told me,' I reply. 'That's not what's happening here. Honestly, I have such strong feelings for him, as soon as we got together, I forgot about my stupid article, and I was never going to write about him. I don't care if I lose my job.'

'This family is already a mess,' Eva tells me. 'We screw up and we hurt each other. Max isn't like the rest of us. He's made different. Do you know what you look like right now? You look like a Ray.'

I suppose she's right. Max liked me because I wasn't like his family. All of this must make me seem like an absolute nightmare, someone who uses people to get where she wants. Someone like Paige.

'I'll go and find him and apologise,' I tell her. 'I'll explain, and I'll make everything right.'

'He isn't quick to forgive,' Eva says. 'Not after everything that's happened. Max needs space to heal, real space – the last time he was hurt, he moved thousands of miles to London.'

I nod in acknowledgement before making my way out of the marquee and hurrying back to the suite. I deeply regret the sky-high heels, now that I'm trying to get from A to B through the various textures of the gardens.

Finally back at the suite, I kick off my shoes. There's no sign of Max downstairs. He isn't upstairs either. I try to call him, but he doesn't answer. I look around again. Some bits of his are still here but his case isn't. Shit. I open the drawer under the TV, where he leaves his valet pass for safekeeping, along with our passports and, shit, the pass and his passport are missing too. He's gone – gone home, I think.

Well, that's what I need to do too. I'll call Addison when I'm certain she's awake, because, to be honest, the time difference still has me all messed up, explain, see if she'll book me an earlier flight home. God knows when that will be, but I doubt it will be today. It's the least she can do for me, seeing as though she gave me this assignment. If she thinks I'll write about it, she'll certainly agree.

I cannot believe I've messed this up. I managed happiness for, what, twenty-four hours? It's a personal best in recent times, sure, but it's not great, is it? He's got a head start on me but I'm not giving up. I just can't believe it's going to take me so long to catch him up.

35

It's true what they say, jet lag really is worse when you get back home. I know there's science involved, when it comes to travelling east but, to be honest, I think it's also to do with that fact that when your plane finally touches down on UK land, you come back down to earth in more ways than one. Back to reality, back to the grind, back to the mess you left before you went. But I haven't come back to unwashed mugs and clothes all over the floor (well, I have, because: my housemates) I've come back to what I don't think I'm being overly dramatic in calling the ruins of my life.

Max isn't answering his phone. I started trying to call him the second I realised he had gone. Then for the rest of the day, and then all day today before my flight, but he isn't picking up. I have no idea where he lives and, with it being a bloody weekend when I did get back, it wasn't even like I could try to collar him at work. So I've had to wait until now, Monday morning, to head into the office and try to find him. I've spent the whole time thinking about what I'll do when I see him, running scenarios in my head, fantasising about it going well, panicking when I think about how badly things could turn out. From tearful grovelling at his desk to accidentally bumping into him in the lift and hitting the emergency stop, trapping us in there together like we were on the day we met... except I just took the lift to the ByteBanter floor completely alone, without a hitch, so grovelling might have to be the one.

'Hello,' I say brightly to the receptionist. 'Can I see Max Ray please?'

'Max isn't here,' she tells me.

'Do you know when he'll be in?' I ask.

'Just a sec,' she says, before looking over my shoulder. 'Hey, Timmy.'

Timmy stops in his tracks.

'Where's Max today?' she asks him.

'Oh, he's gone,' he replies, raising his eyebrows, as though it's some juicy piece of gossip.

'Gone?' I say. 'Gone where?'

'Erm, he quit,' he tells me, kind of nervously. I suppose he doesn't know whether he should be telling me or not.

'He'll be working his notice, right?' I say.

'Nope. He's gone back to work for his dad,' he explains. 'The Ray family are basically our royals, so the bosses agreed to let him go without working his notice period. How the other half live, eh?'

'Oh,' is all I can say. 'Well, er, thanks.'

I head back to the lift before making my way upstairs to my desk. It's weird, sitting down, looking over at the empty space where Cora used to sit. I messaged her, telling her I was home. She replied saying she had managed to use her unused holiday to basically cancel out her notice period, so we made a plan for later, so I could tell her about everything that has happened.

I glance at Addison's office door. She isn't in yet. When she does get in, I'm sure she'll be grilling me about everything that has happened, asking me about the article, probably telling me what I *have* to write about if I want to keep my job. I already know what she's going to say. She's going to tell me to write about Max, about lying for him, pretending to be his fiancée, and how badly it went. It won't be an informative article, it will be pure entertainment, and Max will be the punchline.

Well, if an article about my holiday is what Addison wants, then that's what she's going to get. I'm going to write her an article right now. I'm not sure she's going to like it, though…

36

I sit in the swivel chair opposite Addison's desk, twirling from side to side, my hands sweating because, boy, am I nervous. I try to wipe away the little smudge marks on the piece of paper I'm holding but I only seem to make them worse. Come on, Addison, where are you?

Eventually she walks in, dumping bags of shopping on the floor before taking a seat at her desk. It's only then that she even notices me.

'Frankie, look at you,' she says. 'Love the tan, it really suits you.'

'Thanks,' I reply.

'So, it all went a bit tits to the sky?' she says in a sympathetic tone that couldn't sound less sincere if she tried. She pokes out her bottom lip for effect. 'I want to hear *all* about it.'

I didn't tell Addison much to get her to book my return flight, just that Max had left, it had all gone wrong, and that I needed to get home ASAP. I told her I would give her the gory details in person, to be honest, because I wasn't sure how motivated she would be to have work fund my probably expensive early return if I gave her the goods up front.

'Well, I've written the article,' I tell her. 'It's all in there.'

Addison is unloading a Pret bag on her desk.

'I've got meetings all afternoon,' she tells me. 'If you want me to read it now, you're going to have to read it to me.'

I hate reading my own work to people.

'Read it later, it's okay,' I say, standing up.

'No, come on,' she insists. 'I want to hear all about it now, it will make my lunch break more fun.'

I sigh, sit back down, slump back a little and cross my legs like the kid who doesn't want to read out loud to the class and begin.

'My name is Frankie George, Love & Dating writer, and I owe the men of London (and, more recently, a few others in various locations in Maui) a huge apology. A large part of this job has always been trying out different methods of finding love and, with each one I've tried, I've done everything in my power to make sure I never found it. Only swiping right on people I wasn't instantly attracted to, mentioning marriage in the first message, only using pictures on my profile that I didn't look remotely attractive in – I became the poster child for a hopeless millennial, trapped inside a dating app, laughing at everyone around me, pretending I was there for more worthy reasons.

'But in all of this, in my constant attempt to find love, all I have ever been doing is rejecting it. And so came my latest idea: meet cutes. Trying to meet people the old-fashioned way, like the weird, wonderful and clichéd ways you see on screen. When it came to setting up these meetings, I was hopeless – at home and away – but while I was so caught up in these meetings, there was one thing I neglected to realise: I was checking off every romance trope in the book with someone very special, and I can't believe I missed it. I mean, for crying out loud, the first time I met him we were stuck in a lift together, how did I miss that?

'The cliches that I was trying so desperately to force with

everyone else were already there with him. Workplace romance, a zigzagging alternation between friends-to-lovers and enemies-to-lovers, the fake romance trope and, unbelievable, we even found ourselves in the good old "there's only one bed" situation. It was all there, right under my nose, and I was doing my usual, ignoring it, doing everything I could to continue to prove to myself that love was never going to happen to me. Well, it did, and I missed it and, for what? To keep a job that can only be done by a single girl?

'And so, with this article, I want to apologise to every man I've messed around, every man I never gave a genuine shot, but most of all I want to apologise to the most incredible man I've ever met. I blew it and I'm sorry. And, with that, all that's left to say is that I do want to find love, and I can't do that while I'm writing articles about how to stay single. This isn't just an article, it's my final article, and my resignation. I hope you've found my articles funny, at least, or that you found a way to take something from them. If ever there was a time to listen to me, then that time is now. Don't reject love just because you're scared of it. And finally, from one tragic romantic to another, I love you.'

I place the piece of paper down on Addison's desk in front of her. She's frozen in time with a chunk of sandwich in her mouth.

'Obviously I've submitted the article through the usual portal,' I say. 'This one is for you. Let me know if you need something more formal for my resignation.'

Addison finally swallows.

'You're resigning?' she exclaims. 'But you're the only person in this office who is willing to go that extra mile to create quality, genuine content.'

'That's the thing, though, it's not genuine content, and I'm not willing to do it any more,' I say. 'So, yeah.'

'I'm not going to change your mind, am I?' she says.

I shake my head.

'Bloody hell, it's going to be just me and the cleaner left.' She sighs. 'Okay, well, yeah, I suppose we can print it, it will probably go viral, so that's good. We'll be replacing you, though. If you're not willing to do this, someone else definitely will.'

'That's okay by me,' I say.

'Okay, get back to work, I suppose,' she says. 'While I can still tell you to do it.'

I head back to my desk and sit down, placing my head in my hands. It's the right thing to do, of course it is, but right doesn't pay the bills and it doesn't get Max back either. But, for now, it's all I have. At least there will be other jobs, other flats. I can't imagine there will be another Max, but at least now I have the problem of potentially being made homeless to distract me, which is just great. I suppose I'll have to move back in with my parents, get a job back in Surrey somewhere, try to start my life again. This is not how I imagined my life being at thirty-four. Not at all.

37

'I can't believe you did that,' Cora blurts, her jaw practically in the overpriced espresso martini on the table below her. 'I can't believe you just quit like that.'

'Oh my God, don't,' I insist with a smile. 'I'm worried that, any minute, it's going to sink in. I'm going to understand the gravity of quitting my job, without another one lined up, and realise that it not only means that I can't afford my new apartment, but also that I probably can't stay in my current home for too long, not without finding another job and... blah!'

I blurt that final noise dramatically, as though I'm clearing my throat of a horrible taste. The reality does leave a bad taste in my mouth, though, it's a bitter pill to swallow, admitting what a mess I'm in. And the fact I've just paid seventeen pounds for a cocktail in a fancy bar isn't lost on me, but it's probably going to be my last expensive cocktail for a while, so just let me enjoy it.

'Well, we got our jobs at the same time,' Cora comments. 'I suppose it's sort of nice that we should lose them at the same time too.'

'I'll drink to that,' I reply, raising my glass, clinking it with hers.

I still have to work part of my notice, minus the holiday days I haven't taken, but these after-work cocktails, having chats like this with Cora, are making me think about how much better life would be if I didn't have to work.

'This is the life,' I say with a sigh. 'My holiday with Max gave me a taste of the high life, I don't know how I'm supposed to go back to being skint.'

I'm joking but it's true. We all know rich people exist but, now that I've spent so much time around them, pretending to be one of them, my sad little life really does seem bleak in comparison.

'You should never have let him go,' Cora tells me.

'I know,' I reply. 'Although we weren't actually getting married, so I wasn't set to become a rich Ray, I was always just pretending.'

'That's not what I mean,' she says.

Even though it's a Monday night, the bar is busy enough to be on the noisy side. Cora gets up from her seat opposite me and takes the one next to me, leaning in so I can hear her clearly, without drinkers on tables either side of us listening in.

'Frankie, you should never have let Max go,' she clarifies. 'All the pictures and texts you sent me while you were away, obviously you were having an amazing time, but the way you would talk about Max, come on, I've known you for years, you've never been like this about a boy before. You clearly love him.'

I take such a big gulp of my cocktail it hurts me all the way down.

'It's all so messy now, Cora, I don't think it matters what I think or feel,' I reply. 'He's gone back to California. His mum warned me this would happen. She says he needs space when he's hurt.'

'Screw that,' she insists. 'Call him again. And again and again.'

'That goes against my teachings,' I joke. 'But if space is what he needs, I can do that, for a bit, at least. I've really hurt him. He let me in, and I misled him. I wasn't expecting to fall for him.'

Cora wraps an arm around me and gives me a squeeze.

'Well, as the only one of us with a job interview, I think perhaps I should be the one who buys us the second cocktails we swore we wouldn't have,' she tells me with a smile.

'Yes, let's prep for it,' I insist. 'I've got loads of practice interview questions for you, none of which involve me quizzing you on your seduction techniques.'

'Damn, that was all I practised,' she jokes. 'Back in a sec.'

I'm so lucky to have a friend like Cora who I can talk to, and I know she has my best interests at heart, but perhaps space is what Max needs at the moment, so that's what I'm going to give him. The urge to try him again is overwhelming but I should let things calm down for a few days. Perhaps we'll both see things more clearly then.

* * *

One drink turns into two, then three, then... who's counting, right? I'm not counting anything right now. Except the three Coras dancing in front of me. I'm pretty sure the one in the middle is the real one. I narrow my eyes to check.

It's nice being in the bar with her, drinking, dancing. Honestly, who needs men? Not me. Not either of us. Men have cheated on us, disappointed us, broken our hearts. Why do we even bother? In fact...

I take my phone from my pocket and punch a message to Max.

If you're not going to speak to me then fine, be like that, it says a lot about who you are and I'm not interested in people like that. I don't ever want to hear from you again. Delete my number and leave me alone. Good luck with your new life.

38

'Are you going to be able to keep paying your rent?' Laila asks me.

'Give her a break,' Travis says.

'Sorry, just... someone who lived in my houseshare rage-quit their job and they couldn't afford the rent, so we had to replace them,' she explains.

'Laila...'

'It's fine,' I tell Travis. 'Erm, no, without an income, paying rent isn't something I'll be able to do. But I'm good for a couple of months. In the meantime, I'll just look for something new.'

I did call my parents, after I quit, to tell them about everything that happened and, honestly, I totally understand how Max ended up telling his parents that he was engaged, because when you hear their voices, all you want to do is make them proud, not worry them or let them down in any way, so I couldn't quite bring myself to tell them. That's when I decided to give 'operation find a new job' a go. This is London, I'm sure there are loads of jobs for writers, and I am absolutely not rolling my eyes as I say that.

'Your article was badass,' Travis tells me.

'Yeah, it was,' Laila adds. 'Seriously cool.'

'Thanks,' I say. 'I sent a link to Max when it finally went live yesterday. I haven't heard anything, though.'

'How long has it been?' Laila asks.

'Three weeks,' I reply. 'So, that's that, I suppose.'

I don't tell them about the absolutely mortifying drunk text I sent him basically telling him to piss off. It's embarrassing enough that I wrote and sent it. It's even more cringe inducing that he did as I asked. Who could blame him, though? I wouldn't reply to a crazy outburst like that either.

'I'm sorry to hear it,' Travis says. 'Listen, don't worry, we won't tell anyone about you quitting, so no one else here will put any pressure on you.'

'Thanks,' I reply.

My phone vibrates on my lap. It's been going crazy all day, thanks to my article being shared far and wide. I think people are really appreciating the honesty and that I'm cutting through the bullshit. I also think I'm impressing people by living out their fantasies of quitting their job in a spectacular way.

Can we meet?

'You're not going to believe this,' I blurt. 'It's Max. He's just asked if I'm free to meet. He must have read my article.'

Shit. I spent so long trying to contact him, when I first got back from holiday, I was so worried he would never speak to me again, but now, since I've stopped trying to reach him, the thought of interacting with him petrifies me. And it's such a blunt message too. I can't read between the lines because there's only one bloody line. I don't know how worried I need to be.

'Oh my God,' Laila squeaks. 'That's amazing!'

'Shit, I look awful, I'm sweaty from the Tube after a day at work, I'm in my scruffy stuff...'

'Go get glammed up and go get your man,' Travis says, before laughing at his own choice of words.

'Yeah?' I say. They both nod. 'Yeah, okay!'

I hurry to my bedroom and fling open my wardrobe. I know exactly what I'm going to wear. A brave face and the sexy black Alexander McQueen dress with the zip I wore on our first date.

I reply, letting Max know that I'm free. He replies with a time and an address.

This is the last thing I expected to happen today, but I've finally got the second chance I needed. Now all I need to do is not blow it... again.

39

I arrive outside the building where Max said we should meet. I adjust my dress – it's shorter than I remember it being on holiday – and head inside.

'Yes?' the man behind the desk says.

I glance around the room, looking at the names of businesses on the wall. This is a high-rise full of offices. Why would he want to meet me here?

'Name?' the man prompts me.

'Sorry,' I say. 'Frankie George.'

'Wait there a moment, please,' he replies.

I do as I'm told. Eventually a young woman steps out of the lift.

'Frankie George?' she calls out.

I give her a wave.

'This way, please,' she says.

I have no idea what's going on, but I follow her into the lift. She takes me upstairs to the UK offices of Optecho and suddenly it all makes sense. I remember Max mentioning that they had a London office. When I'd heard Max was going back to work with his dad, I assumed it would be in California. Now that I know that he's still here in London, I can't stop smiling.

'If you just want to take a seat for a moment,' the woman says. 'He'll be ready for you in a moment.'

'Okay, thanks,' I reply.

She looks my dress up and down, but her face gives nothing away. Perhaps she likes it. Or perhaps she thinks it isn't an appropriate thing to wear in an office but didn't know I would be meeting Max here.

My heart is in my mouth, waiting for him to walk out of that door, worrying about what his expression will be like, if he's pleased to see me, if it's a good thing or a bad thing. The optimist in me thinks that he wants me back but the pessimist with the megaphone thinks he's going to finally confront me. And now I'm even more terrified.

'He's ready for you,' the woman says. 'That door over there.'

I take a deep breath, straighten out my dress and head for the door. Here we go.

I walk through the door with my head held high and a big dumb grin on my face and... it's not him. It's not Max. It's a fifty-something fella flanked by a young man and a woman about my age.

He stands up and offers me his hand to shake.

'Frankie George?' he says. 'Lovely to meet you, take a seat.'

'Erm, okay, thanks,' I reply, shaking his hand before doing as I'm told. I try to cross my legs but my dress is too short, so I quickly place my feet on the floor, lest I *Basic Instinct* them.

'How are you?' he asks me.

'I'm well, thank you,' I say. 'You?'

He laughs.

'Yes, I'm well too, thank you,' he says. 'So, tell us a little bit about yourself.'

'Erm...' I take a moment to wonder what the fuck is going on, but I've got nothing. 'What specifically would you like to know?'

'Anything,' the man says. 'Everything. Where are you from? What do you do for fun? Tell us about your work.'

'I'm from Surrey,' I say, because I don't know what else to do. 'I like to watch TV, read books, go to the cinema – I'm a bit of a media junkie in my free time. And my work... I'm a journalist for a women's magazine and website, writing about love and dating.'

'Is journalism what you studied?' he asks curiously.

'No,' I reply. 'Media and marketing.'

Whaaat the hell is going on?

'And your notice period,' he continues. 'What's that like?'

'My notice period?' I repeat back to him. 'From work?'

He nods and... oh my God. Is this... is this a job interview? It is. I'm at a bloody job interview and I'm wearing the world's smallest dress.

'Just a week to go,' I reply. 'Although my boss did say they could be flexible, if I found a new position.'

And I'm joining in now. Incredible.

'Well, Ms George, I have to say this interview is more of a formality,' he explains. 'Your freelance work for Optecho, working alongside Max Ray, speaks for itself. Although he does also speak highly of you, as does Mr Ray senior, the man himself.'

He smiles at me. I can't smile back. I can't do anything right now.

'Ms George, it's my pleasure to extend an offer in the room for you, pending one final interview with the team you will be working with,' he says, holding out a piece of paper. I scan my eyes over it quickly. It's a marketing job. 'You would, of course, have to relocate to the Silicon Valley area. I know we love our commutes in London, but that would be a stretch, wouldn't it? We would, of course, offer you accommodation somewhere local to the head offices in sunny

California until you were ready to find a place of your own. Take the offer away, think about it and, when you've decided, just call the number on the bottom of the page. Sound good?'

I nod. All I can do is nod.

'Okay, then,' he says with a smile. 'We hope to hear from you soon.'

I walk back out to the lift, out of the building, down the road, with no idea where I'm going, in fact this isn't even the right direction. I stop and look at my job offer. There it is, in black and white, a position at Optecho, making far more than I do now, living somewhere hot and sunny, doing something I would enjoy so much more than leading men on via Matcher. But I can't just up and move to California, can I? And what about Max? He'll be there. I mean, he wouldn't have put me forward for the job – basically handed it to me – if he never wanted to see me again. I need to go home and think about this. Actually, no, I need to call Cora and have her meet me at a bar. The decisions I make now will dictate the rest of my life. Do I take the job and the sunshine and the chance to maybe try and win Max back? Or do I cut my losses, try to find something new, or even somewhere new? It doesn't have to be here or California, I could go anywhere.

Of all the times I have needed to not screw things up, this one has to be up there. I really need to think about what I'm doing here. Normally I would go with my gut but today my gut has nothing. Perhaps a little booze will make it more chatty. I'm just hoping the right answer will come to me at some point because, right now, I have no idea what I'm going to do.

40

Another day, another long-haul flight. Honestly, who am I these days? The girl who hasn't been on holiday in years is suddenly on her second international trip of the year.

It's more than just a trip, though, it's an opportunity, not just to bag myself an absolute dream of a job (not only welcomed because I'm unemployed, but because I was really starting to hate what I was writing) but it's also the chance I have been waiting for to finally speak to Max again. After he went cold on me, and I went nuclear on him, our only interactions have been when I sent him the article and when he sent me the stealth invitation to the job interview.

It's a long flight, from London to LAX (admittedly the second time felt much longer than the first) so I decided that would be my time to figure out what to say to Max when I finally saw him. Except it turns out that I, the girl with the fear of heights, really enjoy flying, so it's hard not get swept up in the flight, and everything that comes with flying first – see how naturally I said that? Honestly, I could get used to this. I was so busy going through my interview prep too, which means I didn't really come up with anything to say to Max when I finally see him, and I'm at LAX now. Obviously my flight was paid for by Optecho, seeing as though I'm here for a job interview, and they've sent someone to pick me up, apparently, I'm just trying to spot them now, so at least I'll have the drive to figure out what to say. I don't have much choice now, I'll have to come up with something, so let's hope it's a long drive.

I must admit, it's kind of cool, looking for the driver holding up the card with my name on it in the airport. Me. My name isn't a name-on-a-card kind of name. Eventually I do spot my name, though, and when I look up to greet my driver, I realise it's not a driver at all. It's Max.

'Oh, hi,' I blurt, my heart in my mouth, my stomach either jumping for joy or shaking with fear. I feel sick.

'Hi,' he replies. 'I know we're not on the best terms, but I expected more of a greeting than that, good or bad.'

He looks good. Of course he does, he always does, but frustratingly he looks even better because I know he's not mine any more – if he ever really was. He's dressed smart but casual. Neither like a driver nor like he's on his way to the office.

He's smiling but he's right. That was an odd reaction to seeing him.

'Sorry, I didn't mean anything by it, just... they said I was meeting a driver, I wasn't expecting to see you,' I explain. 'I'm supposed to be here for a job interview. It doesn't look good for the company, if they're sending people like you out on jobs like this. Perhaps I need to consider my options.'

You can't beat a joke for breaking the ice.

Max smiles.

'Would you believe me if I said I asked to come and meet you?' he says.

'Not really,' I reply. 'After that text message I sent you...'

Sometimes it can help to own your embarrassing moments,

right? Admit when you made a mistake and move on from it. It's still absolutely mortifying, though.

'You did seem pretty angry,' he points out.

'I was pretty drunk,' I admit. 'Autocorrect really carried me.'

'It didn't seem like you,' he says. 'But neither did using me for an article, so... Look, let's not do this here, let's get going to our meeting, we're running late.'

I am suddenly reminded that I am here for a job interview.

'Yes, sorry,' I reply, shaking off the awkward, trying to get back into business mode. 'Do we have far to go?'

'Not exactly,' he says. 'Follow me.'

Max leads me through the airport to the same pizza joint where we ate the first time we were here together. There's a table waiting for us, with our exact same order already laid out.

'Erm...' is about all I can say before I laugh.

'This really is a job interview,' he insists. 'You're in California now, everything is a lunch or a dinner, so let's start as we mean to go on.'

I could definitely get used to that. Everything is better when you're eating, right?

'Am I going to get a fair shake, with you interviewing me?' I ask with a smile as I take my seat. I suddenly feel so much more relaxed. This is the Max I'm used to. 'Surely you're going to be slightly biased?'

'Which way?' he asks with a cheeky smile.

'Erm, I'm not actually sure,' I admit.

'I promise to be fair,' he insists as we take our seats in the booth. 'And we may as well eat while we chat. This a business lunch. So, I'm only on board while I get my – *our* – project off the ground. I need to assemble the right team and you were in on the ground floor, so it only seemed right to offer you a job.'

'You haven't taken a full-time job?' I say. 'I thought you moved here.'

'Initially I'm just here to get the project started,' he replies. 'After what happened with us, I figured we both needed a little time to clear our heads. The way we met, the time we spent together, the not total honesty between us, the lies we were telling everyone – we didn't stand a chance. Then I got your message. I thought, if I threw myself into work, let things calm down, then maybe we might be able to find a way to start again from the beginning. Do it right this time.'

Now I really do feel at ease. Max isn't wrong. And while this does feel a little bit like a job interview, it's clearly about so much more. It's about getting us back on track, starting from scratch.

'It was all too much too fast, wasn't it?' I reply. 'Nought to engaged in a week.'

'Exactly,' he says through a relieved smile. 'And I'm sorry if I overreacted when I found out about your job. Old insecurities, feeling like I was being messed around, and if I'm being honest, I was worried about how I would look if you did write it. But when I read your article, it really put things into perspective.'

'I should have told you from the start,' I insist. 'I should have done a lot of things differently. But I did quit my job. And I'm here hoping I can make amends with you. We did really hit it off, initially, and I do miss you. It would be a shame if we couldn't even be friends.'

My heart is pounding inside my chest. I hadn't planned on being so honest. My brain did not co-sign the release of information that just came from my mouth.

'I miss you too,' he admits.

'So, you haven't just up and moved your entire life to California?' I check.

'No,' he replies. 'Well, not yet. The offer is there if I want it, and

I'm thinking about it, but I was waiting to see who was on my team first.'

I realise he's talking about me and the look on my face must be a telling one. It's like Max knows exactly what I'm thinking.

'The reason we didn't stand a chance is because we never got to do things normally,' he says again. 'I wish we could go back to the beginning, meet again, have a normal first date, and you not have to meet my family until way, *way* down the line. If we could get a little bit of that normality back, there might be hope for us. Although I do see the irony, that I'm telling you all this, while simultaneously encouraging you to take a job in a city where you only know me, working for my family.'

I laugh. He's not wrong.

'Perhaps we could work out a way to make both things work together,' he suggests. 'We do make a pretty good team. And did I mention that I miss you too?'

God, he's cute. That smile, those puppy-dog eyes. I think what I love most of all about Max is his inability to give up hope. No matter what happens, no matter what he goes through, no matter how women treat him or how terribly his relationships turn out, he still puts himself out there, he still wants to find love, and he still takes chances. He's braver than I am. When faced with similar, all I've ever done is hide behind my job.

Seeing that look of hope in his eyes fills me with something similar. He makes me want to take chances too. He makes me feel like I *can* have love if I want it. Hope isn't the only thing he makes me feel.

It's not a very me move, but it's one that feels right. I lean forward, over my pizza (and you know you've found yourself a good man when he comes second to pizza), and I kiss him. In another development that is even more unlike me, I feel tears prickle my eyes as we kiss. It's not that it's a bad kiss, it's an incredible kiss. I really have missed Max more than I can explain. It sounds wild, given the short amount of time we've known each other, but when you know, you know, right? I'm overwhelmed to be given a second chance with him but terrified of what's going to happen.

'Kissing you is all I've been able to think about for weeks,' he tells me the second I let him go. 'I realise what a big deal it is, me asking you to move here and start again with me, when we don't know each other all that well. If you don't want the job, that's okay. I'll be done here in six months to a year. I'll come back to London, we can see how things go. All we can really offer each other is a chance. I'm sure I don't need to tell you that life isn't how it looks in the movies. There's no happy-ever-after unless you work for one, right?'

He's right again. The one thing I never realised, when I was attempting all my meet cutes, is that these epic movie romances aren't realistic. Relationships are work – pretty much forever. I want to make it work with Max, but I can't just move to California to see if it works out, can I? But long-distance relationships are hell, and if we wait another year, then who knows if we'll even both still be single? I will be, obviously, but surely someone like Max will be snapped up.

I need to think long and hard about what I do next. Do I take the safe option and go back to London, alone, and try to pick up the pieces of my life, or do I shoot my shot, and move to sunny California to give things a go with Max, see if we can make it work this time? Whatever I do, I'm not going to figure it out before I finish my pizza.

'At least I've booked your return flight for a week's time,' Max says, reading my mind. 'So you've got plenty of time to figure out what you want to do. You never know, I might just make you fall in love with the place.'

Maybe he will. We'll have to wait and see.

41

TEN MONTHS LATER

As the snowflakes fall down around me, I twirl around like a little kid. It's amazing, how perfect it all looks. I've never seen anything like it.

I scoop a little up in my hand, keeping quiet, trying not to make a sound. It's just hard not to get excited. I can't believe this is my job.

'Right, yeah, I think we've got it,' the director calls out.

I hurry over to him.

'So, what do you think?' I ask him.

'Okay, tell him he was right, it's perfect,' he replies.

'You can tell him yourself,' I say. 'He's behind you.'

'Steven, buddy, how are you?' Max asks him. He shakes his hand before kissing me.

'I was just telling Frankie, you were right, the camera is perfect,' Steven tells him. 'Perfect for catching the multi-angle shots we need.'

'Well, when you're a perfectionist, who thinks audiences will be able to see continuity errors in the way the snowflakes fall...' Max teases.

Steven gives him a light, playful punch in the stomach.

'Are you guys still on for tomorrow night?' he asks.

'We certainly are,' Max replies. 'We've got to dash but we'll see you there.'

'Yes, see you soon, Steven,' I say as we exchange cheek kisses.

Max places his hand on the small of my back as he escorts me off the set, back out on to the warm streets of Los Angeles.

'It's so strange, walking from the snow to the sun,' I say with a laugh. 'I'll never quite get used to it.'

'You'll get used to it eventually,' he tells me, pulling me close for a kiss. 'Everything here is so fake that it's normal.'

'Do you know what I won't get used to?' I say. 'All the bloody lunches and dinners. It's always a lunch, a dinner, all the time, with everyone. I never thought I'd get sick of lunches and dinners.'

'Then I shouldn't remind you that we've got a dinner with my family tonight,' he says, squeezing me.

'Your dad is getting an award,' I point out. 'That's a bit more than a dinner.'

'There will be plenty of dinners next week, when we jet off to Maui for the annual Ray family holiday,' he reminds me.

'Don't get me wrong, taking this job, moving here, and finding you waiting with open arms after reading my super-pathetic article and realising I'm just a big dummy is obviously the best decision I've ever made,' I say, taking a much-needed breath before continuing. 'And I'm so relieved that I was able to smooth things over with your family.'

'But?' Max prompts me, sensing the 'but' that is on the tip of my tongue.

'*But...* I'm worried that going back to Maui is going to drag everything back up, everyone is going to remember what a stink I caused last time, and it's going to be awkward,' I say with a sigh. 'We're so close to it all being a distant memory. Going back there once a year is going to be like picking at old wounds.'

'Well, did I tell you Albi won't be there?' he starts. 'He's decided to take the yacht to the Bahamas for... something. Who knows if that's true? It's certainly a lie that he's sailing it himself. But – with the tiny bit of drama from the party last year – you've given my mum an excuse to talk my dad into renewing their vows *again*. She's thinking of making it an annual thing.'

I laugh.

'Everyone loves you,' he tells me. 'It was my fault no one got to meet the real you last year. They know you now, you're part of the family, and the business would be lost without you, so at least you know they'll always value you that way.'

He may be joking but he isn't wrong. I've made myself invaluable to them. Who knew that tech marketing was my calling?

I climb into Max's swanky hire car. He's pretty much the only person in his family who drives himself, which I like. I don't think he would ever spend a lot of money buying a car, but he does enjoy hiring them for trips. He isn't quite as 'money' as the rest of the Rays.

I pop open the centre console, looking for a tissue, but all that is in there is a ring box.

'Oh my God, Max, look,' I tell him, showing him what I've found when he eventually joins me. 'Whoever had the car before you left this in here.'

I can't resist opening it up to take a peek.

'Oh, wow,' I blurt. 'Look at that. It's incredible. I bet this cost someone a fortune. The size of the diamond! You should call them, let them know, someone must be sick with worry.'

Is it bad vibes, to try on someone else's ring? Is there some superstition I'm not aware of, that's going to curse me single for the rest of my life? I know it's probably in poor taste, but what harm can it do? This isn't a romcom movie. It isn't going to get stuck on my finger or anything like that.

'Wait, stop,' Max insists, snatching it from me as I go to try it on.

Wow, perhaps there really is a curse.

'Fine, fine, you're right, it's probably weird,' I admit. 'It's just, well, the nicest ring I've ever seen in my life. It's kind of like you riding around in this car. It's not yours, you just want to try it, see how it is, then give it back.'

Okay, so it's not exactly the same, I'm just making excuses. Perhaps it was an out-of-order thing to do.

'Look, this isn't how I saw this going in my head, at all,' Max starts. He puffs air from his cheeks. 'Frankie, will you marry me?'

Max closes the ring box before opening it up again, proposal style.

'Oh... my... God...' I blurt.

For a moment, I just stare at him.

Max looks terrified.

'It's customary to say more words than that,' he encourages me as the panic sets in. 'Or it seems like a "no".'

'No! I mean, yes,' I blurt. 'Yes, yes, yes. Sorry, I'm just stunned. Yes!'

Max exhales so forcefully he practically blows the ring back to me.

'Okay, now you can try it on,' he says as he hands it back.

It fits me to perfection. Of course, I still have the first ring that Max gave me, on my right hand, but it feels so incredible to finally have a ring on *that* finger.

'I love it,' I tell him. 'And I love you.'

I grab his face and give him ten excitable tiny kisses before kissing him properly.

'I had this whole thing planned,' he tells me when I release him. 'I booked a restaurant, I had this whole speech written, I was going to have the waiter bring the ring with dessert to surprise you – this big romantic gesture. I can't believe I just asked you in the car.'

'That all sounds amazing but all I need is you,' I reply. 'It doesn't matter where you ask me. It was always going to be a yes.'

'I can't believe I'm engaged,' he blurts as his face erupts with a gigantic smile.

'You can't believe it?' I reply. 'You knew it was coming!'

'Well, at least on this holiday you will be my actual fiancée,' he points out.

'I don't know if that's better or worse, for putting last time behind us, but I don't think I care,' I reply, looking at my ring again. 'We'll never top last time, will we?'

'What are you thinking, that it's not Hawaii if we don't cause trouble?' he asks with a laugh.

'Maybe,' I reply. 'Perhaps we could see if that offer to get married there is still good from your dad?'

I'm *definitely* kidding.

'And miss forcing them to go back to Surrey?' he says. 'Are you kidding me? My dad is so reluctant to go back to the UK, I want to make him do it, just to see if they arrest him the second he lands. Something must be up there.'

'Max, you are wonderful,' I tell him.

'Because I want to see my dad arrested?' he replies with a chuckle.

'No, because you are kind, loving, sweet, and incredibly handsome,' I say. 'And because you gave me this absolutely sick job.'

'Oh, that wasn't me,' he insists. 'By all accounts, you turned up for the interview basically naked and charmed them all by yourself.'

'I owe a lot to that dress,' I say to myself with a smile. 'I wish I'd brought it with me tonight.'

'Save it for Maui,' he says. 'We can recreate that night. Just remember the part that goes underneath it.'

'Oh, I have something like that with me tonight,' I tell him. 'We're staying in a hotel, it's standard procedure, is it not?'

'And this is just one of the many reasons I'm marrying you,' he tells me. 'That and because I didn't have to learn a new name.'

'Right, come on, let's go get a celebratory drink somewhere,' I insist. 'Then I need to wash the fake snow from my hair and get ready for the party tonight.'

'I'm tired just thinking about it,' Max says, yawning for effect.

I can't quite believe that this is my life now. This time last year, I had a job I wasn't happy with, I hated where I lived, I was bored, lonely and kind of bitter. I was trying so, so hard to turn things around, to make life better, and then even when I met Max, I carried on down the route I thought I needed to take. It just goes to show that sometimes, if you try too hard to force something, you just push it further away, and that the missing piece of the puzzle could be right there under your nose (or a few floors below you at work, at least) just waiting for you to find it. Don't ignore what's around you because you're so focused on what you're trying to move closer to. You never really know if that person you end up stuck in a lift with may just be the love of your life.

ACKNOWLEDGMENTS

To be writing the acknowledgements for *another* book is nothing short of amazing. This really is the best job in the world, but I couldn't do it without the love and support from so many amazing people.

I'm so lucky to have my brilliant editor, Nia, Amanda and the rest of the fantastic team at Boldwood on my side. They really do such a wonderful job with my books – more than I ever thought possible.

A huge thank you to everyone who reads and reviews my books. Without you I definitely wouldn't be doing this. It means so much to me to have so much support and to receive so many lovely messages. I love hearing from you so please keep them coming.

Extra special thanks go to my family and friends for all their endless love and encouragement. Lynsey, the B to my S, xoxo. Darcy, my right-hand girl. Sammy, quite possibly my new biggest fan. Thanks to the amazing Kim and the wonderful Audrey for always being there for me (and for the best publication-day presents). Thank you to James and Joey for all their help with everything, ever.

And finally, as always, huge thanks go to my husband, Joe. He's always willing to chat about the people and places that only exist in my head, and he doesn't mind when I glue myself to a computer for hours at a time. My happy endings got a hell of a lot better the day I met him.

MORE FROM PORTIA MACINTOSH

We hope you enjoyed reading *The Meet Cute Method*. If you did, please leave a review.

If you'd like to gift a copy, this book is also available as an ebook, digital audio download and audiobook CD.

Sign up to Portia MacIntosh's mailing list for news, competitions and updates on future books.

http://bit.ly/PortiaMacIntoshNewsletter

Discover more laugh-out-loud romantic comedies from Portia Macintosh:

ALSO BY PORTIA MACINTOSH

One Way or Another

If We Ever Meet Again

Bad Bridesmaid

Drive Me Crazy

Truth or Date

It's Not You, It's Them

The Accidental Honeymoon

You Can't Hurry Love

Summer Secrets at the Apple Blossom Deli

Love & Lies at the Village Christmas Shop

The Time of Our Lives

Honeymoon For One

My Great Ex-Scape

Make or Break at the Lighthouse B&B

The Plus One Pact

Stuck On You

Faking It

Life's a Beach

Will They, Won't They?

No Ex Before Marriage

The Meet Cute Method

ABOUT THE AUTHOR

Portia MacIntosh is a bestselling romantic comedy author of over 15 novels, including *My Great Ex-Scape* and *Honeymoon For One*. Previously a music journalist, Portia writes hilarious stories, drawing on her real life experiences.

Visit Portia's website: https://portiamacintosh.com/

Follow Portia MacIntosh on social media here:

facebook.com/portia.macintosh.3

twitter.com/PortiaMacIntosh

instagram.com/portiamacintoshauthor

bookbub.com/authors/portia-macintosh

Boldwd

Boldwood Books is an award-winning fiction publishing company seeking out the best stories from around the world.

Find out more at www.boldwoodbooks.com

Join our reader community for brilliant books, competitions and offers!

Follow us
@BoldwoodBooks
@BookandTonic

Sign up to our weekly
deals newsletter

https://bit.ly/BoldwoodBNewsletter

Manufactured by Amazon.ca
Bolton, ON

27645201R00157